Daring to Soar

Diane Valentine

BLACK ROSE writing™

ISBN: 978-1-61296-547-5

PUBLISHED BY BLACK ROSE WRITING

www.blackrosewriting.com

Printed in the United States of America
Suggested retail price $17.95

Daring to Soar is printed in Palatino Linotype

I want to thank Kathie Giorgio,
and the members of the
Wednesday Afternoon Workshop at
AllWriters' Workplace & Workshop.
Thanks also to my husband, Don,
and the rest of my family and friends.
A special thanks to Evalyn Fulmer, for her support.

Daring to Soar

I

Judy Evans looked out the plane's window, trying not to think of the black hard plastic box in a shopping bag, stowed in the overhead compartment. Instead, she focused on the frigid Wisconsin winter she was flying to, leaving behind a blazing Arizona sun.

This can't be happening to me. Sixty is too young to become a widow. Leaning against the seat, she hoped sleep would block out reality.

Suddenly, there was a twang in her ear. "Howdy, ma'am."

"Pardon?" She blinked a couple of times. She must be dreaming. Next to her sat a caricature of a cowboy, the kind from the old black and white movies she watched as a child.

"I'm Dusty Hoffman." He put out his hand.

"Dusty Hoffman." She repeated it slowly. Why did that name sound familiar?

He winked at her. "Don't get me mixed up with that actor feller, Dustin Hoffman. My real name is Henry, but my friends call me Dusty."

Judy felt embarrassed. "I'm sorry." She gave his hand a polite shake.

"No need to be sorry. Happens all the time." He shrugged. "And what's your name, pretty lady?"

"Judy Evans." Was this guy going to talk all the way to Milwaukee? This was the last thing she needed. She didn't want to talk to anyone.

Just then, a young woman sat down on the aisle seat. Dusty started the routine with her. Then he introduced Judy like they were old friends.

The young woman leaned forward and smiled at Judy. "Pleased to meet you."

Judy didn't say anything, but gave a smile. Then she leaned against the seat and closed her eyes. Dusty droned on to the other woman.

Judy felt the plane start to taxi. She opened her eyes to watch the earth fall away. She closed them again and half listened to the flight attendant give the instructions about emergency procedures. Dusty never stopped talking.

She pretended to be asleep when the attendant came by with drinks. Maybe the plane would go down and she wouldn't have to go through the next few days. No, that would be so unfair to their four children and the rest of their family and friends.

Try as she might, Judy couldn't sleep. She remembered just a few mornings ago. Steve gave her a kiss as she walked out the door to meet some of the other women for the daily walk. She knew Steve would be out golfing by the time she got back. It was all a part of their daily routine. But it would be anything but routine. One of golfers, Ed met her as she got back.

"I'm sorry Steve collapsed on the sixth hole, I'll take you to the hospital where the EMTs took him." Ed was visibly shaken.

Judy went into the unit and grabbed her purse. Neither of them spoke all the way to the hospital.

There, they were met by the doctor and several of the golfing group. "I'm sorry, ma'am. There wasn't anything we could do. Your husband may have died before he collapsed. Even if he'd been in the hospital when this happened, we couldn't have saved him." He took a breath, "would you like to see him?"

Judy nodded.

"I'll come in with you, if you'd like," one of the men offered.

"No, I'd like to see him alone." She was shown the way to a small room. Steve's face wasn't covered. She caressed it and told him she loved him. Then, she kissed his mouth and forehead. She couldn't take any more. She left the room without a backward glance.

She signed some papers. "He wanted to be cremated."

"I'll take care of that for you," Ed volunteered. Judy let him.

"I'll drive you home," offered another of the golfers.

Home. That sounded so strange. It would never be home again without Steve.

Back at the RV Park, Judy knew she had family to call but didn't know who to call first. She went to the desk and there was Steve's sweatshirt hanging over a chair. She picked it up and buried her face in Steve's scent. Smothering huge sobs, she sunk on to the couch until she cried herself out. Get control of yourself, girl, she though. She took the address book and phone back to the dining room table.

Judy made the phone calls. She sounded cold and remote as she did. She didn't want to break down. A few hours later, Ed came over. "Did you make arrangements to fly home?"

"No, I didn't get around to it yet." She knew he saw her red puffy eyes. Home was still Wisconsin, though they had wintered for the past few years in Arizona.

"Would you like me to do that for you?"

"That would be nice. Do you know how soon Steve..?" She couldn't finish the sentence.

"Day after tomorrow." He turned to go, "If there is anything else either my wife or I can do for you, just let us know."

"Thanks for everything. And, yes I'll let you know."

That evening and the next day, Steve's golfing buddies stopped by to offer their condolences. Judy was deeply touched. She occupied most of the time packing and cleaning. She'd take all of her clothes with her. Steve's, she would just leave. She didn't walk with the other women. She just couldn't face them, instead, she walked in the evening, by herself.

When Ed and his wife came to take her to the airport, he gave her the bag containing the plastic box of Steve's ashes.

So many thoughts raced through Judy's mind. All the arrangements to make. The children and her sister did most of the initial phone calls. But there were more decisions ahead. How was she going to handle it all without Steve?

Finally, the sign for fastening their seat belts came on. The temperature in Milwaukee was twenty degrees. Oh, crap, she forgot to bring her winter coat. She always kept one in Arizona in case they had to make a trip up to Wisconsin during the winter.

The young woman got up and retrieved her briefcase from the overhead. The cowboy stood and reached in and handed Judy her package. "Hey, lady," he said in a loud voice. "You didn't do much shopping."

That shocked Judy out of her lassitude. "Those are my husband's ashes. He died a few days ago."

The cowboy stopped grinning and reddened around the ears. "Sorry, lady." He disappeared down the aisle.

Feeling the eyes of the other passengers on her, she wanted to disappear. Judy felt the dam of emotions start to break. She had to get out of there before it did.

Just as she started down the walkway to the terminal, an elderly woman put her hand on Judy's arm. "You have my sympathies, dear. I lost my husband too."

She smiled at the woman and murmured, "Thanks," before hurrying on.

II

Judy was much relieved when she saw her sister, Sandra, and Sandra's husband, Brad, waiting for her as she emerged into the concourse.

Sandra threw her arms around her. "I'm so sorry, Judy." The two women wept openly. Sandra pulled back a bit. "Did you reach Kathy?"

Kathy was their sister who lived in Colorado. "She can't get away on such short notice. Besides, the air fare would be out of sight."

Brad interrupted, "Do you have your claim check? I'll go get your luggage and meet you at the car."

While trying to hold on to her package, Judy fumbled with her purse. Sandra took the package from her. "Here it is." Judy handed him an envelope. He dashed into the crowd. Judy knew

Brad couldn't handle watching them cry.

Sandra handed the bag to Judy. "What's in here?"

"Steve's ashes," Judy almost whispered. She could see Sandra take a deep breath and swallow. "Sandra, I forgot to bring my winter coat. I have one at the condo, but not with me today." She knew she was babbling, but couldn't help herself.

"Judith, how could you forget your coat? It's winter in Wisconsin." She waved her hand dismissively, "That's okay. We're parked right next to the elevator in the parking ramp. The car should still be warm. We just got here. Besides, I have an extra jacket in the car you can use."

Oh, sure, Judy thought, I can wear your size six coat on my size fourteen body, but she didn't say anything. Sandra would give the shirt off her back to anyone, but then tell everyone she did.

"How was the flight?" Sandra asked as they walked toward the ramp.

"Okay, I guess. At least I was able to get a direct flight. Those stopovers in Denver or St. Louis are not my idea of a good time." She paused. "This whole thing is not my idea of a good time." She managed a weak smile.

Sandra put her arm around her shoulder and gave her a squeeze. "I know, honey."

But she doesn't know, Judy thought. How could she? Her husband is alive, even if he is a jerk. She knew the thought was unkind, but at the moment, she didn't care.

"I talked to Kevin this morning. He and Grace will be getting in late tonight. I told them we'd come and get them, but he said not to go through all that trouble. They'd rent a car and get a room at one of the nearby hotels."

That sounded like Kevin. Her son-in-law always seemed to

keep himself at arm's length when it came to the family. That also meant keeping Grace away, too. They were living in the Atlanta area. Far enough away so Grace couldn't see the rest of them easily.

"What about Ellyn?" Judy hadn't been able to reach her younger daughter before leaving Arizona.

"She's probably waiting for you at the condo." Sandra pushed the elevator button. "Clark and his girlfriend should be there, too." She paused, "You're going to have a full house. Do you want to send some of them over by me?"

It would be easy to allow Sandra to take over, but Judy had to do this herself. "No, that's okay. I was just wondering about Andy and Tammy and the kids?"

"Andy is taking a week off. He and Tammy have been at the condo since you called." The elevator doors opened. They rode in silence. At each floor the doors opened, Judy felt the blast of cold air.

"Here we are," Sandra said as she took hold of Judy's sleeve. "We're the Suburban next to the post. Brad just bought it."

The two women hurried across the traffic lane, causing cars to stop. Sandra had one of those remotes to open the car door. They both crawled in and slammed the doors behind them.

"My jacket is right next to you."

Judy draped it across her. It did feel good. Sandra reached over and started the engine. Within minutes, the car was warm.

"What's the weather forecast for the next few days?" Judy asked.

"Cold. Maybe some snow the day after next."

The rear door of the van opened up and her brother-in-law put in her two suitcases and slammed it shut.

Once behind the wheel, he said, "Let's get out of here before the traffic gets any worse."

"I'm sorry I couldn't get a different flight." Judy felt that twinge of guilt for putting him out. Brad had a way of doing that to her. She hoped that Sandra wouldn't have to hear him complain about this for weeks.

"Some things can't be helped." Sandra reached back and patted her leg.

Why did it have to be Steve who died? Why couldn't it have been Brad? Sandra would be better off without him. Stop thinking those thoughts, Judy said to herself. She closed her eyes so she couldn't see the cars whizzing by as Brad impatiently wove in and out of traffic. She was glad Sandra's jacket was covering her hands so no one could see her white knuckles.There was no one in the condo's gatehouse. "What good is it to have a guard house if it's empty?' Brad asked.

"Some days, there is someone." Why did she always feel so defensive about every remark Brad made? "Just pull into the drive. I'll just set the luggage on the walk and take it in myself." Heaven forbid she put him out any more than necessary.

"Don't be silly," Sandra said. "We'll help you in with it. Besides, I want to see Ellyn."

Judy saw the muscles in Brad's jaw tighten, but he said nothing.

Brad placed the bags in the foyer. "I'll wait for you in the car."

Sandra gave a little shrug.

"How can you stand that?" Judy said when he closed the door behind him. She put her things on the table.

Before Sandra could answer, there was a pounding of feet on the stairs. "Mom! Aunt Sandra!"

Judy's youngest child flung her arms around her. "Oh, Mom.

I'm so glad you're home. I guess I still need my mom."

Judy gave her a big kiss. "And, I still need my little girl."

"Andy and Tammy left when I got here. They'll be back later." Then, Ellyn hugged Sandra"Hi, sweetie, I just wanted to see you. Uncle Brad's waiting in the car," Sandra said.

Ellyn made a face.

"He's not so bad. See you tomorrow." Sandra gave her niece a kiss on the cheek and left.

Ellyn shivered. "I can't imagine sleeping with him."

"You're not to imagine sleeping with anyone," Judy said as she hugged Ellyn.

"Oh, Mom." There was a teasing exasperation in Ellyn's voice. Then she burst into tears. "It all seems so unreal. I miss Dad already. If he were here, he'd be making some sort of weird joke."

"It's like a bad nightmare." Judy fished for a tissue in her pocket.

The phone rang. Ellyn leaped to get it. "Sure, she's right here.' She handed the receiver to Judy and mouthed, "Grace."

"Hi, sweetheart, when did you get in?" Judy didn't feel as cheery as she tried to sound.

"About two hours ago. Kevin decided we'd drive." Grace's voice sounded flat.

"I'm glad to hear your voice, but I'd rather see you. Are you coming over soon?"

"Kevin thought we should rest first. It'll also give you some time to be alone."

"Honey, you tell Kevin that you two can come right over. I need you here." She heard a muffled sound.

Then, "Mom, Kevin said we'll be there in about an hour."

Before she could ask where they were staying, Grace hung

up.

"What's up with Grace?" Ellyn asked.

"Kevin wanted to give me some time to relax before they came over."

Ellyn shook her head, but said nothing.

"I'm going to make a pot of tea." Judy rubbed her upper arms. "I have to get warm." She went into the kitchen. Ellyn sat at the table while Judy put on the teakettle.

"When do you plan on going back to school?" She rummaged in a cabinet to find her tea. Ellyn didn't say anything, so Judy looked at her.

"Mom, I was going to tell you and Dad over the phone this weekend."

"Tell us what?"

"I've decided to take a semester off." She held up her hand. "Now listen, Mom, I'm not sure if teaching is what I want to do." Ellyn went on. "I'm going to Africa to work in a mission school."

"Africa?" Judy sat.

"Mom, I've been thinking about this for several months. I have everything arranged. I knew you and Dad..." She stopped and looked at her mother.

Judy needed to keep her hands busy so Ellyn couldn't see them shake. She took out several tea bags and tore them out of their packets. "Go on."

"I'm sorry, Mom. I didn't know Dad was going...going to...die." With that, she burst into tears again. She flung her arms around her mother.

Judy held her close. "I know, honey, I know." She patted Ellyn's back.

When Ellyn let go of her mother, Judy handed her a Kleenex

and took one herself. "When are you supposed to leave?"

"Next week. Actually, a week from today."

"That's pretty soon." Judy sounded calm, but there was turmoil in her brain. How much more could she take? First, Steve dying unexpectedly and now Ellyn traipsing over to Africa.

Ellyn said, "I could maybe go a couple of weeks later, if you need me."

Judy thought for a moment or two. She would be alone, utterly alone. That's selfish, she chided herself. The children have to have lives of their own. This was bound to happen someday, but why now?

"Mom? Are you okay?" Ellyn's voice broke.

Judy gave her head a little shake to clear her mind. She smiled. "I'm sorry, I just got lost in thought. There isn't any reason why you need to change your plans. You'll be here for the service. I can get along fine." She saw the relief on Ellyn's face.

"Are you sure, Mom?"

Judy nodded. "I'm very sure." She poured water into the pot and let the tea steep. "I want to put my suitcases in my room and change clothes."

Ellyn jumped to her feet. "Here, let me help." She stepped in front of her mother and grabbed a suitcase in each hand.

Judy took the package and purse she'd left on the hall table, and followed Ellyn. Ellyn flipped both suitcases up on the bed."There you go. I'll leave you alone. Let me get you a cup of tea first." Ellyn was gone but a minute or so before she brought in a steaming cup of tea. After setting it on the nightstand and closed the door behind her.

III

Now where do I put this, Judy thought as she looked around for a place to set the bag containing Steve's ashes. For the time being, she set them on his dresser.

She kicked off her shoes and sat on the bed. This is so unreal, she thought. This can't be happening to me, to us. It happens to others, but not me. Bone tired, she just wanted to crawl into bed. Ah, but there were other things to do. Standing up, she opened the smaller case. She took the stacks of her underwear, she put them in the drawer. From the other case, she took tops and pants to hang them away.

There were all of Steve's winter clothes hanging at one end of the closet. The shock was physical, like a blow to her stomach. Everything seemed so normal, but nothing was. It took all her strength to hang up the clothes before she sank to the floor in tears.

The phone rang, but she didn't answer it, Ellyn did."Mom, its Mrs. Gray from church."

I don't want to talk to anyone now, Judy thought, but she picked up the phone on the nightstand and said, "Hello, Janet."

"Oh, Judy, I'm so sorry to hear about Steve. We all are," the voice on the other end gushed sweetly.

Judy gritted her teeth. This was just the start of what she'd have to endure for the next several days. "It's nice of you to call. Thank you."

"I'm going to bring over some food. Several others from choir want to know if there's anything you need."

To be left alone, Judy thought, but instead, she said, "I haven't got anything organized yet. I just got home a short time ago."

"Well, if there's anything at all, just let someone know."

"Thanks for the offer," Judy said.

"I'll be over within the hour with the food. Bye."

Judy went into the bathroom and rinsed her face with cold water before looking for Ellyn. "Janet Gray is coming over with some food. Could you please see her? I really don't want to see her or anyone right now.'

"You know I can't stand that woman." When Judy didn't say anything, Ellyn continued. "Okay, I'll be a grown up for now and handle it for you."

Judy patted her arm. "Thanks." .

Back in her room, Judy worked quickly to finish unpacking. If she worked fast, she might not have time to think.

There was a knock on her door. "Mom?"

"You can come in."

Ellyn opened the door a crack. "Clark and that bimbo are here."

"Ellyn!"

"Well, she is."

Judy let out a sigh. "I'm coming right out." Another thing to confront without Steve.

Clark held his mother in a tight squeeze. "I can't believe Dad's gone."

She could feel the wetness of his tears on her neck. "I know, dear." She couldn't say anything more for fear of losing control.

"I'm sorry too," came a small, childlike voice.

Judy saw Tina standing next to Clark. She tried to give the girl a smile. "Thank you."

"I put our bags in the downstairs guest bedroom," Clark said.

Judy took a deep breath. "Tina can stay in Ellyn's room with her. You can have the guest room."

"Mom! That's not fair. We're living together. I'm an adult." Clark's face got red.

"You know the rules."

"You're such a hard ass." Clark glared at his mother.

"Shut up, Clark." Ellyn rounded on her brother. He shut his mouth with a snap.

Judy said a silent prayer of thanks and left the kids to work things out. She could see them in the hall mirror and hear the three of them talking.

"Listen, I'm not real fond of Tina sharing my room." Ellyn turned to her brother's girlfriend. "No offense, Tina. But this has always been the rule around here. Just because Dad isn't around any longer doesn't mean Mom's going to change the rules."

"Maybe we can go stay at a motel." Tina whined.

"We don't have any money," Clark barked at her. She shrunk back. His voice gentled as put his arm around her. "Sorry, I didn't mean that, honey. We'll only be here for a couple of days."

Judy closed the door to her room behind her. "Damn you, Steve."

The doorbell rang. There was a murmur of voices, but Judy couldn't hear what was being said. The front door slammed. She couldn't settle down so she went to the kitchen.

"Did I hear the doorbell?"

"Mrs. Gray just brought over a casserole and some jello." Ellyn poured herself a glass of milk. "And Sue from across the street brought over a salad. Says she'll call you next week to shop or go to the movies or something."

"That would be fun." Judy rummaged around in a drawer. "I'm going to put this paper and pen on the counter. When someone brings over something, just write it down. I'll have to send out thank you notes after the funeral."

"No problem. By the way, I think everything is cool with Clark and Tina now."

"Thanks, honey." Judy opened the refrigerator door. Not much inside.

"I got milk and bread, but I didn't know what else you might need." Ellyn sipped her milk.

"I think I'll go to the store and get some groceries." Judy took her winter jacket out of the closet. "Just take messages. I'll call them later."

Taking her keys and purse, she went into the garage. She got into the driver's side of the Buick and adjusted the seat. I won't have to worry about doing this anymore. She sat there. What was she planning on doing? Oh, yeah, she was going to the store and buy some food. She pressed the button and the garage door slowly went up. She started the car and glanced in the rearview mirror. Clark's car was parked on the street.

She drove the ten blocks to the supermarket. The parking lot was jammed with people stopping in on their way home from work. She had to park in the farthest row. The cold air was bracing.

Once inside, Judy wheeled the cart to the produce section. She picked up a head of lettuce and looked at it and put it down. She put a bag of apples in the cart. What else should she get? Milk. So she went to the dairy section and put in a gallon of milk, along with a carton of eggs and a bottle of orange juice, the kind with lots of pulp the way Steve liked it. But he wouldn't be drinking it. It went back in the case.

What else? Cereal. Crackers. Bread. Lunch meat. Judy wandered from one end of the store to the other. Suddenly, she felt panicky. With only twelve items, she could use the express checkout. She wrote a check and handed it to the clerk.

"I need your check cashing card, ma'am." the clerk said without even looking up.

Things were closing in on her. Judy dug around in her purse. "I forgot it. Can you use my license?"

The clerk sighed and wrote down the numbers of Judy's driver's license.

Once inside the car, she started the engine and rested her forehead on the steering wheel. She longed for the warm Arizona air. She could just drive there instead of going home. But the kids and everyone would have the police out looking for her. She glanced at the clock. She had already been gone over an hour. She shifted the car into reverse and backed out of the stall. Slowly, she drove out of the lot and toward home.

IV

Two cars were blocking the entrance to her garage. What jerk is parking in my drive? She slammed the door and stormed into the front door.

"Some idiot blocked me out of my garage. Clark, please bring in the groceries," she yelled. She hung up her coat in the closet and turned to see her daughter, Grace, and her pastor. Her face burned. "Oh! I'm sorry, sweetie." She gave her daughter a big hug. Grace must have come home while Judy was out.

"That's okay, Mom."

Pastor Lynn put her arms around Judy. "I'm so sorry to hear about Steve. I came over as soon as I knew you'd be home. Sorry about the car."

"Pastor Lynn, I'm so embarrassed. I didn't recognize your car." Judy would have liked to crawl into hole.

"Don't give it a second thought." She reached in her pocket and handed a wad of keys to Clark. "Please go move my car and then pull your mother's car into the garage."

Clark did as he was told.

"Now, come and sit down," Pastor Lynn said as she sat down and patted the spot next to her.

Judy smiled. Thank God for Pastor Lynn.

"Grace, why don't you go make a pot of tea? Your mother looks like she could use one. I know I could."

"Now, tell me what happened." Pastor Lynn took Judy's hand and held it between her two warm ones.

Judy took a deep breath. She told about the morning Steve died without going into every little detail.

Pastor Lynn handed Judy a tissue. Judy didn't even realize she was crying.

"One of the men helped me make arrangements for Steve and the flight...well." She gestured helplessly.

Grace came in with a tray and set it on the coffee table.

"Thanks," Judy and Pastor Lynn said together.

"I'm going down by Ellyn if you need me." Grace left the room. Judy heard Clark clanging keys and banging doors.

"Judy, we need to talk about the service." Pastor Lynn reached into her briefcase and pulled out some papers.

"I know. It'll have to be soon. Grace and her husband need to head back to their jobs, as does Clark." Judy poured them each a mug of tea.

"Did Ellyn tell you about her plans?" Pastor Lynn adjusted her reading glasses.

Judy sighed. "Yes, but I haven't had much time to think about it."

"I understand."

The two women discussed the memorial service, date and time, scriptures to be read and music played. It all seemed so cut and dried to Judy. Steve's picture would be placed on the communion table and his ashes would stay at home.

"What about interment?" Pastor Lynn put the papers in a stack.

"I'll see to that in the morning. The cemetery has a place for ashes. I'll let you know."

Pastor Lynn stood. "If there is anything more I can do, just call." She added, "Any time, night or day."

"Thanks."

Pastor Lynn's keys were on the hall table. She gave Judy another hug. "We'll all be praying for you and your family."

Judy could hear the children's voices coming from the lower level family room. She probably should have consulted them about the service. Oh, well, she'd tell them about the plans. If they wanted something changed or added, they could call Pastor Lynn.

Before she could join her children, Tina came up the stairs. "Mrs. Evans. I mean, Judy." She burst into tears.

"Let's go into the living room," Judy took Tina's hand and led her into the other room. They sat on the sofa. "What's wrong?" Judy always thought of Tina as a wild, self-centered girl.

"This brings back memories of when my brother was killed in a cycle accident." More tears.

Judy handed her the box of tissues from the end table.

"Thanks," she sniffed. "It happened last year. But I want you to know how sorry I am about Clark's dad. I know Clark was a prick about us sleeping together here." She made a sweeping gesture, "But I like it that you have rules. My family doesn't care what I do." Tina dried her tears and gave Judy a dazzling smile.

"Thanks for sharing this with me." Judy hugged her. Maybe Tina wasn't as ditzy as they all thought. "Now, let's go down and see what the others are doing."

The kids were all leaning over a photograph album. Ellyn looked up. "We're going to put together a collage for Dad's service."

Judy didn't care one way or the other, but she forced herself to smile. "That will be nice." She noticed her son-in-law sitting away from the others. "How's it going, Kev?"

"Okay." He flexed his shoulders and shifted in his chair.

So much for conversation. Normally, Judy would have tried to draw him out, but not today.

"Hey, Mom, look at this one. Dad's in a leisure suit." Clark hooted.

"And you're in go-go boots." Grace pointed to the same picture.

Ellyn jumped up. "I have some poster board in my room."

Judy couldn't help but watch the dynamics going on. Her children were renewing the old bonds. Even Tina fit in. If Kevin didn't keep a tight rein on himself, he could join in the camaraderie and enjoy it.

"Hey, Mom!" came a shout from upstairs.

"We're all down here," Judy shouted.

There was a rush of feet down the steps. Andy came and encircled his mother. "I'm so sorry." he whispered in her ear.

"I know, dear."

Her daughter-in-law put her arm around Judy's shoulders and Andy released her. Tammie gave her a warm hug. "Is there anything we can do? My parents send their love."

"That's sweet of them." Judy felt she was conversing in trite little sayings.

"Gramma!" Judy was thrown off balance by a pair of arms wrapped around her knees.

"Careful, Katie, or I'll accidently step on you." Judy picked up the four year old.

Katie looked straight into her grandmother's eyes. "Are you sad?'

"I'm very sad, but you make me feel a whole lot better." Judy snuggled her face in the little girl's neck and gave her a kiss. "Why don't you go help Aunt Ellyn with some pictures?"

She hadn't noticed the baby in her son's arms. They must have passed him around during the hugs. "I'll take Drew upstairs with me. You can stay down here and help." She took the infant. After removing his snowsuit, Judy lay him on a blanket on the floor. Funny, it had only been a month since she saw him, but he had grown so much.

Judy went into the kitchen and opened the refrigerator. It was crammed, but nothing appealed to her. She went to the phone and ordered pizza. She took out enough money to cover the cost of it, putting several bills on the table by the door.

The baby began to fuss so she rocked him. Happy sounds drifted up from the basement to her. Tears stung her eyes and she held the baby closer.

When the doorbell rang, Clark bounded up the steps to answer the door.

"I ordered pizza. The money is right there on the table." She talked only loud enough for Clark to hear, not wanting to wake the now sleeping infant.

"What do you want me to do with these?" Clark had the pizza boxes in his arms.

"Take them downstairs. There are plates and napkins on the bar and drinks in the fridge down there."

Clark started to leave, then said. "Aren't you going to eat?" There was concern in his voice.

"I just got Drew to sleep."

"Mom, you need to eat something." How could this man go from being a petulant little boy to a caring adult in the matter of hours?

"Oh, you talked me into it." Holding her grandson, she went down to join the rest of her family. The girls set up everything in minutes. There was no need to tell everyone to dig in, except for Kevin.

Grace put a couple of slices of pizza on a plate and brought it over to him. "What would you like to drink?"

"A beer." He took a big mouthful of food. Grace brought him a beer. Then, she sat down next to Ellyn. Andy put the baby in the carrier.

Judy sat on a bar stool next to her granddaughter.

"I love pizza. It's my favorite." There was tomato sauce smeared from ear to ear.

"It's one of my favorites too." Judy took a bite. She had been hungry and not realized it. When was the last time she had anything to eat?

Ellyn held up the poster of pictures. "I think we have all we can get on here. We were wondering if we could take the wedding picture of you and Dad from your dresser and the family picture from the wall?"

"Sure." Judy gladly let the children take over. "Will you also take down the picture of your dad? You know, the one we had taken just before Christmas. We're going to have it in the front of the church for the service."

"What do you think of the poster?" Ellyn asked. She brought it over to her mother. Judy looked at it. Funny how one's life could be summed up with just a few photos.

"Good selections. You covered his life very well. Grace, you and Kevin don't have to stay in a motel. You can use your dad's office to sleep in. The sofa makes into a fairly comfortable bed.

Sandra also said you could stay with them."

"Kevin and I are staying at that new motel right by the shopping center and freeway."

"Nonsense. You don't need to spend that kind of money." She knew what Sandra told her about the arrangements but was going to offer anyway.

Grace lowered her voice, "Kevin and I talked this over and this is what he wants."

Judy shrugged. "Well, the offer stands for anytime. You can always change your minds."

"Thanks, Mom," They both turned to see Kevin standing a few feet behind them.

"Grace, I think we should go. It's been a long day and I'm tired." Kevin stood up.

"I was hoping to stay a while longer." Grace started to clean up supper.

"You can come tomorrow."

Grace didn't say anything more. She set down the plates and went upstairs. Judy followed. Grace shrugged into her coat and kissed her mother on the cheek. "I'll see you tomorrow. Ellyn's picking me up early tomorrow morning so Kevin can sleep in. Thanks for supper."

Judy stood there for a moment, lost in thought. What was going on with Kevin and Grace? Grace always had such a sparkle and a mind of her own. Judy wanted to have a chance to talk to her oldest child alone.

"What's with Grace?"

Judy jumped. She hadn't heard Ellyn come to stand beside her.

"Maybe she's just tired."

"Yeah and I'm Daffy Duck."

"Come on, let's go and see that poster again."

V

Everyone was in a better mood in the morning. Clark whistled as he came upstairs to the kitchen. "What can I help you with, Mom?"

"I was just sorting through the mail that's stacked up." Judy threw an envelope on the floor beside her. She looked over the top of her glasses. "There are plenty of things for breakfast, but you'll have to fix it."

"Did you make any coffee?" Ellyn appeared in the doorway.

"Help yourself." Judy motioned toward the counter by the sink. "Where's Tina?"

"Snoring." Ellyn laughed.

"She is rather loud, isn't she?" Clark said. Then he looked at his mother.

"Just not under my roof." Judy didn't even look up.

"Does ESP come with conception of the firstborn or the birth?" Clark asked.

Clark and Ellyn laughed. Judy just shook her head and grinned.

Tina joined them. "What's so funny?"

"Good morning," Judy looked up.

Clark went over and gave Tina a kiss. "Want some juice or coffee or something?"

"A glass of juice will be fine." Tina sat down next to Judy. "You always have so much fun. My mom is so busy, she hardly ever talks to me."

"Your mom has a high pressure job and does her best." Judy knew about Tina's mother. She raised Tina by herself and provided very well for her.

Tina sighed.

Judy stacked the mail and stood up. "I'm going to my room and take a shower."

Things seemed so normal. Sitting in the kitchen, going through mail, the kids coming in and talking. Steve usually was gone by the time the kids got up.

Closing her bedroom door behind her, Judy went into the bathroom. Once in the shower, her mind kept whirling. What needed to be done today? Not a whole lot. Pastor Lynn would complete the plans for the memorial service. There was enough food in the house. The house was clean and the laundry was pretty much caught up. The day stretched before her, looking dull and boring. She was restless. Maybe she should go for a long walk.

The phone was ringing when she got out of the shower. Then there was a knock on her door.

"Mom, it's Aunt Sandra," Clark said.

"Okay, I'll take it in here." She wrapped the towel around her and sat on the edge of the bed. "Hi, sis," She heard the click as the other phone hung up. "What's up?"

"How are you doing?"

"Fine."

"Did you sleep good last night?"

"Not too bad." The truth was that Judy never was a good sleeper. She had suffered with bouts of insomnia ever since she was ten years old.

"What are your plans for today?"

"I have no plans, though I was thinking about going for a long walk."

"I have to find a dress. Want to come along?"

Judy debated for a moment. Would she be better off pacing around her house and listening to the kids or pacing around the shopping mall and listening to her sister? "When are you picking me up?"

Sandra chuckled. "I knew you would say that. We can have lunch at that new tearoom afterwards. I'll be by in a half hour."

"Great. Now I'm sitting here, wearing a towel and freezing."

"See you!"

Judy wondered what she should wear. Her sister always looked chic, even when she was painting the house. If they were going to the tearoom, jeans would probably be out of place. Khaki pants and a navy jacket would do. Next to the jacket was Steve's suit. A wave of sadness enfolded her and she flung herself across the bed, weeping. She would have to get rid of his clothes and other personal items, but not right now.

She splashed cold water on her face and hurriedly got ready to meet her sister.

"I'm going with Aunt Sandra to the mall. Then we're going to have lunch someplace."

"Where's your cell phone?" Clark asked his mother.

"In my purse, but I think it needs charging. I so rarely use it."

"Here, take this one in case we have to get in touch with

you." He thrust a cell phone into her hand.

"I'm going to be gone only a few hours."

"Mom, just take it." Clark spoke with his new authority.

"Okay."

"Grace called while you were in the shower. I'm going over to get her in a little while," Ellyn said.

"Well, I hope Kevin goes and sees his old buddies instead of coming." Clark helped his mother on with her coat.

Judy didn't even want to enter that conversation. She knew that Clark and Ellyn only tolerated Kevin for Grace's sake.

There was a beep of a horn and Judy saw Sandra's car in the drive. "Gotta go." She fled out the door.

While Sandra tried on dress after dress, Judy wandered around the mall.

"Are you sure you don't need a new dress?" Sandra asked several times.

"I have a couple of outfits at home." Judy didn't want or need a new dress.

Sandra just shrugged and bought two dresses and a pair of pants.

The tearoom wasn't as fancy as Judy imagined. There were several women in wearing sweat suits and sneakers. When they were seated, they ordered iced tea.

Sandra leaned in her chair. "Now what are you going to do?"

"About what?" Sandra always spoke in riddles.

"About the house, I mean, condo? And what about the place down in Arizona?"

"I haven't really thought of that."

"Are you going to be okay financially?"

"I should be with my school pension, Social Security and

other assets." Judy filed a mental note to go over finances when she went home.

The waitress brought their drinks. Sandra emptied two packets of Sweet & Low into her tea. Then she stirred her tea for a long time. The clink, clink, clink about drove Judy over the edge.

"Will you cut that out?" Judy put her hand over Sandra's.

"Sorry." Sandra put a straw into her tea. Again, she twirled the ice around, creating the clinking noise.

I give up, Judy thought. "You know, I don't have to make any plans right away anyway."

They ordered lunch. They talked about benign topics like the weather and the new addition to the library.

"When was the last time you ate anything?" Sandra asked.

Judy realized she had wolfed down her sandwich in a matter of a few minutes. She swallowed the last bite. "We had pizza for supper last night."

"You have to eat to keep up your strength."

They both laughed. They had an obese uncle who used to eat only to "keep up his strength."

"I'll try." Judy wiped her mouth with a cloth napkin.

Sandra dropped Judy off at the house. "I'll see you tomorrow at the church...unless you need me sooner."

"No, that's okay. The kids are all here. Thanks for the diversion and lunch."

The children were sitting in the living room and were very quiet.

"What's going on?" This was not normal for her children. It was way too quiet. She hung her coat in the closet.

"The kids are napping," Tammie said.

"Mom, I want you to see this." Clark went over to where

Grace sat. She tried to pull away from him, but he pushed up her sweater sleeve.

Hideous bruise marks were visible across the room.

"Honey, what happened?" Judy went to take a closer look.

"Kevin did that to her," Clark said through clenched teeth.

Judy tried to look Grace in the eyes, but Grace wouldn't meet her mother's gaze, she just yanked her sleeve back down. "Is Clark telling the truth?" She knew Clark wouldn't lie about that. Still, she wanted Grace to answer for herself. She felt sick to her stomach.

Grace uttered a weak, "Yes."

"Tell her everything." This time, it was Andy.

Grace swallowed. "Kevin pinched me when I didn't move fast enough yesterday."

"Tell Mom the rest of it," Ellyn prodded. Judy's head began to ache.

"He shoved me down last night."

Andy went over and pulled up Grace's pant leg, revealing a scraped knee which also was bruised.

"But he said he was sorry," Grace said without conviction, as she stared at the floor.

"I take it this isn't the first time he's hit you?" Judy tilted Grace's chin so she had to look into her mother's eyes. Grace didn't need to say anything for Judy to know it wasn't.

"We're not going to let her go back," Clark said.

"But he'll get real angry."

"No matter how angry a man gets, he has no right to hurt you," said Tammie. Judy was amazed at the rancor in her daughter-in-law's voice. Tammie was always so calm.

"We'll take care of that," Ellyn said.

So far Judy hadn't said much of anything. Her children were

suddenly adults and acting like it. They had circled the wagons around one of their own. She was proud of them, but extremely concerned about what Kevin might do.

"But my job," Grace said.

"We need nurses here too," Tina chimed in.

"You bet we do and I'll bet they get paid better around here," Ellyn said.

"But what about my clothes and other things?"

"They're just things," Clark said.

"Kevin will be mad." Grace grimaced.

"You can have my room. I'm going to do some missionary work in Africa. I'm leaving in a few weeks," Ellyn said.

"Yeah, you can keep Mom company," Clark said.

All eyes went to Judy. Things were beginning to spin out of control. Steve was gone. Ellyn was going to Africa. Now Grace was in an abusive marriage. She was always Steve's special child, Daddy's little girl.

"That would be fine. I'm not sure what I'm going to do, but it would at least work for the time being." Judy spoke slowly. There was no way she could deny any of her children under the circumstances. She had no idea how she was going to come to grips without Steve, and now this.

"See? I told you Mom would be great about this," Clark said to Grace. He got up and gave his mother a hug. "Hey, Andy, let's go over and get Grace's belongings out of the hotel room and away from that lowlife."

Judy's heart sank. She was afraid that one of her sons would lose his temper, and how would Kevin react?

"Don't worry, Mom, we'll be good little boys and not beat up the big bully." Andy raised his right hand.

Judy had to be by herself for a while. She was about to hit

overload. Too much at one time. "I'm going to take a nap."

"Okay. We'll answer the phone and everything," Tammie said.

"Let's go down and rearrange the room so you have room for your things, Grace," Ellyn said. "Tina, you and Tammie can help."

The four young women went downstairs. Judy could hear them chatting about moving this and putting that in a different place.

In her room, Judy took off everything but her bra and panties and slipped on her robe. She covered herself and plumped up her pillow a couple of times, trying to get comfortable.

"Oh, Steve, why did you have to die? I need your help coping with our children." The tears slid down her cheeks and into the pillow. "I don't know if I can make it without you."

She fell into a deep sleep. Dreaming of such disconnected events, she woke up confused and dazed. Everything felt out of sync. Then she remembered Steve was dead. She would be alone.

Aware of the bustling about on the other side of the door, Judy lay, trying to ignore it, but finally she looked at the clock. Seven A.M. Oh, my gosh. She'd slept through the night. It was morning! After putting on her slippers, Judy went into the kitchen.

"Hi, Mom," Ellyn said brightly. "I hope we didn't wake you up."

"I was awake anyway."

Grace was huddled up in the kitchen with her hands wrapped around a cup of something hot. From the aroma, it was probably hot chocolate.

"That was some nap you had," Ellyn said as she poured her mother a cup of coffee.

"I can't believe I slept until morning. I've never done that before in my life. I feel a lot better than I did. Must have needed it." She took a sip of the hot liquid. She turned to Grace. "How are you doing?"

"I've been better." Grace took a spoon and stirred her drink.

"We all have." Judy took another sip.

"Did you ever try and sleep three women in one bedroom?" Ellyn wrinkled her nose.

"Many times. You forget there were three of us girls and two boys in a three bedroom house." Judy said. She had told them the story of growing up in a big family and only three bedrooms and one bath.

"Yeah, I forgot."

Judy looked around. "Tina still sleeping?"

"No, she and Clark got up this morning for a jog. They should be back any time."

Ellyn went over to the phone. "I guess I can put this back now." She hung up the receiver.

"What was that all about?"

"Kevin called me several times last night." Grace said.

"Finally, I'd had enough," Ellyn said.

"I certainly hope someone didn't need to get in touch with us in an emergency." Judy thought it rather strange the phone hadn't woken her up. She didn't remember hearing it ring at all.

As soon as the phone was hung up, it began to ring. Ellyn answered the phone and handed it to her mother.

Judy put her hand over the mouthpiece, "Who?"

"Aunt Sandra," Ellyn answered. "I'll go turn your phone on.

I shut the ringer off before you took your long nap." That explained that.

"What's going on?" Sandra asked before Judy had a chance to say anything.

"What do you mean?"

"I've been trying to get you last night and then again this morning. Who's the gabby one?"

"We had the receiver off. What do you want?" Judy didn't mean to sound so short.

"What time should we be at the church this afternoon?"

"Three."

"Fine. Now why was the receiver off?"

"I'll tell you later." Judy looked over toward Grace who was rinsing her cup out in the sink.

"You don't want someone to overhear you?"

"That's right. We'll see you then." Judy was glad Sandra was so quick to pick up on the tone of her voice. It was like ESP they'd had since they were kids.

The front door banged open. Clark and Tina came gasping in.

"Wow, am I out of shape or what?" Clark collapsed on a chair with Tina next to him.

"You're not panting as hard as Clark," Judy said.

"I've been running twice a day and Clark hasn't been doing it at all."

"I've been pretty busy, but I'm going to get to it now." He bent over and took off his shoes. "I don't want to be like Dad."

"What a dumb thing to say!" Ellyn exploded.

"I didn't mean it the way it sounded," Clark defended himself.

"Oh, just shut up before you say something even worse," Ellyn snapped.

Judy turned so he couldn't see the tears well up in her eyes. She knew Clark didn't mean to remind her, but the words hit hard. She had worried over Steve's health for so long. He wasn't much overweight, but just out of shape. Golfing was almost all the exercise he ever got.

"I'm going to take a shower," Tina said as she got up.

"Yeah, me, too." Clark picked up his shoes and stood also.

"Not together. Coordinate it with your sisters." The words came out so fast. It was like when they had all been teenagers.

"No problemo," he called over his shoulder.

Taking her coffee with her, Judy went into the living room to watch the "Today Show". Things seemed too normal. Even what she was doing, was normal. Life was going on just like nothing happened. Didn't everyone know that she had lost the love of her life? Her soulmate. She would be alone to cope with everyday problems. She curled her feet around her on the sofa and dragged on the afghan, tucking it around her feet.

The phone rang, one of the kids answered it. There were some angry shouts from downstairs, but she couldn't understand what was being said. She got up and went to the head of the stairs. "What's going on?"

"That was Kevin. He wasn't in the room when we got Grace's things yesterday," Clark answered, "and I told him in no uncertain terms what he could do."

I'm sure you did, Judy thought.

"If he even shows his face around here, I'll rearrange it."

"Just cool down," Judy said and went to watch TV.

She didn't need anything else to happen right now. All she

needed was to have Clark hauled up on charges of assaulting Kevin. Actually, she was more worried about Kevin seeking revenge on one of the family. Secretly, she feared what he might do if crossed. Well, she would know soon enough.

The day went quickly. The phone rang often. Well-meaning friends and neighbors dropped off food and offers to help if she needed it. Judy wished she could go to sleep and wake up when the whole funeral and was over.

VI

They walked into church together. It was an odd feeling to know the service was to remember Steve, but he wasn't here. His ashes remained at home, in the bedroom he and Judy shared. She felt aware and alert all during the visitation and service, but she couldn't remember much of what happened afterwards. She couldn't have told anyone who was there or who wasn't.

There was a light supper put on at the church after the service. Ellyn brought her mother a plate of food. She nibbled a bit on a sandwich and some chips. Had she eaten a cookie? She didn't know, nor did she care. Tomorrow morning they would put Steve's ashes in the mausoleum.

It was almost midnight when they returned to the condo. Without any more than a "Goodnight," they all went to their rooms.

Judy was exhausted. She laid her clothes over a chair. After putting on a flannel nightgown, she brushed and flossed her teeth. The only light came from a street light and the moon coming in the bedroom window. She didn't want the glare of the bright lights over the mirror.

When she got into bed, the sheets felt cold. After wiggling around to get warm, she gave up. There was an old quilt on the top shelf of the closet. It was heavy, but it would keep her warm. Another bout of wiggling to try and get comfortable. She was wide awake. Her mind raced. Her hand was sore from the many handshakes. If only she could cry and release some of the tension. But no tears came.

She got up and took some aspirin. That sometimes helped her relax. Then back to bed for another session of tossing and turning.

There was a sharp rap at her door. Judy struggled under the weight of the quilt to look at her clock. It was eight.

"Hey, Mom, what time are we supposed to be at the cemetery?" It was Ellyn.

Judy cleared her throat. "Ten. I'm going to get up and take a shower before I come out." She threw the bedding aside and sat on the edge of the bed. She hadn't felt like this since her college days when she drank too much beer. No, this was worse.

A shower helped to revive her. She dressed in a pantsuit and comfortable shoes. It would be cold in the cemetery. Hopefully, Pastor Lynn would be brief with her comments. Judy was relieved by Pastor Lynn's suggestion of having the internment private.

Everyone was there, eating in the kitchen.

"I fixed you some eggs and toast," Grace said as she dished up some food and handed it to her mother.

"Coffee will be fine." The thought of food nauseated Judy.

"Mom, you have to eat something," Ellyn said.

Clark played the trump card. "Dad would be upset."

Her children were becoming her parents and it was starting

to rankle her. Steve was always on her case about not eating when she was upset.

"Okay. I'll at least give it a try." She took a forkful of scrambled eggs.

"Would you like some jam for your toast, Mrs. Evans?" Tina asked.

"She prefers honey," Clark said.

"Either one will be fine."

"I'm going to take my shower now. Everyone else has taken theirs." Ellyn got up and put her dishes in the sink.

"Clark and I'll clean up the kitchen," Tina said. Clark made a face, but didn't say anything.

Good for you, Tina, Judy thought. Maybe there's hope for him yet. She managed to eat about half of the eggs and a piece of toast.

"Now drink your juice." Clark said as he pointed to the glass of orange juice by Judy's plate.

Judy was going to say that she didn't like orange juice in the morning, but changed her mind. She was annoyed at Clark's patronizing tone but let it go. She gulped down the lukewarm juice and smiled. "Thanks for everything." She quickly took a drink of coffee to kill the taste of the juice.

"Can we all get into the Buick?" Clark asked.

"I'm sure we can. Parking is at a premium at the cemetery," Judy answered.

Ellyn came into the room with a towel wrapped around her head. "Aunt Sandra made reservations at a restaurant afterwards."

"When did she tell you that?" Then Judy looked at her daughter. "Did you turn off my phone again?"

Ellyn looked guilty. "Mom, you need your rest."

"I don't care. Just don't do it again." Judy sighed and took another sip of her coffee and then took the mug and went into the living room.

She could hear the soft murmur of voices coming from the kitchen where Clark and Tina were loading the dishwasher. They sounded like good friends. The edge she saw in Clark a couple of days ago had vanished. He hadn't changed since he was little. Always one to see how far he could go, but then taking the limits in stride.

Judy brought her coffee cup into the kitchen. "Here's the last thing."

"Do you want to run it while we're gone?" Clark asked.

"I don't see why not." Judy left the kitchen and went to finish getting ready.

Judy carried Steve's ashes out. She wanted to hold them on the way. They all crowded into the Buick. Clark insisted on driving. Judy was glad he did. Ellyn had a lead foot and Grace was so easily sidetracked, it made everyone nervous.

"Andy, Tammie, and the kids will meet us there," Grace said.

"I know. He told me last night," Judy answered automatically. She did remember something from the night before after all.

Everyone was so quiet. Judy usually had the radio on whenever she went someplace, but she had shut it off when she went to the store the last time. Nobody made any attempt to turn it on. There had always been an argument about what kind of music they would listen to.

The cemetery was at the edge of town and only a ten minute drive. Still, it seemed a lot farther than that. Already there were many cars. I thought this was going to be a small gathering, Judy mused.

"We're supposed to park right up front." Clark drove the big car up to the front of the line and parked.

Why do we have to park up here, Judy thought. We're not going anyplace. Steve's ashes are going in the mausoleum. Oh, well, she wasn't going to ask any questions. Frankly, she didn't care where they parked.

Sandra came up and put her arm around Judy's waist. "How ya doing, kid?" she whispered.

"Fine," Judy gave her a half grin. They both knew she was lying.

Andy and Clark walked on each side of her. The young women followed behind.

"Granma," came a small voice from behind.

Judy stopped and turned. Katie's round face was ringed by the hood of her jacket. The little one held out her arms. After she handed Steve's ashes to Clark, Judy took her and held her close. A security blanket. No, more like a talisman.

"Are you sad?" The little face was nose to nose with Judy's.

"Yes, I am." Judy fought tears.

The family continued to walk. Some man in a black wool topcoat opened the doors of the small building for them. "Mrs. Evans." He nodded his head in greeting. It was the cemetery's director. Clark handed him the package with Steve's ashes. "I'll transfer these to the urn you selected." Judy just gave him a little smile and went on.

There wasn't much room in the mausoleum. Pastor Lynn was already there. She gave Judy an embrace and rubbed her back for a moment. "Is everyone here?" she asked. Judy nodded. "Then let's start."

Pastor Lynn read a couple of scriptures while piped in organ music played in the background. Can the music, Judy thought.

Pastor Lynn gave a prayer and nodded to the director. He led the way to a glass case. With a key he unlocked it and place the urn inside. Then closed it. Pastor Lynn gave a benediction.

Why had she let them talk her into putting Steve's ashes in here? Maybe she should have scattered them someplace. Too late now.

Then they were all moving into the cold outdoors. Judy's feet were numb.

"We're going to the Steak Ranch. Anyone who wants to can join us," Sandra announced in a loud voice.

"We'll see you there." Andy gave his mother a kiss on the cheek and went to join his wife and children.

"Granma," Katie called.

"You can't go with Grandma right now. You have to sit in your car seat. We'll go to the restaurant and then you can see her," Judy heard her daughter-in-law say.

"Grace." A deep voice spoke behind them. It was Kevin. "I came to get you. We need to leave now to get to work tomorrow." He was smiling and carrying a small jeweler's box. "Here, I bought this little token of apology, darling," He popped open the box as he handed it to her, A small diamond pendant lay on dark blue velvet. "I love you so much." Charm was oozing out of every pore.

"She's not going with you." Clark pushed aside Kevin's hand and stepped protectively in front of his sister.

"She can talk for herself." Kevin never took his eyes off Grace. "Come, sweetheart, or we won't be home in time to go back to work."

Please, God, not here and not now, Judy prayed silently. She didn't want anything more to happen. She didn't want Clark to take a swing at Kevin. And she certainly didn't want Grace to go with him, either.

Grace stepped around Clark, but she stayed just out of Kevin's reach. "I'm not going back with you."

"What about all your belongings?" Kevin kept smiling. "And the wonderful life we have together?"

"Sell everything. Give it away. Or keep it. I don't care." Grace's voice was barely audible, but there was a firmness to it.

Judy was amazed at the strength her daughter was showing.

"What about your job? And my school tuition?"

Ah-ha, Judy thought. Now the truth is coming through.

"I can get a job here. There's a big demand for nurses anywhere in the country." Grace took a breath. "As for your schooling, ask your parents. Besides, you shouldn't be spending money you don't have." She pointed to the necklace, then walked over to the car.

Kevin took a step forward, but Clark stepped in front of him, blocking his way. "Leave her alone," he said so softly, Judy was sure no one else heard.

They got in the car and drove away. Kevin was still standing in the spot.

"So he wants your money," Ellyn said.

"I guess that's it." Grace reached for a Kleenex.

"Do you have much?" Ellyn asked.

"No, not really. Most of my important things, like pictures and books, are here with Mom and Dad." She paused. "He's probably pissed to think we won't be buying the house we looked at."

Judy cringed at the vernacular her daughter used, but said nothing. The girls talked about plans Grace would have to make, but Judy barely listened. She stared out the window. This is really happening to me, she thought. I'll never feel the

49

warmth of Steve's body next to mine. Never have the long talks about this and that. No more irritations about little habits, like laying wet towels over wooden chairs or throwing away the newspaper before she read it.

"Mom? What are you thinking about?" Ellyn asked, snapping Judy out of her thoughts.

"Your dad and how life will be without him."

Ellyn patted her shoulder. "I know, Mom. I know."

No, you don't really, Judy thought. Not until you've gone through it and even then, it's different for everyone.

The restaurant had reserved a separate room for them. A few friends and family members were already there. Sandra had Judy seated at the head of the table.

"I'd rather be in the middle," Judy said. She could talk to people easier that way. And right now, she needed to be in the midst of those who meant so much to her and Steve.

For a while, Judy was able to push her grief to the back of her mind.

"This is the latest picture of the twins." Someone handed her a wallet. Two little faces grinned toothlessly with drool on their chins.

"They are so cute." Judy meant it.

No one mentioned Steve. It was like he never existed. They probably didn't want to remind her and have her break into tears.

Pastor Lynn said a short grace and the waitress came in to take their orders.

Judy was hungry. She ordered a large Cobb salad and iced tea. "I've had enough coffee for today," she explained when her sister seemed startled by the order. "You're having a coke."

Sandra nodded. "You're right," and then continued on with

her conversation with a cousin who sat next to her.

Judy's salad was too big, so she had it boxed up to take home. It'll be a good supper, she thought. Just a glass of wine, some bread and the salad. Just like when Steve was gone for a couple of days.

VII

The house seemed so empty. Clark and Tina left right away.

"I've got to catch up on the classes I missed and so does Tina," Clark said as if he had to explain their departure. "I'll call when we get home." He kissed his mother and said, "Love ya."

Tina gave her a hug. "Thanks for letting me be a part of your family."

The words struck Judy like a punch, though she didn't say anything. She was too choked up. She remembered the conversation they shared the first night she was home.

"I'm going to help Grace make some order out of the guest room. Clark probably left it a mess," Ellyn said.

Judy had to laugh. Of her four children, Clark was probably the most meticulous of all. Even if Ellyn thought she was. "Do whatever you want. I'm going to finish going through the mail. A lot has piled up since we...I got back." She put her salad in the refrigerator and sat down at the kitchen table.

She put the bills in one stack, cards and letters in another, a pile of ads and catalogues and everything else in another stack. She got up and got a glass of water. Then she went to find the checkbook. She knew she was stalling.

Finally, she opened the bills. Ellyn usually forwarded the bills to them, but hadn't yet. Almost everything was deducted automatically from their account. All she did was subtract each from the balance. She hadn't thought about finances until now. She remembered someone saying something about accounts being frozen. What about the life insurance policies they paid on all these years?

Judy went to the desk and pulled out the insurance file. There was also a copy of their wills. She better call a lawyer on that one. Together, they had a decent income, but Steve's would be gone now. It was already after four. Probably no one would be in the office any longer that day.

She set the checkbook and bills aside. Next, she went through the ads and catalogues. They all went in the wastebasket. There was a large stack of cards and letters. She took them into the living room and set them on the coffee table. Then she went in and changed into her robe and slippers.

Judy knew she was bouncing from one thing to another, but couldn't seem to help herself. She went and got her coffee and a letter opener. She couldn't believe what she found. There were letters and notes in many of the cards, all telling her how sorry they were about Steve's death. They were from students she had and some from Steve's former students. Old neighbors and long forgotten friends. Tucked inside many of the envelopes were checks and cash. Who would send cash through the mail these days, Judy wondered.

After making a list of gifts of money, Judy tucked the checks and cash into an envelope and put it in her purse. She found the list of people who brought over food. She hoped the children were diligent about recording everything. She stapled the two lists to a third list of those who sent flowers and plants. Maybe she could get the girls to help write notes So much to do. She went and watched TV.

"Mom, where's the newspaper?" Grace called from the kitchen.

"We stopped getting everything but the Sunday paper and quit that while we were gone." Another thing to do. Call the newspaper and start Sunday delivery.

"Can I take the car and go buy one?"

"The keys are on the hall table." Damn, now she'd have to share the car with Grace. What an awful way to think, she told herself. She'd have to make arrangements to have the minivan driven from Arizona.

She flipped through the channels. Nothing interesting. CNN would at least give some semblance of intellect.

Ellyn postponed her mission trip a few more weeks. "Thought I'd stick around and hang with Grace until she gets a job. We might not get a chance like this for many years."

"I think I'd really enjoy just to have you both here for a while," Judy said.

The next few days, Judy got very little done. She just couldn't concentrate. She'd make lists and misplace them. She'd look over the list and pick out the easiest task, do it and cross it off. It gave her a small sense of accomplishment. She wasn't fooling herself. She had to get organized and get certain things done.

Resolutely, she sat down at the kitchen table and started to write out thank you notes. I didn't deposit those checks, she thought in a panic. She started to dig through the stacks of papers. Now where are they? I remember putting them in an envelope but where is the envelope? I didn't accidently throw it out, did I? Anxiety set in as she went through the contents of the kitchen wastebasket. Coffee grounds and banana peels stuck to everything. No envelope. She was relieved she hadn't thrown it out, but was still frantic to find the money.

Maybe if I go back to what I was doing, it'll come to me. She wrote several cards and addressed them. There was one address she couldn't find. It was in her wallet. She went to her purse and there was the envelope. She forgot about the address.

Judy put on her coat and went out to the car. She had to get this to the bank. It took a while in line. Must be Social Security check day; elderly people were in front of her. Same long lines were at the grocery store and post office. She didn't really mind. The only thing waiting for her at home, were more thank you notes to write.

At home, she parked the car in the drive, grabbed her purse and packages and went into the house.

"Mom, where have you been?" Ellyn came running into the hall. "We got up and you and the car were gone. Grace has a job interview in an hour. She needs the car."

"She didn't tell me that. I had some errands to run. I won't need the car anymore today." Judy really wanted to say it was her car and her life, but she knew it would only make matters worse.

A short time later, both girls were gone. Grace was going to drop Ellyn someplace and then go on to her interview. Judy felt extremely free with the house to herself, if only for a few hours.

The doorbell rang. Damn, Judy thought. But she went and answered it anyway. It was Calvin from across the street. He and Steve had golfed together for years. Their children were about the same age and his wife, Sue and Judy did many things together.

"Hi, come on in."

"Oh, I just stopped by. Sue thought you might need some help."

"I was just going to have some coffee. Would you like some, too?" Judy headed toward the kitchen and Calvin followed.

As she reached for a mug on a shelf, Calvin came up behind her and cupped her breasts in his hands. He rubbed suggestively against her rear.

"What are you doing?" She jumped and dropped the cup. She tried to dislodge his hands, but he just squeezed more.

"Don't you miss this?" he whispered in her ear.

She struggled and finally freed herself. Whirling around, she looked at his smirking face. "What gives you the right to touch me?"

"I was just going to help you out." He shrugged.

"Get out and don't ever come back here again."

He left without saying another word. Judy started to shake. She collapsed onto a chair and put her head on her arms and wept. Her stomach churned. She never felt more humiliated in her life. How could she have let this happen? How would she ever face Sue again? She went into the bathroom and threw up. Then she took a long hot shower. Try as she might, she couldn't wash off the feeling of Calvin's hands.

Judy tried to think what she had done to provoke Calvin's behavior. Could she have given off some signal he misunderstood? No guy ever came on to her before. She had always been friends with them. She even wondered if Steve had ever behaved like that. No, he wouldn't have. Steve never made suggestive remarks about other women whether in a group or when they were alone. Calvin made comments, even when his wife was present.

"Something wrong, Mom? You look rather pale," Ellyn said when she and Grace got back.

"I'm just fine." Judy smiled. She was too embarrassed to say anything to her daughters.

Over the next few weeks, Calvin's wife, Sue called several times to ask Judy to go out to lunch or shopping. Judy made some feeble excuse each time. The very thought of Calvin made her skin crawl. Soon Sue stopped calling.

Judy thought about telling Sandra about what Calvin did, but she just felt so embarrassed about the whole incident. She tried to push it from her mind. So, she decided to go back to Arizona to close up the park model and bring back the minivan. It needed to be done. May as well get through the sooner the better. She dreaded the thought.

VIII

"I'm going to fly down to Arizona and bring the van back," Judy said to Sandra over the phone a month after the funeral.

"All by yourself?"

"Why not?" Then Judy had an idea. It might be easier if she didn't go by herself. "Unless you want to go with me. I'll take care of all expenses."

"Brad wouldn't like it."

To hell with Brad, Judy thought, but said, "Well, then I guess I'll go alone."

"What about one of the girls?"

"Grace just started a new job and Ellyn's getting ready to go to Africa."

"Yeah, that's right."

"Grace and I are taking Ellyn to the airport on Sunday. I'm going to see if I can get a flight out on Tuesday. I may stay a week or so before coming back. I'll drive the minivan home. There are some odds and ends I need to take care of. Besides, I love the desert in spring."

Sandra sighed. "It really sounds great."

"The offer still stands." Judy held her breath. It would be so much fun for just the two of them. And, most of all, she wouldn't have to be there by herself.

"Well, let me talk to Brad. If you're going to pick up the tab, maybe he won't mind so much."

"Let me know soon."

Wouldn't it be fun if Kathy could join them? With Kathy living just outside Denver, it wouldn't be far for her to go. They hadn't seen each other for over a year. Judy picked up the phone and then put it down again. She better wait until she heard from Sandra.

Much to her surprise, Sandra called back later that day. "Brad said it would be fine with him."

"Great, but doesn't that make you wonder what he's up to?" Judy laughed.

"He's got some project going on at work. But I think the part about you footing the bill was the deciding point."

Mr. Tightwad. "Say, how about if I call Kathy and see if she can come down for a few days, too?"

"That would be fun. I haven't seen her for a couple of years."

"Then I'll do it tonight." Judy had dreaded going to their place in Arizona, but now she looked forward to it. It would be so much fun to show Sandra around and if Kathy could come...

Kathy didn't even hesitate. "You bet. Just tell me when."

"I have to make flight reservations. As soon as I do, I'll give you a call."

"When are you going to join the 21st century and get email?"

"The kids have been on me about that too, but I don't know. I think I'm too old to learn about computers and all that stuff."

"You'd be surprised at what you can still learn."

Judy made the reservations and called Kathy before she let

her children know what she was up to.

"That's cool," Grace said. "I'm glad I'm here. You won't have to stop the mail or anything." Judy let the other three know. Before she left, she had an appointment with her attorney.

"Everything's pretty straightforward with the estate. You should get a new will made as soon as possible," the attorney said.

"As soon as I get back." She paused. "Why don't you draw one up while I'm gone? I can look it over and sign it."

"That wouldn't be too difficult."

For the time being, things might be a bit tight. With Steve's death, his pension was gone. It was almost half of the income. She might have to make some tough choices, but not for now. Now she was going to enjoy a visit with her sisters away from children and husbands. Well, husband. Kathy was single.

It was frigid when they left Milwaukee, but it was different when Judy and Sandra landed in Phoenix. The weather was warmer with a hint of spring. They took an airport shuttle to the RV Park.

Judy paid the driver.

Before they went inside, Sandra turned around a couple of times. "This looks like a postcard. The palm trees and all."

"It sure does. We'll take a day and go out to the desert and take pictures."

Judy had left the unit in good shape, she thought. The unit was hot and stale from being closed up. She switched on the air conditioning.

'Whew! Is it ever hot in here!" Sandra said. She wrinkled her nose. "What's that awful smell?"

Judy opened up the cabinet under the sink "Whew! I must have forgotten to empty this." She took out the wastebasket and set it outside. "It'll cool off in a bit. Besides, it'll be pretty chilly once the sun goes down."

"When did you say Kathy would be here?"

"She said something about dinner time." Judy checked the refrigerator. At least she'd cleaned out everything but a few jars of salad dressing and some mustard. Nothing in the freezer except some ice.

"Anything I can do?"

"Sure. There's a dust rag in the closet over there."

Sandra made a face. "You always did give me that job."

"Privileges of being the older sister." The teasing felt good. Getting away felt good.

"After I take this garbage to the dumpster, I'm going to have to get some groceries," Judy said. No matter what she told people, she missed Steve desperately. She expected to see him around every corner. As much as she loved her sisters and looked forward to this time together, they were only substitutes for Steve.

"Do you want to unpack first?" Sandra jolted Judy out of her thoughts.

"We can or we can leave it until later."

"Who's going to sleep where?"

"Well, we can all sleep in the same bed. There is a king-sized one in our room."

"Or?"

Judy flipped a cushion off the sofa. "This makes into a queen-sized bed and the chair makes into a twin bed. Take your choice."

"This is pretty nifty." Sandra looked around. "Are you going to get rid of it?"

"I haven't decided." She hadn't. Much would depend on her

money situation.

"What do you do for fun?"

"There are lots of things." Judy picked up her purse and keys. "Come on. I'll tell you on the way to the store."

The van coughed a couple of times when Judy tried starting it. Then it sputtered to a start. Judy let out a sigh of relief.

As they drove to the main highway, Judy waved to several people.

"Everyone seems so friendly."

"They are." Then she remembered the incident with Calvin. "Wanna grab some lunch?" Judy asked.

"Sure." Sandra said.

Judy pulled the van into a spot at McDonald's. After a quick sandwich, they drove a couple of blocks to the grocery store.

Sandra pushed the cart while Judy threw a few items in it. "Same products as at home."

"Yup. I'll warn you, almost every store you shop in at home is down here. It's weird. Cookie cutter mentality. Sometimes I forget where I am. If it wasn't for the heat and palm trees, I'd think it was summer at home."

"I was hoping to see more of the Southwest flavor around." Sandra said.

"We'll do some sightseeing and find some of the traditional places."

"Kathy ever been down here to visit?"

"No, she's talked about it but hasn't gotten around to it yet. We went up to see her on our way home last year."

Kathy was waiting for them at the unit. After a round of hugs, they went inside.

"I got an early start. This place is pretty easy to find." Kathy sank down onto the sofa.

"Let me put it this away. Anyone for a cold beer or soda?"

They all decided a Coke would hit the spot.

"Did you have trouble getting the time off on short notice?" Sandra asked Kathy.

"I whined a lot."

Judy could just see the act her youngest sister must have put on. She had always been good at getting her own way.

"I have to be to work on Monday." She took a sip of her drink. She set the can on a coaster. "Sorry I didn't make it for the funeral."

"Nothing you could have done anyway," Judy said. "This means more to me."

There was a knock on the door. Judy went to answer it. The woman from the neighboring unit was there.

"Hi, come on in." Judy held open the door. "This is Lola from next door. These are my sisters, Kathy and Sandra. Would you like a cold soda?"

"No, thanks. I just stopped by to see how you were doing. Everyone was so sorry about Steve. You were gone before the news was out. Thanks, also, for those clothes you donated from your husband. " Lola sat down next to Kathy.

"I wanted to go home right away," Judy said. "I packed up Steve's clothes to fill the time. Glad someone could use them."

"So what do you do?" Lola turned to Sandra.

"I work in a nursery."

"I love babies."

"No, a plant nursery. A greenhouse."

"Oh, I get it. And what do you do?" She looked up at Kathy.

"I work for an insurance company in Colorado."

Lola wasn't the sharpest knife in the drawer. Judy hadn't really talked to her much in the past.

"And what about your families?"

"My husband is retired and my children are out on their own."

"I'm single," Kathy said.

"Oh, I'm sorry, dear." Lola reached over and patted Kathy's hand. She looked at her watch and stood up. "It's time for square dancing and I can't be late."

As soon as Lola was out the door, they all started to laugh.

"I'm sorry about that," Judy said when she caught her breath. "I don't know her well."

"What a character!" Kathy wiped her eyes.

"Poor thing. She seems so lonely."

"Lonely? Not by a long shot. The woman square dances almost daily, she plays bridge and shops. She's always on the go."

They unpacked and decided who was sleeping where. Kathy and Sandra would share the sofa bed and Judy would sleep on the fold out chair.

"That way, we won't have to shout to each other during the night." Sandra said.

Judy hadn't wanted to sleep in the big bed by herself as it was. She wasn't sure she could ever sleep in the bed she and Steve shared the last night he was alive. Funny, it didn't bother her to sleep alone in the bed at the condo.

Dinner was at a little local restaurant that featured Southwestern cuisine. Sandra and Kathy each had a couple of margaritas, but Judy stuck to diet coke.

"I'm driving, remember?"

They all ordered something different and then ate off of each other's plates.

Leaning back in her chair, Kathy said, "I'm stuffed."

Sandra just moaned.

There was still plenty of food left, so Judy had the waitress box it up so they could take it with them.

It was twilight when they got home. Judy put the food in the refrigerator. "How about a hike around the area?"

"I'm not sure I can even move." Sandra flopped onto the sofa.

"I'm game," Kathy said.

"We'll need light jackets." Judy went to the closet and hauled out three windbreakers.

"Well, I guess I'll join you." Sandra got up and put on a green jacket.

Judy left on a light and locked the door. "We'll go down this way and circle around. I'll show you the clubhouse and the pool."

The air was cool, but there was no breeze. It didn't take them long to get used to the coolness. They walked down the middle of the street. Occasionally, they would have to move to the side for a car or golf cart.

There was a bridge tournament in progress in the clubhouse and square dancing going on in a pavilion. Between sets, several people came up and offered their condolences. Judy was touched. She and Steve hadn't been coming here but two years and everyone was so supportive.

"Wow, I can hardly stand the reflection off all the white hair." Kathy squinted.

"Get used to it. It won't be long before we're all white like that, too." Sandra laughed.

"Not as long as there's hair dye." Judy had been coloring her hair for years.

On the way, a lizard slithered in front of Kathy and she gave a shriek.

"Are there snakes?" Sandra asked.

"Probably. I haven't seen any, but other people say they have."

When they got back to Judy's, the light was flashing on the answering machine. Judy pressed the button while they hung up their jackets.

"Hey, Mom, just wondering how things are going. Everything's fine here. Talk to you later." It was Grace.

Judy called her. There was no answer, so she left a message. "Hi, Sweetie. Everything is fine here. We're about to turn in. Talk to you soon."

They got ready for bed and switched on the TV. They watched a couple of shows and then the news.

"This is like our pajama parties," Kathy said.

"Just don't do anything to my hair," Sandra said.

"And no prank calls," Judy added. "Let's drive out to the desert tomorrow."

"Sounds good to me," Kathy said.

"Me, too," Sandra agreed.

As soon as the lights went out, they started to talk.

"How's your love life?" Sandra asked Kathy.

"There are a couple of guys I go out with, but nothing serious."

"I'm glad I'm not in the dating scene. There seem to be a lot of weirdos out there." Sandra gave a big yawn.

"You're right about the weirdos. This married neighbor guy came over and rubbed up against me and tried to get me to go to bed with him." Judy said.

"You can't be serious?!" Sandra said.

"It happens to me a lot," Kathy said. "You'll have to be

careful all the time."

"But I'm over sixty."

"They don't care."

It was long after midnight before they fell asleep. Judy had dreams of being chased by Calvin. Damn Kathy. Until that evening, Judy thought it had just been an isolated incident with Calvin. She would have to be on her guard. She hadn't thought about Steve's presence as being so protective-an invisible shield.

The next morning, Judy got up and slipped into her swimsuit. "I'm going down and take a quick swim before breakfast."

"Even before coffee?" Sandra didn't even open her eyes.

"Wait and I'll come, too." Kathy hopped out of bed. She gave Sandra a nudge. "Come on with us."

"I look terrible in a suit." Sandra put her head under the pillow.

"Don't worry about it. Come with us and you'll see what I mean." Judy threw a suit at her. "I'll get us towels."

Sandra groaned and got out of bed and joined her sisters for a swim.

As they got near to the pool, Sandra said, "I see what you mean."

There were people who were twenty years or more their senior in the pool. Wrinkles, flab and cellulite reigned rampant.

"Actually, we're the best-looking ones here," she whispered to her sisters.

A few laps across the pool and Judy was ready to get out. She climbed the ladder and wrapped a towel around her sarong-style. This was a good idea, to have some time with just her sisters. It was maybe thirty-five years or longer since they did anything more than an occasional lunch or shopping trip, just the three of them. There was a special bond, a history which no one else shared.

"I'm ready to go, too." Sandra stood next to her.

Judy waved and Kathy got out of the pool.

"I'm starved. What's for breakfast?" Kathy flung the towel over her shoulders.

"We can zap our leftovers from last night," Sandra said.

Judy ignored her. "I was going to fix us some waffles."

"That sounds better. It's too early for salsa and guacamole."

They took turns at breakfast and in the shower.

"Well, old tour guide, what's on the agenda for today?" Sandra asked.

"I thought we could drive out to the desert. Tomorrow, we can do some other sightseeing and the last day Kathy is here, we can shop."

"What about the night life?" Kathy asked.

"I don't know. We went out so seldom. We went to the movies once in a while. Otherwise, we got together with some of the other couples and played cards."

"Bor-ing!" Kathy rolled her eyes.

"That's where our kids get it from," Sandra said to Judy.

"I actually learned it from the kids," Kathy said.

"I guess we could see if there's a club around here for tonight."

"Fine, and what am I supposed to do? Both of you are single," Sandra said.

Single? Judy never thought of that. She was part of a couple for so long. She just stood there, trying to process it all.

"That's coming from the original party animal," Kathy said.

"That's what got me in all the trouble." Sandra grinned.

Judy remembered what Sandra had been like before she was married the first time and then again after her marriage broke up. Brad was Sandra's second husband.

"Then you'll have to be the chaperone." Kathy gave her a poke in the ribs.

"If Mom could see us now," Sandra said.

"You mean she doesn't?" Judy raised her eyebrows.

Their mother always knew when they were up to something. Judy caught on to some of the tricks after she had children, but not all of them. Her mother definitely had an extra sense when it came to her family.

"Then we'll have to give her something to fret over." Kathy winked.

The day was beautiful. The desert was just starting to bloom. They did some hiking and took rolls of film.

Once they were at Judy's, Kathy collapsed on the sofa. "I'm too tired to go out tonight." Her sisters agreed.

"I'll pop for a pizza," Sandra said.

"No meat or anchovies on mine," Kathy said.

"That sounds good to me," Judy said. Within a half hour, they had stuffed themselves with pizza.

Then, it was time for a stroll around the area. Same as the night before. Several other people stopped them and offered their sympathies to Judy.

"I can't believe how friendly everyone is," Kathy said.

"And how everyone knows everyone else's business," Sandra said.

"Didn't you get bored down here?" Kathy asked.

Judy chewed on her bottom lip. Did she dare admit it? "Yes, it gets monotonous after a while. I read a lot. Steve loved it, though. He golfed almost every day."

"Are you going to keep the place?"

"I haven't decided yet. I really like getting out of the cold winters, but I miss everyone. And now with Steve gone..." The words caught in her throat.

"That's okay." Sandra put her arm around her. "Why couldn't it have been my ex?"

Or Brad, Judy thought. That's really unkind of me, but he's such a pain in the ass.

They picked out a couple of interesting places to see the next day. Everything was so far apart. Judy didn't relish all the driving. She was going to have enough on the way home. Kathy would too. Sandra could help out some, but she didn't like to drive.

Several of the women brought over pies, cakes and cookies. It was their way of saying they were sorry.

One of the visitors was a retired minister who asked, "Would you like to have a memorial service for Stu?"

"His name was Steve." Judy tried to sound gentle when she answered him. "It would be nice, but we haven't been coming here very long and besides, I had one for him at home."

"I understand, m'dear, but it's a tradition," the old man said firmly.

"Well, we're leaving day after tomorrow." Judy hoped there wouldn't be enough time.

"Time enough. Tomorrow night at the pavilion at seven. It won't be long."

Judy groaned silently.

"Now what were his favorite hymns?" The minister took out a piece of paper and a pencil stub.

"I don't know. Why don't you just pick out a couple?"

The man gave her a disapproving look, but wrote something

down. "Let me make sure I have his name right. Stu Evert."

"No, Steve Evans."

He wrote down something more. "I'll see you tomorrow night. If you want to add anything, just knock on our door." He jammed the piece of paper into his pocket, shook Judy's hand and left.

"How much do you want to bet he gets the name wrong?" Sandra asked.

Judy shook her head. "No sense betting on a sure thing."

"I agree," Kathy said.

The next day was shopping day. They went to some of the historic areas and to a shopping mall. No one bought much, but they had fun just browsing. Sandra did get a few souvenirs to bring to her family. Kathy found a couple of tiles to bring as souvenirs. Judy didn't get a thing.

Seven that evening, they were at the pavilion. Chairs were in rows and there was a makeshift pulpit in the front. There was a brass urn with flowers which Judy figured were probably silk. She went to a couple of memorial services last year and the bouquet looked familiar.

Someone ushered them to the front row.

"It seems strange to see all the men in western shirts and bolo ties and the women in dresses with full petticoats underneath," Sandra said in a soft voice.

"This will be short," Judy whispered to her sisters who were seated on either side of her. "They don't take much time out of their square dancing time."

There were more people there than Judy had expected. Almost every chair was occupied. The square dance caller played the keyboard for the hymns. Lo and behold, the minister did get Steve's name right.

"Good thing neither of you took me up on that bet," Kathy said later on.

The service was over within a half hour. Several men who Steve golfed with spoke a few sentences. Judy was moved to tears, which surprised her. She had no notion that people even knew who they were.

Afterwards the minister gave her an envelope. "This was collected as a memorial. You're to give it to the charity of your choice."

"Thank you. I'll do that. And, I'll make sure you all know where I sent it."

That night, they counted the money. It was over a hundred dollars, mostly in singles.

"What are you going to do with it?" Kathy asked.

"There is a fund here to help anyone in need. I think it should stay here."

Even though they had to leave early the next morning, no one could sleep. They talked long into the night. There was a chorus of groans when the alarm went off the next morning.

"It's still dark out," Sandra whined.

"It won't be for long. I want to get out of town before the major traffic starts." Judy got up and stripped the bedding off and threw it on the floor.

Her sisters did the same.

"I'll just take it home and do it there." She gathered it up and shoved it in the pillow cases. Then she went through the unit and checked everything over while her sisters showered.

They had coffee and doughnuts for breakfast and the rest of the orange juice.

Judy took her shower and wiped down the bathroom. This time, she made sure the fridge was empty, as well as the wastebasket. She let her sisters load the car and van.

One final look around and she locked the door. She gave Kathy a hug. "This has been fun. Thanks for coming down."

"We should do this every year, just the three of us," Sandra said. "And not for a funeral."

"Next time, it'll be on my turf," Kathy said as she opened her car door.

"Sounds good," Judy said. She stood and watched her youngest sister drive away. She and Sandra waved.

"Well, come on," Judy said.

They made good time. Each morning, they got an early start and then stopped early and found a motel. Sandra drove for an hour or so at a time. They made a couple of extra stops to see some points of interest. Judy was grateful the weather held out. Some of the worst weather could sweep across the plains that time of year.

IX

At home, Judy started to get things in order. She met with her attorney, her tax consultant and her broker. Two things were keeping her from being in financial difficulties. First, she had her own pension and medical insurance. Second, the condo and the Arizona property were paid for. Still, she would have to be careful.

"Did you ever think about going back to work?" Sandra had stopped over one evening.

"What would I do?"

"You could sub. They're always looking for qualified subs."

"I've done my stint in teaching. I don't want to go back in the classroom."

"A greeter at Wal-Mart?"

"From the sublime to the ridiculous."

Sandra shrugged. "I was only trying to help."

"Kathy's been after me to come out and stay with her for a while. Just to see if I liked it."

"Yeah, she told me." Sandra took a sip of her tea and reached for a cookie. "You can't be serious. Everything you have is here."

"Such as?" Judy was starting to feel testy. Everyone had her figured out.

"The kids."

"The kids are all adults. Ellyn is in Africa. She plans on being gone for at least six months. Besides, everywhere I turn, I see Steve."

"You can't run away from memories."

"No, but this would give me a chance for a new start, or at the least, a new direction."

"I don't know what I'd do without you around."

"Ah ha. That's the whole thing." Judy finally figured out what her sister was getting at.

"Okay, I admit it. I'd be lost without you. My kids aren't around much and Brad...Well, Brad, I'd rather not have around much."

"Sorry, kiddo, but you're stuck with the guy."

After Sandra left, Judy took a mug of tea into the living room and flicked on the TV. Grace was working a double shift at the hospital. It was nice to have the place to herself. She hadn't really given much thought to Kathy's invitation until she was talking with Sandra. She certainly wasn't needed around here. Grace was working and her divorce was proceeding slowly but surely. Clark and Tina were planning on getting married in two years. Why would anyone have such a long engagement?

It was time for Judy to do something for herself. For the first time in her life, she was free. She did feel a bit of guilt when it came to Sandra. But Sandra brought on her own problems. After her divorce, she met Brad. Soon she let Brad move in with her and her kids He was Sandra's senior by fifteen years and had health problems. Nothing terminal, just chronic. He was chronic. What did her sister ever see in him? Sandra felt obligated to marry him after living with him for almost a year. Poor basis for a marriage, in Judy's mind. But then again she hadn't been in Sandra's shoes. Better not be too critical, she told herself. Things can haunt you if you're not careful. After all, she was single.

The more she thought about it, the more the idea of visiting Kathy appealed to her. She didn't say anything to her children or even mention it again to Sandra. Instead, she made plans even before she called Kathy.

That night, she had trouble getting to sleep. When she finally did drift off, she dreamt about Steve. He told her to go on with her plans. She should be more adventuresome. Something he'd told her for years. The dream was so real, she woke and reached for him.

"Damn it, Steve, just when we were living our dream retirement you had to die..." She punched her pillow until she was worn out. Then she wrapped her arms around his pillow. There was just a faint smell of his favorite aftershave. It gave her comfort and she relaxed some.

After a shower and some coffee, Judy decided to pack up Steve's clothes. Carefully, she folded shirts and pants and put them in some boxes. She was bringing the extra hangers down to the laundry room when Grace woke up.

"Packing up Dad's clothes." It was more of a statement than a question.

"I figured no time like the present."

"Would you like some help?" Grace offered.

"No, this is something I feel I need to do on my own," Judy said. "But you can help me load up the van when I'm ready."

Grace put her arms around her mother. "It must be rough. I know how sad I feel about Kevin and he was a jerk."

Judy smiled though there were tears in her eyes. "I love you."

"And I love you." Grace kissed her mother's cheek. "I think I'll grab something to eat and go back to bed. Just let me know if you change your mind."

"I will." Judy felt so proud of her daughter. It was comforting to have her around. She missed Ellyn. "How do you like the P.M. shift?"

"It's not quite as hectic as the day shift."

Next, Judy tackled Steve's dresser. His underwear, socks, and other clothing filled another couple of boxes. The smell of his aftershave was stronger. It was a comfort as before. She found an unopened bottle tucked among his sweats. She debated about what to do with it. Then she put it into the box. There was a partial bottle in the bathroom. That one, she would keep.

Judy taped the last box and carried it into the hallway by the door to the garage. She went into the bathroom and threw away Steve's toothbrush and other items, except for the aftershave. She opened the bottle and placed it on a shelf.

After a quick bite of lunch, Judy called Kathy at work. "Is the offer still good?"

"You mean it?" Kathy giggled. "Of course I mean it. When?"

"I have a couple of things to take care of before I leave."

"Are you going to fly or drive?"

"I thought I'd fly. I can always rent a car if I need to."

"Just let me know a few hours ahead of time. There are clean sheets on the guest bed already."

"I'll call you as soon as I've made my reservations."

"Did I understand you saying you were going away?"

Judy spun around. Grace stood in the doorway.

"I'm going to spend some time with Aunt Kathy," Judy said. "I wanted to see if the offer was still good before I mentioned it."

"How long are you going to be gone?"

"I'm not really sure."

"A few days? A week? A month?"

"I have no idea. It may just be a short visit."

"You're not planning on moving there?" Grace stared at her mother.

"I don't plan to. Do you mind staying here by yourself?"

"I guess I'll be okay." Grace's voice was choking. "At least for a while."

"I'll be back. It's not much different than Dad and I being gone all winter." Judy could see the tears forming in her daughter's eyes and was surprised by her daughter's reaction. But, then again, Grace was going through her own hell. "Grace, I'll be only a phone call away. Remember Aunt Sandra's nearby."

Grace put her arms around her mother. "I'm sorry, Mom. I know it must be hard without Dad. I know how hard it is for me without Kevin, even though he abused me"

Judy hugged her. "You'll be just fine. We'll both be just fine." She fervently hoped it was true.

Within a week, Judy took care of all the business, bought her ticket and got a good supply of traveler's checks. She phoned each of the boys and had Andy send an email to Ellyn. Ellyn replied, saying she was glad her mother was taking the time to get away.

The day before she left, she and Sandra had lunch.

"So you're really going." Sandra took a bite of her tuna sandwich.

Judy tasted her French onion soup before replying. "You bet. I'm looking forward to meeting some new people and different scenery."

"Have you decided how long you're going to stay?"

"I bought a one-way ticket."

Sandra choked on her coffee. "You what?"

"One way."

"Who else knows this?" Sandra wiped some coffee off her chin.

"You're the only one."

"You mean Kathy doesn't even know?" A smile began to form.

"You got it."

Sandra raised an eyebrow. "Do you plan on moving there?"

"No, probably not, but I'm going to start to be more spontaneous."

"More impulsive." Sandra poked the air with her fork.

"I have everything arranged so my bills will be paid from my checking account. My lawyer has all the paperwork done for the estate and my new will. There is no reason why I shouldn't live like a vagabond for a year or so."

"You mean you might not stay with Kathy all the time?"

Judy shrugged. "I have no plans whatsoever except that I am flying tomorrow to spend some time with our sister."

When they got up to leave, Sandra handed Judy the tab. "Here. You can pay today."

Judy took it. "Trying to make me feel guilty?"

Sandra snorted. "I'm not sure anyone can get you to do that."

Grace was just leaving for work when Judy came home. "I guess I won't see you before you leave. I have a double shift tonight."

"No, I'll be leaving about six in the morning."

"How are you getting to the airport? Are Aunt Sandra and Uncle Brad taking you?"

"No, I have the airport shuttle coming. It's easier that way." Judy hung up her coat.

"Is there anything I have to do?"

"You can make sure the plants are watered. And forward any mail other than junk."

"Can do." She kissed Judy's cheek. "Take care and let me know when you get there. I'll let the others know."

The house seemed so big and empty. Judy flicked on the TV for some noise... A cup of tea sounded good, though she was still full from lunch. Mentally, she ran through her list. She couldn't think of anything she forgot.

When the tea was ready, she poured it into a big mug and went into her bedroom. There was only a bit more she still needed to pack. What was she going to do all night? She set the mug on the dresser.

Steve, why did you do this to me? For over thirty years, we talked about everything and made all the decisions together. We bounced ideas off each other and came up with much better ideas than we could have come by alone. Tears stung her eyes. For all her bravado with Grace and Sandra, she was scared to death of the future. It loomed out there with no form. A blank landscape. *Getting away from here is the only answer. It will give you time to think.*

She sipped the tea and finished packing. Just before closing her suitcase, she took one of Steve's handkerchiefs and poured some of his aftershave on it. It was like taking a part of Steve with her. She tucked it in, along with his picture, and zipped the case shut. She wondered how long the fragrance would last. Then she lugged the suitcase into the hallway. The rest could go in the carry-on.

Judy wasn't hungry for dinner, so she fixed herself a bag of microwave popcorn. There was one soda in the fridge. She sat and watched the evening news and some ridiculous reality show. When she finished the popcorn and drink, she went in and took a long hot bath. It was pretty early to go to bed, but there was nothing else to do.

She checked and rechecked the alarm. Judy was afraid she would oversleep. So she was afraid to go to sleep. She tossed and turned for several hours.

Her alarm went off and she got up in plenty of time. One quick look in the hall mirror while she waited for the shuttle. The concealer did a good job of minimizing the dark circles under her eyes.

X

There was little activity at the airport. Most of the people were dressed in suits and carrying briefcases. It took little time for Judy to get her bag checked. She bought a cup of coffee and a sweet roll and went to wait for her flight to be called. The board said it was on time.

The plane was only half full and she sat by herself. She couldn't help but remember her last flight. In a few hours, she would be in Colorado. She leaned in her seat and dozed off in spite of the coffee.

There was a short layover in Denver before Judy would board a smaller plane to fly into the airport nearer Kathy's. When they landed, she went and retrieved her bag and then found the airport shuttle. Kathy told her she couldn't meet her, but would see her after work. She should just let herself into the condo and make herself at home.

The shuttle brought her to a gated development. This was a different place than she and Steve went when they visited Kathy last year.

Kathy had given Judy the combination to the front door. The

door opened like magic. She brought in her luggage.

Color was everywhere. Mauve and yellow and soft green and lavender. It was like stepping into a garden. Not only that, but there was a coziness. Kathy surprised her with this. But now that Judy thought about it, how much did she really know about her youngest sister?

There was a note on the hall table.

Welcome to my humble abode. Make yourself comfortable. You can have the loft for a bedroom. Help yourself to anything you can find to eat. Worked late last night, so not much in the cupboards. I'm leaving early and will pick up some stuff on my way home, but I'll call later on.

Love, Kathy

Judy looked up and saw a railing around what looked like a loft. There was a spiral staircase leading up. She took her things up the stairs. What she saw took her breath away. I could get used to this, she thought. The area was huge and centered against one wall was a brass bed covered in a quilt. The quilt was the same kind of color profusion as the rest of the house. She could look over the railing into the great room. The other side had two skylights to let in the sunshine. There were doors on either side. She opened one. A walk-in closet. She crossed the room. A wonderful bath with a sunken whirlpool tub and a separate shower. The same color scheme.

I wonder how much a place like this goes for? She wished Steve could be there to see this. Tears filled her eyes. Snap out of it, she told herself. You can't go on wishing for something that just can't happen.

She unpacked and hung the clothes away. They didn't take up much room in the closet. Good excuse to do some shopping while she was out there. Her toiletries went into the bathroom. Then, she put both cases into the closet and went downstairs to do some exploring. The first place was the kitchen. She realized she hadn't eaten much and was starving.

Kathy's cupboards were like Old Mother Hubbard's or almost. She did find a can of soup and some crackers. The milk was in a solid mass in the bottom of the carton. Judy refrained from throwing it away. Who knew what Kathy might say if Judy took over some chores?

She was eating when the phone rang.

"Hi, Sis, how was your trip?"

"It was okay."

"Did you find everything you need?"

"I'll get by. Say, why didn't you tell me about your place? It's wonderful."

"I thought you'd like it. I'll pick up dinner on the way home." There was a pause. "I have to go. I'll be home about five."

Before Judy could say another word, there was a click.

After cleaning up her dishes, Judy finished her exploration. Kathy's room was on the main floor. It, too, had its own luxurious bath. On the far end of the great room was Kathy's office. A huge fireplace was flanked by soft leather sofas on the other end. A powder room was between there and the kitchen.

Several doors were closed, but there was a set of French doors that opened onto a deck. The view was spectacular. That was the only word Judy could think of. A valley with mountains in the distance. The door off the kitchen, opened into a garage.

Kathy told her she would be using her share from their

mother's inheritance to buy a condo. She and Steve bought their condo and the place in Arizona. Sandra used her share to pay off debts Funny, how three women who were raised in the same family had such different lifestyles.

In the distance, there was a golf course. She could see someone swinging a golf club and then a white ball went flying. She walked away. Steve would spend hours at a driving range. Would everything remind her of Steve? She turned away.

Back in the loft, she found the book she brought with her. After throwing off the quilt, she stretched out.

"Hey, Judy! Where are you?"

Judy sat up and looked around. It took her a moment to realize where she was. It was dark outside.

"I'm up here," She got up and leaned over the railing. "I went to read and fell asleep."

"Come on down. I stopped at this Chinese restaurant and got us dinner."

"Just give me a minute or two." Judy went into the bathroom and splashed water on her face. Then she brushed her hair.

"Smells good." She seated herself at the kitchen table.

"What do you want to drink?" Kathy opened the refrigerator door.

"Not milk. I checked it out earlier."

Kathy picked up the carton and gave it a few shakes. "I can see why. Sorry about that."

"Steve and I have that problem in Arizona but not when the kids are around."

Kathy gave her a startled look, but made no mention of Judy's reference to Steve. "I'll make us some tea." Kathy put a teakettle of water on the stove.

"Fine."

The food was wonderful. Neither of them said much during the meal.

"There's enough for your lunch tomorrow or do you want to go into town with me in the morning?"

"I think I'll just stay here tomorrow."

After Kathy left for work the next morning, Judy took a stroll around the complex. All the houses looked alike until she began to notice little things. Some had window boxes or rock gardens. Each had a different window treatment she could see from the sidewalk.

Kathy called about lunchtime. "There's a temp job just posted. Are you interested?"

It was rather sudden. Judy thought about working up to something. "What is it?"

"A file clerk for about a month. The gal is on maternity leave and the work is just piling up."

Judy hesitated.

"You could drive with me so you won't have that worry."

"Sounds tempting. Can I let you know tonight?"

"Sure. I'll let HR know that I've talked to you, just in case."

Judy thought about little else all the rest of the day. First, she thought it might be too soon. She wasn't sure she wanted to be tied down. Then she thought she could really use the money. Besides, she didn't have anything to keep her busy and she would probably get bored. A month wasn't any big commitment. She'd know if she wanted to find a real job. By the time Kathy got home, Judy decided to take it.

"I forgot to tell you the job is only eight dollars an hour." Kathy hung up her coat.

"That isn't any big deal. It's only for a month." Judy went into the kitchen and Kathy followed.

"What smells so good?"

"I made a chicken stew. You certainly don't have very much to work with." Judy motioned for Kathy to sit down.

"I don't eat much at home." She spread the napkin on her lap.

Judy set the pot on a trivet on the table.

Kathy tasted the food. "Hmmm, I don't think you should take the job. I could get used to having a dinner like this waiting for me."

"I've decided to take it if they'll have me." Judy sat down and helped herself to the stew.

"Great! You can come in with me tomorrow. That'll give you a chance to see something too. After work on Thursday, I have a business women's meeting and you can join me. We meet at a café and grab a sandwich or salad then."

"Is all that you do, just work and go to meetings?" They hadn't had much time to talk.

"Pretty much so."

"No men in your life?"

Kathy blushed. "Maybe I've sworn off men."

"This sounds interesting."

"They mess up your life and your mind. They're usually only interested in one thing. Now that I'm over fifty, they aren't even interested in that."

"You sound so cynical. Who hurt you so much?" She didn't really know her sister at all.

"It was a long time ago. Besides, I have more fun with my women friends."

"Oh?"

"I'm not a lesbian, if that's what you're thinking." Kathy took a forkful of food.

"So what if you are? It makes no difference to me." That was true. She remembered all the arguments she and Steve had about homosexuals. He had such a different view of this subject. It was like he was so uncomfortable around gay men.

"Do you think you'll ever be interested in another man?" Kathy asked. "I know it's rather soon, but you have a future."

"I haven't really thought of it. Probably not. There are some very good points to being single."

"See what I mean?" Kathy pointed her fork at her. "Sandra would have been better off if she had never married that fink of a Brad."

Judy nearly choked. "I agree." Kathy was always cagy about her personal life, even when they were kids. She felt Kathy might just be hiding something, maybe a boyfriend? Just a gut feeling.

That night, Judy lay and gazed out the skylight above her bed. Would she find anyone she would like to be with? She shuddered as she remembered the creepy experience with the neighbor. Not all guys were like that. For the time being, she was content to let life just happen to her. She'd have a job for a month, after that, who knows.

She couldn't believe how nervous she was about interviewing for a job, even a low-level one like a file clerk. It had been thirty years since her last interview.

"Wanna take a cup of coffee with you for the ride in?" Kathy took out a stainless steel commuter cup.

"No, I'm nervous enough. Maybe tomorrow." She checked in

her purse to see if she had everything.

"There's nothing to be afraid of," Kathy said.

"Fine for you to say. This is a whole new ball game for me. For many years, I've dealt with six-year-olds."

"And their parents."

Judy laughed. The kids had been a snap. The parents were the challenging part.

The drive into town was not very long, but just too exciting for Judy. She never taught at a school more than ten minutes from where she and Steve lived. Judy thought long commutes were a waste of time. She was grateful Kathy was doing the driving.

Kathy pulled into the parking garage and parked on the ground floor. "The company owns the building and we can park here and take the elevator without going outside." Kathy pointed. "The elevator is over there on the right."

Judy could have guessed that with all the people heading toward one corner.

"Your interview is at ten. You can stay in the employee's lounge until then."

Judy followed her sister to the elevator and then out of it and down the hall.

Kathy pried the top off the travel cup. "I'm going to rinse this out and get some fresh stuff. Help yourself to coffee or, if you'd rather, there's a water cooler over there." She came over to Judy. "Don't worry. You'll do fine."

Judy took a deep breath. "Keep telling me that."

Before Kathy left her, she gave directions to HR. "If nothing else, ask someone. We've all been through the getting lost phase."

"I think I can find that."

Kathy gave Judy a hug.

Judy had two hours to wait before her appointment. Someone left a paper so she read it, cover to cover. She leafed through a couple of magazines and catalogues. She'd have to get a couple of new outfits if she got the job.

The personnel office was easy to find. Judy went into the waiting area.

"Are you Judy Evans?" asked a woman behind the desk.

"Yes." Judy's mouth felt dry.

The woman got up and motioned for Judy. "Come right this way."

Judy followed.

"Judy Evans to see you."

Another woman was seated behind a big desk. "Thanks, Sally." She stood up. "I'm Meg Farnsworth, head of HR. Kathy told me about you yesterday. I'm glad you came in." They shook hands. She motioned for Judy to take a chair opposite her.

"I have an application for you to fill out. I, also, need to make a copy of Social Security card, your driver's license and your birth certificate."

"I don't have my birth certificate but I do have my passport with me." Judy took the clipboard offered to her. She took the documents out of her purse and handed them over. I have to see about some papers.

"You can stay right here." Meg closed the door softly behind her.

The application was simple enough. Her hands sweat as she wrote. They required a drug test. This was a lot of work for just a month-long job. When she finished, she sat and waited for

Meg to return.

"Hi, you may have thought I wasn't coming back." Meg came breezing into the room and handed Judy her papers. "Always something new in the insurance business."

Meg sat down and took a few minutes to scan it.

"I haven't had much job experience," Judy said.

"Having only one job for these many years is very unusual." She looked up. "Do you know the alphabet?"

Judy laughed.

"You're hired. All you have to do is pass the drug test."

"That's it?" Judy couldn't believe she had been so nervous for this.

"Pretty much. Can you start tomorrow?"

"Yeah...I guess so...I mean, yes, I can."

"Good. I'll have Sally make the arrangements for you to take the drug test." She lowered her voice. "All you have to do is pee in a bottle."

"Where do I have to go?" Judy felt a moment of panic. She didn't want to have to drive Kathy's car someplace.

"We use the clinic across the street." She pointed out her window.

"That's good. I just got in and don't know my way around."

Fifteen minutes later, she was in the clinic office, being shown into a restroom by a lab tech. "I'll just set your purse here. I'll be right outside the door. You can wash your hands out here when you're finished" The tech motioned to a counter with a sink outside the small restroom.

In the room, the only thing there was a toilet with blue water. When she was finished, she asked, "What's with all the routine?"

"You would be amazed at the lengths some people go to try and beat a test." The tech shook her head.

"This whole thing is so new to me," Judy said as she picked up her purse.

"I'll send over the results to Meg as soon as I can."

Judy left the building and headed across the street. She looked at her watch. The whole interview and lab test took less than an hour.

Somehow, she found her way to the lounge. Now she was ready for a cup of coffee. She even bought a doughnut out of the vending machine. Sugar was always good for stress.

Kathy came into the lounge "Well, did you get it?"

"Sure did. Even went for the drug test." Judy stood up and put on her coat.

"Celebration lunch is in order then." Kathy went over to the coat rack and got her coat. "What do you want? My treat."

"It really doesn't make much difference." Judy didn't really care. Almost any cuisine was fine with her.

"Well, we had Mexican and Chinese. What about American?"

Judy laughed. "Fine."

"There's this little place not too far from here." Kathy looked at her watch. "We got out just before the crowd."

The place was just a couple of blocks away. It was rather nondescript on the outside, but inside was like stepping back in time.

"My gosh, are those linen tablecloths?" Judy asked.

"This place is first class. Nothing is too good for my sister who just got a job." Kathy stepped up to the hostess and asked for a table for two.

"Right this way." The hostess took two menus and walked into the dining room. The sisters followed. A vase of real flowers graced every table. Marble pillars framed a fireplace. Crystal chandeliers hung from the high pressed-metal ceiling.

"Can I get you anything from the bar?" the hostess asked.

"Mineral water with a twist." Kathy said.

"Make that two," Judy said.

"You can have some wine if you want. I just have to go back to work." Kathy shrugged out of her coat.

"I'd rather not. Mineral water is fine with me."

"What are you going to order?" Kathy opened her menu.

"Your server will be right here to take your order."

"What are you going to do for the rest of the day?" Kathy asked after they were served.

"I don't know. What do you suggest?" Her food was wonderful.

"The library is two blocks down that way." Kathy pointed one way. "And the museum is two blocks that way." She pointed in the opposite direction.

"You know, I should get some clothes for work."

"There are a couple of little shops around. Or if you'd like, we can stop at the big shopping center we passed on the way in."

"Why don't I see what I can find this afternoon, but I think we should stop at the mall anyway."

"Sounds good." Kathy had the server put the leftovers in a box. "I'll store it in a fridge at work. We can have it tomorrow for lunch."

"You mean no one will take it?" Judy remembered the people who would take someone else's lunch at the school unless there was a skull and cross bones on it.

"I have a tiny fridge in my cube."

"Oh." Judy walked with Kathy to the office building. "See you at five."

She hadn't felt so excited and alive for months or maybe even longer. A new job, albeit for only a month. A new community. A whole new life and identity. She wasn't going to think beyond the day.

The library wasn't like every other library. It was brand new with a view of a wooded area and a stream. Judy took a deep breath. All libraries smelled the same. She was only there for a short time. Just enough to look around. On the way to the museum, she found one of the shops Kathy told her about.

The shop was posh. The thick carpet and chamber music made her wonder about the prices. She looked at a couple of hang tags. Wow! She was right. She wandered toward the rear of the shop.

"May I help you find anything?" A female voice came from behind a rack of dresses.

"I'm just browsing," Judy said. There was a sale sign over a couple of round racks in the back. She found her size and started to look. There was a cotton knit pantsuit in burgundy with a long tunic top. The price wasn't even bad. It was different from anything she wore to school. There it was slacks, even jeans and sweaters.

"Could I try this on?"

"There's a fitting room behind those coats." The clerk pointed.

Judy hated trying on clothes, but if this fit, she would have herself an outfit. Either she had lost a lot of weight or the garment ran large.

"How did it fit?" The voice was outside the door.

"It's too big. Otherwise, I really like it."

"I'll see if we have one in a smaller size."

Judy rehung the set.

Sure enough. Within a few minutes, two outfits of the same style were handed in through the door. Each was a different color.

Sneaky way of selling. If one fit, she'd be tempted to buy both. Damn, they both fit. Still she wasn't about to buy two. She decided on sticking with the burgundy.

"Anything else I can show you?" The voice had a body. A young woman about college age, as far as Judy could guess.

"No, I think this will be all for today." Judy handed her the Visa card.

"Are you here for a visit?" The clerk folded the pants inside tissue paper.

"Yes and no. I'm here visiting my sister. But I just took a month long job."

"What will you be doing?" The clerk did the same with the tunic top.

"File clerk at the same company my sister works for."

"This will be perfect for that." She put both pieces into a shopping bag. "Have you ever worked before?"

Judy laughed. "I was a first grade teacher for over thirty-five years. My husband and I retired a couple of years ago."

"Is he here with you?" The clerk punched in some numbers on the computer.

"No, he died earlier this year."

The clerk finished the transaction. "My deepest sympathies."

"Thank you," Judy said.

"I hope you enjoy your stay here. And come back any time." the clerk handed Judy the bag.

"I might just do that."

Outside, Judy thought about the conversation. She was able to talk so matter-of-factly about Steve's death. It surprised her. Was she supposed to act and feel this way after only a few months?

A block down the street was another shop. She went in, but didn't find anything to interest her. She finally got to the museum. She had about an hour to prowl around until she had to go to meet Kathy.

The museum was like most small-town museums. There were displays of local history, some of Colorado history and then some pieces someone must have brought from a trip abroad. It was well done and she found a small gift shop tucked away in an alcove. She bought a book on Colorado history. Then it was time to leave.

She got to the building lobby just as Kathy got out of the elevator.

"Hey, what's in the bag?"

"A pantsuit I got in that little shop about a block from here." Judy held out the bag and Kathy read the name.

"Wow! You do go all out.'

"Actually, it was a good deal, and besides, it's in a size smaller than I usually wear."

"Still want to stop at the mall?" They made their way with a dozen other people to the parking ramp.

"Sure, why not."

Kathy popped the trunk on her car and Judy put in her bag.

"I thought I could find some Colorado souvenirs for my kids. T-shirts, coffee mugs, you know, the usual."

"I think there's a shop like that at the mall." Kathy exited the parking ramp and merged into traffic.

"I did buy a book about Colorado. Thought I'd bone up on what's around."

"The place is getting to you, isn't it?" The light turned red and Kathy laid on the brakes.

"I'm enjoying myself, if that's what you mean."

"I've invited several people over for a buffet on Saturday night. That way, you'll get to meet some of my friends."

"That does sound like fun. I'll get to find out just what kind of a person you really are. Not the person who shows up every few years to play sister."

"Oh, I handpicked these people. They will only give you glowing reports about me."

The mall was like a shopping center in any city. Judy found another outfit and a couple of extra tops.

"I think there's a T-shirt boutique off that way."

So they went down a side hallway. Not only were there T-shirts, but baseball hats, sweatshirts, and mugs, things with Colorado emblazoned on them. Judy bought something for everyone, including herself.

By the time they got home, Judy was exhausted.

"There are a couple of messages on the machine," Kathy said as she walked by her desk. She reached over and hit the play button. Judy went into the bathroom.

"Hey, Sis, there's a message from Grace wondering when you're coming home," Kathy said when Judy came out of the bathroom.

"It's too late to call her tonight. Was that all she said? I'll call her in the morning. On second thought, it might be Grace's night off."

"The other message was from HR. I didn't erase that message if you want to listen to it.

"Your drug test came back negative."

"That's a relief."

"Are you on some drug that would cause a problem, like coke or LSD?"

"Oh, come off it. Every time you take a test, you always expect something strange will show up."

"Always the optimist." Kathy said as she left the room.

Judy punched in her home phone number. It rang several times before an out of breath Grace answered.

"Where did I get you from?"

"And hello to you too, Mom."

"Sorry. You left a message for me to call you."

"I just wanted to tell you that I found an apartment closer to the hospital. I'm moving the end of the month. How much longer are you staying with Aunt Kathy?"

"That's fine honey. But you know you can stay as long as you want to. I'm going to be here for at least a month. I took a temp job as a file clerk for a month. It's the same place where Kathy works."

"That sounds like it could be fun."

"It'll be different. Now if you need anything, let me know. Is your apartment furnished?"

"Partially. I'll ask before I take anything." They talked for a few more minutes before hanging up.

Judy went into the kitchen where Kathy was unloading the dishwasher.

"What was the big deal with Grace?"

Judy sat down at the table. "She found an apartment closer

to work."

Kathy sorted the silverware into the drawer. "Did you expect her to continue to live with you?"

"Not really, but I did think she'd stay there until I got back."

"Did you tell her about the job?"

"Yeah and she seemed okay with it." At least Judy hoped she was.

"Well, I think I'm going to bed. Does that alarm clock on the night stand work?"

"I think so, but I'll make sure you're up in plenty of time if it doesn't."

Judy went into her room and got ready for bed. Then she washed her face and brushed her teeth. She decided to wear the burgundy pantsuit in the morning, so she cut off the tags.

She was excited about having a job. Just being with people was going to be fun, though the work was probably boring. She'd love to share this with Steve.

She crawled between the sheets and switched off the light. What would he say? He'd probably be encouraging. He'd also give her a bad time about not having enough to do. The truth was that she didn't have enough to do. What was she going to do with the rest of her life? She could stay with Kathy now and work for the month, but then what? Back home? Back to Arizona? Maybe she should travel to Europe. That wouldn't be much fun by herself. She'd want someone to share it with.

There was no need to worry about sleeping through the alarm. Judy didn't sleep that night. She got up, made a pot of coffee and took her shower before Kathy got up.

Judy started coffee while Kathy showered. She fixed them some toast.

"Hey! This is great to have something to eat ready for me," Kathy said.

"Well, I was so nervous about today, I couldn't sleep. Probably shouldn't have coffee."

"You'll do just fine." Kathy patted Judy's hand.

"Feels like the first day of school, both as a student and a teacher."

Judy's hands were sweaty as she watched Kathy maneuver through the traffic on the highway. Finally, they got to the parking ramp where Kathy parked the car.

"I'll meet you in the lounge about twelve thirty," Kathy said as they entered the lobby.

"See you then," Judy answered. They took the elevator to their floor. Kathy went right and Judy went left.

Within an hour, Judy knew what she was doing. The work wasn't difficult. Just rather dull. The first day, she spent most of the time in the file room. She took time for lunch with Kathy and then returned to the mountain of files. Judy did get exercise climbing to put something on the top shelf and then, crouching to put a file on the bottom one.

Various people came in to get needed files. They would chat for a few minutes with Judy before going to their office. Sometimes Judy would have to help them find what they were looking for. Everyone was helpful and friendly.

The day went by so quickly. The mound of manila and red and blue folders grew instead of shrinking. This was like a treadmill with an ever-increasing incline.

"How'd it go?" Kathy fastened her seatbelt.

"Not bad. Time sure went fast." Judy leaned against the car

seat.

"Did you make any progress?"

"No. The piles just grew bigger and bigger."

"Everyone has been holding on to their cases or they would never find them in that mess." Kathy flashed her employee card at the garage attendant.

"I can understand that." Judy realized she was starving. "What are we going to do about dinner?"

"We can stop and get a steak or chops. It won't take much time."

"What do you do for fun in the evenings?"

"Laundry. Cleaning. Reading."

"That sounds exciting."

"Remember, tomorrow night, after work, I have a dinner meeting with my investment club. You'd be surprised at how interesting it can be."

Judy dozed off and slept until Kathy pulled into the garage."I didn't realize I was so tired." Judy yawned. "I didn't realize you even stopped at the store."

"How did you manage to keep up with first-graders all those years?"

"I dunno. Guess I'm just out of practice. Climbing up and down that ladder to reach the top row of files is more exercise than I'm used to."

"You're getting paid for step aerobics."

They both laughed and went into the house.

Kathy was right. Dinner was ready in less than an hour. They had baked fish, salad, mashed potatoes and broccoli.

"I even have dessert." Kathy went to the freezer and brought out a pint of ice cream.

"Hey, you're good. Where did you learn all this? Certainly

not from Mom." Their mother had been an awful cook.

"Some of the ideas, I picked up in college, but most from coworkers. They have families and need to get things done in a hurry."

Judy remembered those days when the kids were all at home and she was working full-time. "Your coworkers are quite friendly," Judy said as she started to clear the table.

"I knew you'd like them. That's one of the reasons I'm still there. I had to take a pay cut when the company was bought out a couple of years ago."

"I didn't know that." Judy was learning more about her sister.

"I didn't want to worry anyone. Mom was sick at the time." Kathy shrugged.

"Tell me about your investment club."

Kathy explained how each month they contributed twenty-five dollars as dues. They would discuss certain stocks. They took turns doing the research. Finally, they would vote on what to buy or maybe sell. "We make some money and reinvest it."

"How well do you do?" Judy and Steve never had much to do with investments. Their teacher's pension had been administered by the state.

"Generally better than the stock market. We invest in goods and services we use. Sometimes, I invest on my own with some of the most promising."

"Makes sense to me."

"I have been able to make a bit and stash it away," Kathy said.

That evening Judy did the laundry while Kathy ran the vacuum.

"Remember when you used to assign us jobs?" Kathy

wrapped the electric cord around the holders on the vacuum.

"Yeah. I hated to dust, so that's why you got the job all the time. I got Sandra to do it when we were in Arizona a few months ago." Judy couldn't suppress the grin.

"And you made Sandra clean the bathroom."

Now they both grinned.

"Hated that job too," Judy said. "There were advantages to being the oldest girl."

The next day went pretty much the same as the first, except the pile of files did go down. Kathy was right about people hoarding them.

After work, the two sisters walked a couple of blocks to the restaurant where Kathy's meeting was.

"We get the table over there." Kathy pointed to a long table off to one side. A reserved sign was in the middle. Several women were already sitting there with drinks.

The women greeted Kathy and Kathy introduced Judy to them.

One young woman asked Judy where she was from. Another asked how long she planned on staying. Soon, Judy chatted away with the others like old friends.

The food was okay, but nothing special.

"They are so accommodating, we like to meet here," Kathy whispered in Judy's ear.

Several women arrived after the meal and had coffee.

As soon as the waitress cleared the table of plates, the meeting started. Checkbooks came out and there was the sound of pen scratching and paper tearing. One of the women collected the checks and wrote something in a book.

The meeting was interesting enough for Judy. She wondered if there were any investment clubs back home. The group was supportive of each other. It would be a challenge to learn a new thing. And it was something apart from the life she shared with Steve.

They were only in the restaurant about two hours.

"That went fast," Judy said as they walked to the parking garage.

"Most of us have to get up for work early. Some have to take kids to day care before they even come to work."

The light was flashing on the answering machine when they got into the house. Kathy pressed the play button.

"What's the meaning of taking a job? Aren't you coming back?" It was Sandra.

Judy groaned. She'd been waiting for this call. Grace must have talked to her aunt. She wondered why it had taken Sandra so long. "Damn. What time did she call?"

Kathy looked at the caller ID. "About an hour ago." Kathy poised her finger over the play button. "Want me to play it again?"

"Once is enough." She debated whether to call Sandra right away or maybe take a bath and get ready for bed first. Or maybe just wait until tomorrow. Stop being so evil, she told herself. She took a shower and get ready for bed first. But she knew it was two hours later than where Sandra was so she didn't want to wait too long.

Her hands were cold and sweaty as she punched in Sandra's phone number.

"Hello." It was one of Sandra's kids. Judy wasn't sure which one. They all sounded alike.

"Hi, honey, this is Aunt Judy. Is your mom handy?"

Whoever it was didn't take the receiver away from their mouth when they yelled, "Mom! It's Aunt Judy!"

Judy winced. Her ear rang.

"Hi, I was wondering what took you so long to call." Sandra sounded out of breath.

"Hello to you, too. Kathy had a meeting after work and I went with her."

"What's this about you getting a job?"

"A temporary job. Only for a month. Grace must've forgotten to tell you." Judy tried to sound cool.

"I thought this was a vacation."

"It is. But what was I going to do all day? Sit around and eat bonbons?"

"I don't know."

Judy could hear some sort of commotion going on in the background. "What's going on?"

"Brad just came home. When are YOU coming home?"

"I don't know. There is nothing pressing. I'm usually gone at this time of the year anyway." Judy was beginning to hate this conversation. Why should she have to defend herself?

"Well, I thought with Steve's death and all..." Sandra was huffing.

"That's precisely why I am visiting Kathy. Remember, I told you about the one-way ticket. This will give me time to think about what I'm going to do next."

"And working. We're worried about you."

This conversation was going nowhere fast. "I want to relax a bit before going to bed. Talk to you later." Judy hung up before Sandra had a chance to say anything more. Judy went into the living room and sank into a chair.

Kathy looked up from her book. "The usual?"

Judy nodded.

"See why I don't go home often?"

"You're a coward."

"You're damned right I am. You don't butt into my business, but Sandra does enough for both of you. And when Mom was alive..." She threw up her hands and her book slammed to the floor. "Well, let's not even go there."

"I didn't realize how bad it was. Steve always acted as a buffer."

The phone rang and Kathy got up to answer it.

"If it's Sandra, I've gone to bed." Judy got up and headed for her room.

"Hello?" Kathy said and sat down on the floor. "Why, hi yourself." She put her hand over the mouthpiece and whispered, "It's for me."

"I gathered that much." Judy went into her room and closed the door. She couldn't help but wonder who Kathy was talking to. A man, maybe?

She opened up the bed and stacked two pillows. She found her book and lay down. This was a new habit, reading in bed. Well, at least she hadn't done this since she was a kid.

Judy was about to put her book away when there was a knock on her door. "Hey, Jude, you still awake?"

"Sure, come on in." Judy closed her book and sat up with the pillows bracing her back.

Kathy came and sat on the edge of the bed. "How would you like to go on a date Saturday night?"

"A date? Good God, why would I want to do that?" She was caught completely off guard.

"The call was from a guy I date off and on. He wants me to go out Saturday night, but I don't want to leave you home alone. So I asked him if he had a friend."

"Kathy, you didn't?" Judy felt her face get warm.

Kathy grinned and nodded her head. "Yes, I did and yes, he has."

"But..."

"But what? You're single. It's time you had some fun."

Judy hesitated. She hadn't thought about dating again. She hadn't been very good at it when she was young and now she was old. She twisted the wedding band she still wore.

"Humor me," Kathy said. "Don't think of it as a date, but that you're making sure I behave myself."

Judy giggled. "Your chaperone? I guess if you put it that way. It might be fun. And then if it's not, I can blame you."

"And I'll blame Mark." Kathy got up and blew her sister a kiss. "Nighty-night." She switched off the light just before she closed the door. "You could take off Steve's ring."

Gone was any thought of sleep. In a way, it was exciting to go on a date. Then she thought of Calvin. Her stomach lurched. No, but if he was like that, she'd kill Kathy and Mark. Where were they going? Did she have the right clothes to wear? She hoped Kathy wouldn't slip and say anything to Sandra about this. She'd have a bird.

The rest of the week went by quickly. She was busy for eight hours at work. Still, occasionally her mind strayed to what this date would be like.

"Do you know where we're going on Saturday night?" Judy tried to sound disinterested.

"There's a bluegrass festival going on in a nearby town."

"I like bluegrass."

"They have these festivals all over Colorado during the nice weather."

"Oh." That sounded simple enough. "What are we supposed to wear?"

"Pants, sweater, flat shoes."

"I can do that."

"You'll do just fine. You'll like Mark."

How does she know? Judy wondered. The whole thing sounded pretty casual. Still, she just knew that this blind date was going to be bad news.

XI

Saturday morning, they slept in. The sun was dazzling and the temperature was fairly warm.

"Care to go for a walk?" Kathy asked as they sat and sipped coffee at the kitchen table.

"Sounds great."

"Then we can go over to the mall. I want to have my nails done." Kathy looked at her hands.

"I think the last time I had my nails done was for Andy's wedding."

"You should try it."

"Maybe I will."

Before they went to the mall, Judy took off her ring and left it on the dresser. She felt naked and unfaithful to Steve. She was tempted to put it back on, but hurried out of the room instead.

At the salon, the nail technician tried to talk her into acrylic nails, but Judy didn't want that. Besides, she had some friends whose nails got funny after having that done. Inspecting the job, Judy saw the line where her ring had been. Tears stung her eyes.

When they got to Kathy's place, they had a bowl of soup and

a sandwich for lunch. Judy was so nervous, she almost couldn't choke food down. She looked at the clock. In a few hours, she would have her first date in years--decades. She was glad they were meeting the men at the park.

On the ride into town, Judy twisted her phantom ring and hummed along with the radio to quell her nerves, but it didn't help. Kathy concentrated on the road. There was a lot of traffic.

Two men were waiting when Judy and Kathy walked up. Each man had a couple of lawn chairs in quivers on their backs. One man went over and gave Kathy a quick kiss. "This must be Judy. I'm Mark." He gave her a firm handshake. He turned to the taller, older man standing next to him. "This is Joe Barker. You already know Kathy and this is her sister, Judy."

Joe shook hands with both women. "Pleased to meet you. Mark has told me all about you."

"Come on. The music will be starting soon." Mark took Kathy's arm and walked ahead of Judy and Joe. Mark took care of the tickets and pointed the way they had to go. "The company I work for gave me the tickets."

Judy and Joe didn't talk Judy wanted to say something, but her mind was a blank. Very unusual. She was good at small talk.

They unfolded the chairs. "We usually just throw a blanket down, but the ground gets pretty hard after a while," Mark said. He and Joe placed the chairs so the sisters were next to each other.

"Thanks." Judy gave Joe a smile. He'd overdone the Brute cologne, but it didn't matter. She was glad it wasn't the same scent Steve used. He was clean and his hair looked freshly cut. She looked down at his hands. Clean, but he had the look of work. I wonder what he does for a living? He, also, was lean and muscular. Steve had been short and very slim. Stop making comparisons, she told herself.

"How do you like the area?" Joe asked when they sat down.

"Fine, what I've seen of it so far."

Silence. Judy knew she would have to make an effort to get to know more about him.

"Do you want something to drink?" Mark asked. "The concession tent looks pretty empty right now."

After deciding what they wanted, Mark and Joe went to get the orders. Soon the men were back and the four settled in.

Kathy leaned forward and asked Joe, "I forgot where do you know Mark from?"

"We both used to work for the same company. Before that I had a small company, but I sold it. Now I just do consulting. I'm a mechanical engineer. I do trouble shooting and repair equipment. My motto is have wrench, will travel"

Judy was thankful her sister was doing the talking.

"Oh." Kathy sat back.

Judy took a deep breath. "Where do you go?"

"Mostly remote places. Sometimes I bring in a crew to help."

Silence. Judy could feel her armpits start to sweat. The guy seemed nice enough, but shy. Or maybe he was disappointed in her. Maybe she could say she had a headache so she could go to Kathy's. No, that wouldn't be fair. She had to act like an adult. She looked at her watch. Four more hours and she'd be done with this.

The music started and Judy found herself really enjoying it. Joe would tell her something about the group who was playing or about the piece from time to time. She relaxed a bit.

Later on, she and Kathy went to the restroom.

"So what do you think of Joe?"

"He seems nice, but rather quiet." Judy hadn't really formed an opinion.

"You're not very talkative yourself. Is there something wrong?

"Not really, but it's been a long time since I dated."

Kathy nodded, "I can understand that."

"What do you know about him?"

"Mark says he's brilliant and loaded."

"Loaded?" Judy wasn't sure she knew what Kathy was getting at.

"Mucho money."

"Oh." Big deal. She wished Kathy hadn't told her that.

Joe smiled at her when she sat down next to him.

"Anything exciting happen while I was gone?"

"A new group is setting up." Joe pointed.

After a couple of hours, Kathy and Mark led the way to a sports bar across the street. Joe took Judy's hand. "So we don't get separated."

His hand was big and rough and not sweaty. She liked the way it felt to be holding hands.

"I think Mark made reservations for us to get a table."

Joe was right. Mark and Kathy were already seated by a round table off to the side. Kathy waved to them as they walked in.

Judy was glad Mark had a table for them. The bar was already crowded. She sat next to Kathy and hung her coat over the chair.

"I'm buying this round. What's everyone having?" Joe said.

Mark and Kathy wanted Coors, but Judy ordered a diet Coke.

Before Joe could make it to the bar, a waitress came over and took the order. Joe sat down next to Judy. The noise level of the baseball game on the big screen got pretty high. It was hard to carry on a conversation. The waitress brought their drinks and a basket of chips and a bowl of salsa.

"Why don't we finish our drinks and find a different place? The noise is giving me a headache," Joe said.

"There's that all-night diner on the edge of town," Kathy said.

"Sounds good to me. I could stand a piece of pie," Joe said.

When they got up to leave, Mark said, "Joe, you take Judy with you. Kathy and I'll take her car."

Joe looked at Judy. "Fine with me," she said.

The air was crisp and fresh when they got outside. The odor of cigarette smoke and fried food hung on their clothes.

Joe took a deep breath. "Better already."

"I know what you mean," Judy said.

The four walked to the parking ramp. "My truck is on the street," Joe said.

"And mine is in the garage," Kathy said. Mark had his arm around Kathy's shoulders.

The two couples parted.

"I've got a pickup or we could have all gone together."

They walked to the end of the street. Some pickup. Judy never saw such a big truck.

With a remote, Joe unlocked the doors. He went over and opened the door for Judy. "Just put your foot there and grab onto the bar and pull yourself up."

Easier said than done, Judy thought. But she did as instructed and was in the seat on the first try. Joe closed the door after her. What a view. What a dashboard. It looked like an airplane cockpit. It smelled like a combination of new car and Brute.

Joe got in and started the truck.

"I've never been in such a fancy truck," Judy said.

"I practically live in here. Sort of a mobile office." There was a certain pride in his voice. Mozart boomed over the speakers. He reached over and turned down the volume. Somehow, she pictured him liking country and western.

"So what do you do?" Joe said.

"I'm a retired teacher."

"You can't be old enough to retire."

"I retired early. School district gave us a package we couldn't resist."

"We?"

"My husband and I were both teachers."

"Your husband?"

"He died several months ago." There was an awkward silence.

"I'm sorry," he said.

Deeper silence. Judy would have said something, except a large lump was in her throat.

Joe slowed down and made a left turn into a parking lot. "Here we are."

Getting out of the truck was easier than crawling in.

"I don't see Kathy's car," Judy said as she looked around.

"They probably took longer to get out of the ramp," Joe said. He put his hand on her elbow and they went into the diner. "There's another couple coming," Joe said to the hostess.

"Smoking or non?" The hostess picked up four menus.

"Non," Joe and Judy said together.

They followed the hostess to a booth on the far side of the room. They each slid into a bench across from each other.

"Listen. I'm sorry about your husband. I didn't mean to be so tactless." Joe looked her in the eyes. His eyes were dark brown, almost black.

"How could you have known?"

"Just the same. Any kids?"

"Four. Two girls and two boys. How about you?" She began to feel more comfortable.

"Divorced, with a daughter in college."

"Can I get you something to drink?" a waitress asked.

"Hot tea," Joe said.

"Make it two," Judy said. This was getting weird. They seemed to have the same taste in many things. She wondered how old he was.

"Hi, you two." Kathy slid in next to her sister and Mark sat across from her. Kathy looked a bit disheveled and her lipstick was smeared. Mark also wore the same shade of lipstick. Judy grinned to herself, but didn't say anything. Kathy was going to have some explaining to do. There was more to Kathy and Mark's relationship than Kathy led her to believe.

"It was a mess getting out of that traffic," Mark said.

The waitress brought the tea and asked Kathy and Mark what they would like to drink. They both wanted coffee.

"What kinda pie you got?" Joe asked.

The waitress named off about ten different kinds.

"I'll have cherry with a scoop of ice cream," Joe said.

"Make mine lemon meringue," Judy told her.

Mark ordered a sandwich and Kathy ordered a hot fudge sundae.

"Well, how'd you like the music?" Mark looked at Judy.

"It was very enjoyable"

"The next time, we'll get a table and go for the whole day," Joe said.

Next time? Well, she hadn't bombed out.

"What are you doing tomorrow?" Mark directed his question to Kathy.

"Not much," Kathy said.

"How would you ladies like to take a drive and we can show Judy the lay of the land?" Mark said.

"I have some paperwork to catch up on, but I can do it anytime," Joe said.

"Sounds great," Kathy answered before Judy could say anything.

"We'll pick you two up about ten," Mark said.

Their desserts came. Joe mentioned a couple of landmarks Judy might be interested in seeing.

"I'd like to see them again, too," Kathy and Mark said together.

Judy stifled a yawn. "I'm sorry. All of a sudden, I'm really sleepy."

Joe looked at his watch. "It is late." He picked up the tab.

The four of them put on their coats and went to the entrance.

"I'll walk the girls out," Mark said to Joe.

"Here. I'll meet you at the truck after I pay the bill," Joe said.

Judy walked behind her sister and Mark. They had their arms around each other's waist. The lights went on in Kathy's car as it unlocked. Judy got in. In the rearview mirror, she watched her sister and Mark share a long kiss.

"Well, what do you think of Joe?" Kathy asked as they pulled into traffic.

"He seems nice enough. It's rather hard to make any

conclusions after just a few hours."

"He must like you. This is the first time I've known him to be willing to spend the day with any woman."

"How long have you known him?" Judy was curious about Joe.

"A year or so. He just got over a messy divorce. I don't know any of the details. Mark just said Joe really got screwed."

"We'll see what he's like tomorrow." Judy yawned again.

"You don't mind I said we would go?"

"No, I'd like to see some of the area other than the malls." Judy closed her eyes. "How serious is it with you and Mark? You've been holding out about him. Sworn off men, eh?"

"Well, I had, but Mark convinced me to give him another chance." She paused. "You aren't much company after ten, are you?" There was a teasing quality in Kathy's voice.

Judy got out of the car and stretched. "I'm not a night person." She went straight to her room. No brushing her teeth or washing her face. She couldn't wait to get to bed, though she thought her nap would keep her from sleeping. No fear. She dropped right off.

The next morning was drizzly and cool. Judy would gladly have put the covers over her head and stayed in bed.

Kathy knocked on the door. "Come on, ol' sleepyhead."

Judy groaned. Her sister sounded just too cheery. "Okay. I'm getting up." She swept the covers off and sat up on the edge of the bed. Then she flopped over on her pillow. She should have said no last night. It was going to take too much energy to go out today. And then she had to work tomorrow.

***

"Judy, are you up?" Kathy must have been outside her door.

"Can we call them up and tell them we changed our minds?"

"No such luck. They've probably left already. It's an hour's drive, at least."

Judy took her shower and wondered what to wear. Jeans, a turtleneck and tennis shoes. If they were going to be walking around, she wanted to be comfortable. She took a tweed blazer and wore that too. Egads, this was too much work.

"I fixed us some waffles. I put yours in the microwave. You might want to heat them up a bit." Kathy was in the living room, looking at the newspaper. She wore a denim shirt and jeans with half boots.

"Thanks. Am I dressed okay?" Judy opened the microwave and stuck her finger into a waffle. It could use some warming.

"That'll be fine. No one dresses up much around here. I like the looks of the blazer."

Judy ate breakfast and finished getting ready. She had just sat down to read some of the paper when the doorbell rang. Kathy was in her room so Judy got up and answered it. It was Mark and Joe.

"Come on in," She stepped aside. "Kathy is just putting on the finishing touches."

The two men sat down on facing chairs. Mark was dressed in a sweater and cords. Joe was wearing jeans, a plaid shirt and a jean jacket. He also wore cowboy boots. Very nice, Judy thought.

Kathy breezed into the room. She went over and gave Mark a kiss. "I'm ready to go."

The men stood up and moved toward the door.

"I drove. All Joe's got is that monster truck for two," Mark said. Outside was a Blazer.

"She knows that," Joe said as he jerked his head in Judy's direction.

Kathy sat in front with Mark and Joe got in the back seat with Judy. Judy was grateful for the bucket seats.

"Where do we want to go first?" Mark said to no one in particular.

"I thought we could go to the ski slope, but you can't see anything with this kind of weather," Joe said.

"How about to the art museum? They have a new exhibit there," Kathy suggested.

"Sounds good to me," said Joe.

Judy didn't say anything. She didn't know what was around. She did know she wasn't thrilled about doing much outdoors, especially in this drizzle.

"Maybe next weekend will be better weather for looking at the scenery," Joe said.

Next weekend, Judy thought. He's pretty sure of himself.

The museum was great. They only saw a couple of floors before Mark suggested they go get something to eat. "There's that little wine bar on Second Street."

"Are they open on Sundays?" Kathy asked.

"If not, there's a couple of good places nearby," Mark said.

The four of them walked three blocks to the wine bar. It was open. They were serving a brunch buffet.

"Ohh, the food looks scrumptious," Kathy said.

"It does look great," Mark said.

"Then let's go for it." Joe moved toward an empty table.

***

The food was as good as it looked. Judy was glad for the little elastic inserts in her waistband. The walk back to the art museum helped too.

The four of them walked around a couple of more exhibits before closing time.

"How about going to a movie?" Mark asked.

Judy wanted to go home. She was tired and she wanted to call the kids and Sandra yet today. But she didn't say anything.

"I have to fly out early tomorrow, so if you just want to drop me by my car?" Joe said.

That gave Judy courage to speak up. "I want to do some things tonight before I go to bed."

"I'd love to go to a movie," Kathy said. Judy could have strangled her.

"No problem. I'll take Judy home. It's on my way," Joe said.

"Good idea," Mark said before Judy had a chance to reply.

They walked over to Mark's car. Judy got into the back and so did Joe.

"You don't mind, do you?" Kathy fastened her belt.

Judy was somewhat concerned. She didn't really know Joe. However, Mark and Kathy seemed to think he was okay. The incident with Calvin still unnerved her.

Joe must have read her mind. "You'll be safe with me."

Judy managed to give him a weak smile.

A few miles from the city, Mark pulled into a parking lot. Judy saw Joe's truck. There could only be one like it in the world.

"See ya later." Kathy waved to Judy when they got out of the car.

Judy gave her a little wave and followed Joe to his truck.

In no time, they were heading toward Kathy's condo. Judy

was beginning to recognize the highway. Joe popped in a different CD of more contemporary classical music.

"I really appreciate this. I wanted to call my children before it got too late. They are a couple of hours later than we are here." She sounded stupid to herself.

"I understand. I hate these early flights, but that way, I don't have to spend the night. I can get everything done during the business day."

They were silent, but it wasn't an uncomfortable silence. Judy couldn't think of a thing to say, so she didn't say anything.

"Maybe next weekend will be better weather and we can show you some of the sights."

She surprised herself by saying, "I'd like that. It's dark when we leave work so all I see are headlights."

"Do you ski?"

"I'm not an outdoorsy type person."

Joe chuckled.

"The most exotic I get is to hike."

"There are some great trails around here. When the weather dries up, we'll have to go."

Judy didn't tell him she was only going to be there another few weeks. But then again, maybe she would stay longer. Or was there something sinister about his offer? She'd been reading too many mysteries lately.

Joe pulled into the driveway and they both got out. He walked her to the door. "I had a great time. I'm glad Mark suggested this."

"You are?" she thought. "Now what? Do I invite him in?" She didn't have to think very long. Joe turned her around and put his hands on her shoulders and bent and gave her a kiss. A very nice kiss. Nothing pushy or anything. She liked it. She liked him.

"I'll see you next weekend. If Mark and Kathy want to go along, fine. Otherwise, we can go by ourselves." Then he added, "If you don't mind."

"That would be fine with me-either way," she lied. She was nervous. She felt like a teenager, just starting to date.

She stood on the porch and watched him back out the drive. They waved at each other and then she went inside.

XII

The light on the answering machine was blinking. She hit the play button. One from Grace, one from Andy and three from Sandra. For crying out loud, maybe she should stay just to keep from being smothered by them.

Before she called any of them, she decided to make herself a sandwich or something. Then she put on her robe and slippers. It was nice not to have anyone around. She missed her solitude.

Who should she call first? Sandra. Get the thing over with. She steeled herself for another sermon.

Sandra was cheerful and not bossy like she usually was. They talked for a few minutes.

"Can I talk to Kathy for a minute?" Sandra asked.

"She's not here. She's at the movie with a friend."

"Man or woman?"

"Man."

"What's he like? Did you get to meet him? Is it serious?"

Judy felt like a spy. "I don't know much about him. He seems nice enough."

"Well, find out and let me know."

Judy finished the call as quickly as she could. She was not about to tell Sandra that she had been on a date. She was beginning to understand Kathy much better.

Grace was on another call and would call her back. Andy let each of the kids talk for a few minutes. Judy missed them.

"When are you coming home, Mom?" he asked when the kids were done.

"I'm not sure. You know I have a temporary job?" She couldn't remember if she told him or not.

"Yeah. How's it going?"

"Filing is boring, but everyone is friendly so the time goes quickly."

Andy wasn't much of a talker so the call was short.

Judy went to her room to get her clothes ready for the next day. She would take a bath, but wanted to wait until after Grace returned her call. She took her book and went into the living room. She started to read the paper instead.

The phone rang. She got up to answer it. "Hi, Chicky,' she said.

There was a silence and then a giggle. "Is that how you answer all your calls?" It was Kathy.

"I thought you were Grace calling," Judy said, happy it hadn't been someone else.

"You got home safe?"

"Yes. Did you expect me not to?"

"Of course not. Anyway, I'm not coming home tonight. I'm going to stay at Mark's. You can drive in tomorrow and meet me at work."

Judy wasn't sure she was more upset about Kathy staying with Mark or having to drive in by herself.

"Judy?"

"Oh, I was just thinking about driving with all that traffic."

"You'll do fine. Would you bring me some office clothes?"

"I'll bring you clean underwear, too."

"That would be a good thing. See you in the morning." Kathy hung up.

Judy stood in the hall, holding the phone. When it buzzed, she hung it up.

This was something she hadn't even considered. Kathy was going to spend the night with Mark. She wondered even more just how serious this was. What if Joe hadn't taken her home? Would she be sleeping over at Mark's, too, or was she just cramping Kathy's style by being there?

I guess I'll just have to have a long talk with her, Judy told herself.

When Grace did call, Judy was more cautious when she answered the ring.

Nothing new. She liked her new place. So much handier for work. She'd call again next Sunday.

Judy slept better than she thought she would, being alone in a strange place. She woke up early. The thought of the drive in was scary. If she got an early start, maybe she would miss most of the heavy traffic. Steve did most of the driving when they went someplace together.

It was dark when Judy left. There were more vehicles on the road than Judy imagined. Still, she had allowed herself more than enough time. Kathy always gave herself just minutes to spare.

***

In the parking ramp, there were more than the usual parking spaces, but Judy parked where they usually did. That way, she would remember where she parked the car. She grabbed the bags out of the back seat and locked up Kathy's car. What a relief to have the drive behind her!

She was surprised to see Kathy there, waiting for her.

"This my stuff?" Kathy grabbed the tote bag from Judy before she even got an answer. "Come on with me. I have a lot of news."

Judy followed her into the women's room. Kathy took the bag and went into a stall. "I took a shower at Mark's, and he found me a toothbrush."

All the conveniences of home, Judy thought. "So what's the news?"

Kathy's left hand waved over the stall door. "This!" On her hand was a sparkling diamond ring.

"Wow!" Judy couldn't help but gasp.

"We're getting married." The door opened and Kathy came out. She rolled up her jeans and shoved them into the bag.

"When?" Judy was at a loss for words.

"In two weeks. Would you be my matron of honor?"

"Of course I will." Judy threw her arms around her sister. "Isn't this rather sudden?"

"Yes and no. I'll explain it all to you after work. Mark is going to ask Joe to be his best man."

"Are you going to call Sandra and see if she and Brad can make it out?"

"Nope. It'll just be the four of us. I don't want to tell

anybody until after it's over. No fuss. No muss." Kathy pursed her lips.

"Whatever you say." Judy gave Kathy another hug. "I'm so happy for you."

"Now, what about dinner? Do you want to eat on the way home from work or eat in?"

"I'd rather eat in I took a couple of lamb chops out of the freezer."

"Oh, yum. Maybe Mark and I can hire you as our cook."

Judy laughed. "I don't think so."

Judy started early that day and put in her eight hours. She sent a message to Kathy saying she had some errands to do and would meet her at the car.

She really didn't have any errands, so she went to the library and browsed until almost time for Kathy to meet her. Then she hurried to the car. All day long, she thought about Kathy and Mark. How long had they known each other? What did he do? Had he been married before? She would keep a lid on those questions until the ride home.

"Okay, tell me all about what's going on," Judy said as they drove.

"Not until dinner," Kathy said. "I want to see your face when we talk. I can't do that and drive in this traffic at the same time."

Once home, Judy changed her clothes. "I'll start dinner."

"While you do that, I'll get the mail and do a load of wash." Kathy disappeared.

Within an hour, they sat down to their meal.

Judy lifted her wine glass. "Here's to you and Mark." She took a sip.

"Okay. You can start with the third degree," Kathy said.

"To start with, how long have you known him? What does he do for a living? How old is he? Has he--"

"Hold it." Kathy interrupted. She took a sip of her wine. Actually, it was a large gulp. "First of all, we've been dating on and off for five years."

"Five years? How can anyone just date for five years?" Judy and Steve dated for one and that was long enough.

"I'm not going to answer your questions if you keep interrupting me."

"I'll shut up." Judy raised her left hand as if she swore an oath.

"He sells insurance. He's been married before, but no children. He was widowed." Kathy stopped to take a bite of food.

So far, so good, Judy thought. She was going to start with a barrage of more questions when Kathy said, "He's forty-two."

"Forty-two? He's ten years younger than you!"

"So what? If I was a man and he was a woman, the age difference wouldn't make anyone blink an eye." Kathy looked straight at her sister. "I love the shocked look on your face."

She was right, but still... Judy decided to try another tack. "So, why haven't I heard about Mark before? This all seems rather sudden.

"If I had shared this with you or Sandra, you would have been asking all sorts of questions. The miles are my wall of privacy. It was just one of those on and off things." Kathy shrugged.

"Where are you going to live?"

"He has a place in the city. A converted warehouse. Much more convenient than out here."

"But you have this place just perfect."

"Sis, it's just a place to live. I don't have any real attachment to it. I certainly don't spend much time here," Kathy made a sweeping gesture. "Would you like to buy it?"

Judy laughed, "No, as much as I like the place, I have to figure out what to do with the rest of my life. But thanks for offering."

Judy leaned in her chair and looked at Kathy. She knew that this look used to intimidate her. She wondered if it still could.

`"What?" Kathy squirmed some in her chair.

Ah, ha, Judy thought. I still have it. She didn't say anything.

"Last night, he asked me to marry him."

"But why are you getting married so fast?"

"Well, I'm not pregnant."

Judy grinned. "That's a relief."

"We figured why wait? Besides, I want you to be at the wedding and know you wouldn't come just for that. And another thing," Kathy took a sip of water. "If you went now, I know you'd blab it all over and then we'd end up with a big wedding--which neither of us wants. We want to get married on Friday so we can have the weekend for a honeymoon. The pastor was fine with that because he has a wedding rehearsal later that evening."

"Okay, okay. You've convinced me." Judy leaned toward the table. "I just want you to be happy." She reached across the table and patted Kathy's hand. "Let's go shopping for wedding clothes tomorrow after work."

"Sounds great. Nothing fancy. Maybe a suit or dressy dress." She turned to look at Judy. "Now just don't let this slip to anyone at work or when you're talking to family on the phone."

Judy went through the motions they used when they were kids to zip and lock lips shut.

"Good!"

They went on eating dinner.

"You guys going on a honeymoon?" Judy popped their plates into the dishwasher.

"Mark told me he had things all planned. I don't feel right about taking off any more time at the present. We'll probably go away for the weekend."

Judy remembered her wedding. They were married when Steve came home on leave just before he was shipped out to Korea. Even in 1960s, men were being sent to Korea and Germany. They had been grateful it hadn't been Nam, like some of their friends. Sandra was her maid of honor and Kathy the junior bridesmaid. She couldn't remember who was the best man. She thought it was one of Steve's college roommates. The wedding reception had been a picnic in the park. Her parents hired a caterer. For their honeymoon, they spent the weekend in a rustic beach house. It seemed so long ago.

On Friday, Joe called to tell her they would have to postpone their sightseeing plans. He would be out of town until the Wednesday before the wedding. He apologized several times. "Well, I'll see you at the wedding." Joe said after a few minutes.

"See you then." Judy felt rather empty after the call ended. She looked forward to getting out. She went to work during the day. Most evenings, she was alone. Kathy and Mark were busy with arrangements for the wedding. She helped Kathy start to pack up.

Kathy and Mark found a larger unit in the converted warehouse where he lived. Kathy wouldn't move any furniture out until after her place was sold.

"Mark says places sell better with the furniture still in place."

"That seems to be the rule." That's what she and Steve did when they sold the big house.

Wednesday after work, Kathy took Judy over to see the new place. It was within walking distance of her office. They took a freight elevator up to the fifth floor.

"Mark must be here already," Kathy said as she pointed down the hall. One door stood open.

Voices could be heard. Men's voices.

"I wonder who's with him." Kathy started to walk faster. Judy had to almost run to keep up with her.

Kathy went over and gave Mark a kiss as Judy walked in. "Hey, Joe, welcome back," Kathy said.

"Thanks. It's good to be back." He looked at Judy.

She couldn't help grinning at him. She was truly happy to see him. "Let's go down to my place and order a pizza?" Mark said as he held Kathy close.

"I want to see this place first," Judy said.

"Come on. I'll show you around," Kathy said. "Mark, why don't you go and order the pizza? It always takes so long."

"Okay, honey." Mark gave her another kiss and he and Joe went out the door.

Judy got the grand tour, everything from the linen closet to the master bedroom suite.

"Did you ever see such a view?" Kathy opened the drapes in the living room. "We have the same view from the balcony in our room."

The mountains were purple in the background of the city. "It is about the best view I've ever seen."

"About?"

"I love the desert, but I could change my mind."

Kathy didn't reply. "And when you stay with us," she

opened a door, "this is where you can sleep."

The second bedroom was large, but just how large, it was difficult for Judy to gauge. There was no furniture, only the light blue carpet and ivory drapes.

"There's a bathroom over here." Kathy opened one of two doors on the opposite wall.

It wasn't as grand as the master bath, but it was lovely.

"And this is the closet." Kathy opened the other door. There was a walk-in closet. "I think I'll probably use part of this one for storage."

"It's great! The view and all the room. The best thing is that you don't have to battle the traffic every day."

"That's what Mark said when I bought my place. He wanted me to move in with him, but I'm just a bit old-fashioned for that."

They took the elevator down a couple of floors.

Mark's place was in the middle of the building, next to a stairway. Kathy didn't knock but went right in. It was a studio apartment with a loft.

"Now I like this, but I can see why you want a bigger place." Judy looked around. The high ceiling and openness made it look much larger.

"Wanna buy it? I know the owner personally and could get you a sweet deal," Mark said as he handed Kathy a can of Coke.

"Yeah. Sure. Kathy already offered to sell me her condo. I'm in enough trouble with my family for staying out here as long as I am." Judy took an empty chair at the glass topped table.

"You are over twenty-one, aren't you?" Joe asked.

"Yes, but since Steve died, no one gives me credit for an ounce of common sense,"

Kathy went into the fridge and got out a can of Diet Coke for Judy. "See why I stay out here? They'd have my life programmed. Besides, they refer to me as an old maid."

"Well, not for much longer." Mark gave her another kiss.

The buzzer sounded. Mark went to the intercom and pushed a button.

"I got a pizza here for a Mark."

"I'll be right down." Mark grabbed his wallet off the counter and went out. Kathy went with him.

Joe took a swig of his beer. "So your family thinks you need tending?"

"I can't believe it. At first, I thought it was nice to have them care so much, but now I feel that they are smothering me."

"I know what you mean. After my wife left me, my mom wrapped me in cotton. She worried I'd get hurt again." He took another swig.

"Your mom?"

"Yeah, she's eighty-five and still works part-time, volunteering. You'd like her. I'll have to take you out to meet her before you leave."

Little warning bells went off in Judy's brain. Don't get serious. It's far too soon. "We're going to be pretty busy with the wedding coming up." She got up and went to the window. "The view is as nice as from their new place."

"You're right about that."

Judy about jumped out of her skin. She hadn't heard Joe get up and stand next to her. He put his hands on her shoulders and her neck, just below her ear. She gave a little shiver and turned. Without a word, he gave her a long lingering kiss. His tongue just grazed her lips. A quiver went through her stomach. Why am I reacting like a teenager? And, why does it feel so right? She pulled away as Kathy and Mark came in.

"Come and get it while it's hot," Mark said. He took some paper plates and tossed them on the table.

Judy felt her face get very warm. Feeling flustered, she went over and sat, hoping it didn't show. Suddenly, she wasn't hungry at all.

"You feeling okay?" Kathy asked. "I thought you were starving."

"I feel fine. I just don't want to wolf down my supper." She felt Joe's eyes on her, but he didn't say anything.

Kathy seemed to take her word for it. She and Mark chattered away about their wedding and weekend away.

Every time Judy looked up, she saw Joe looking at her. She quickly lowered her eyes.

"Thought your sister might like to meet my mother," Joe said.

"Oh, you'll love his mother. She's a riot," Kathy said. "You take good care of Judy."

"You sound like Sandra," Judy said.

"Who's Sandra?"

"Our other sister," both women said in unison.

Joe said, "I'll drive you home, if you'd like."

"I have to work in the morning, or I'd take you up on the offer." Judy worried about driving in the dark. She could just imagine herself driving around in circles before she found the condo.

"How about if you follow me?"

"I could do that."

Shortly after the pizza vanished, Joe and Judy left.

Judy kept Joe's taillights in her vision. He was easy to follow. He kept a nice steady pace. She was beginning to enjoy Joe's company. He was funny and intelligent. Plus, he was polite.

When they pulled in front of Kathy's condo, Joe parked his truck and got out. "You're safe and sound."

"Thanks. I really appreciate your help."

"This place can get confusing enough during the day, let alone after dark."

"I'm going to leave the car in the drive tonight, instead of putting it in the garage." Judy was groping for something to say. "My job is finished the week after the wedding. I may stay a day or two after, but I'm getting anxious to get home. There are a lot of things I have to put in order."

"Then you won't be here when I get back."

"Where will you be?" Judy suddenly felt lonely.

"I have business in Europe. It'll take more than a week to get it taken care of."

Judy imagined the week after the wedding stretching into a long quiet time. Kathy would be with Mark and Joe would be gone. Oh, well, she would be busy with work.

"Friday, after the wedding, would you go to my mother's and spend the weekend?"

Judy hesitated.

"Separate rooms. No funny business," Joe said as if reading her mind. "My mother is a bit old-fashioned when it comes to certain behavior."

"Sure, I'll go. It'll be a nice to see something more of Colorado."

"We'll leave right after dinner, then."

"Great." Judy debated about asking him in for a drink. What could it hurt? "Would you like to come in for a drink?"

"Naw, I'll walk you to the door, but I have some phone calls to make yet tonight."

True to his word, he walked her to the door. This time, the goodnight kiss was more intense. Judy's knees felt weak.

"Goodnight, Judy," he whispered and left.

Judy went in and closed the door. She didn't put on the light until he drove away. She didn't want him to see her watching him from the window in the door.

Suddenly, she was so lonely. Besides, she was afraid. Was she beginning to fall for this guy? It was too soon. She was vulnerable and she knew it. Those kisses were way too sensuous. Still, she wasn't going to pass up the chance to spend the weekend with him at his mother's. She just wasn't going to let him get too close.

The message light was blinking on the phone. Judy hit the play button. Sandra called twice and Grace once. Neither sounded urgent. She erased the messages and decided to call them tomorrow.

Sleep didn't come. She played the scenes with Joe over and over in her mind. Was she too standoffish? Was she too forward by responding to his kisses? God, she had no idea how to act anymore. When she went through all of that, she started to think about what it was going to be like back home. Her life looked like a big empty space.

It was after midnight when the phone rang. "Hello?" she said with hesitation. Who would be calling her at this hour?

"I didn't wake you, did I?" It was Joe.

"No, I was having trouble getting to sleep."

"Me, too. I made those calls and by that time, I was so wide-awake, there was no use in trying to sleep."

"Who would you be calling this late at night anyway?" Judy knew it was none of her business, but didn't know what else to say.

"I had to call Europe. It's already tomorrow there." He laughed.

"I guess it would be." Judy fluffed up her pillow and put it behind her back as she sat up.

"You won't have any trouble finding your way to work in the morning, will you?"

"No, I've driven it often in the past few weeks when Kathy stayed with Mark."

"Just thought I'd ask." Joe sounded disappointed.

Judy tried to think of something to say. Finally, she said, "Tell me something about where your mother lives. Kathy said she's a dynamo."

"She sure is. She lives on a little ranch. A few years ago, after Dad died, she thought about putting up a smaller house. But she likes the big house and takes care of it with the help of a housekeeper and cleaning lady."

Judy tried to stifle a yawn, but Joe must have heard her anyway. "I think I better let you get some sleep." He yawned. "I think I should too."

"Thanks for calling." Judy was ready to hang up.

"I really have enjoyed spending time with you."

"And I've liked having you show me this part of the country."

They hung up and Judy tried to go to sleep. Now she replayed the phone conversation. Was he interested in her? And if he was, what kind of interest? A one-night stand? Purely platonic? Purely sexual? A lifetime commitment?

***

It was almost dawn when she was awakened by the phone again.

"Hey, are you all right?" It was Sandra.

"Yeah, I'm fine. You know you woke me up." Judy didn't bother to keep the irritation out of her voice.

"Sorry, but when you didn't call, I got worried."

"I got home late and decided to wait until the morning to call back."

"Is Kathy there?"

"No, she spent the night with a friend."

"Same guy as the last time?"

"Knock it off, Sandra. What is so important that you had to wake me up? I have to get ready for work."

"Nothing important. I was just wondering how things were going and when you're coming back. Don't have to get so huffy about it."

"I have a week left on the job. Then I thought I'd stay a few extra days before coming home." Judy was angry with herself for giving in to Sandra's bossiness.

"Well, excuse me for living," Sandra said. "I was only trying to be friendly."

Judy mentally threw up her hands. "That's okay. I just had trouble sleeping last night." That was the truth.

Sandra told her a couple tidbits of gossip before Judy could get her off the line.

She felt like she had been on an all-nighter. Her eyes were scratchy and her throat was dry. And her head ached. Moreover, she had to go to the bathroom.

While in the bathroom, she took a couple of aspirin to relieve her headache. Better get ready for work, she thought.

A shower revived her some. The sun was just coming up when she went into the kitchen to make coffee. She'd better hurry if she was going to beat the traffic.

Kathy was waiting for her in the office building lobby. "Well, what do you think of our new digs?"

"The view is spectacular. Joe and I talked about it last night."

"You and Joe, huh?" Kathy gave her a sly look. "All you did was talk?"

Judy felt her face get warm. Judy knew Kathy was teasing, but she was getting angry. "No, he spent the night and left when I went to work."

"Okay, I'm sorry, it's just that you two would make a great couple."

"Kathy, I was married for a long time and my husband just died a few months ago. I'm not looking for anyone."

"Sorry." Kathy looked so contrite, Judy almost forgave her.

"However, we did make arrangements to visit his mother this weekend after the wedding dinner."

Now Kathy gave her a knowing smile, but didn't say anything more.

"Mark is going to a bachelor party tonight. It's his."

"I thought you guys were going to keep the wedding a secret until after?"

"We were, but Mark made a slip and... well, you know the rest."

Judy just shook her head. She didn't tell Kathy that their coworkers knew too. On Friday, they were giving her a surprise shower.

***

Friday was a beautiful day. The two women hung their dresses in the car and packed small cases with what they needed to get ready for the wedding. "All we need is for someone to steal our stuff," Kathy said. Carefully, she put a sheet over everything so no one would see.

XIII

The shower was scheduled for noon. The day before, Judy bought a skimpy nightgown for Kathy as a shower gift. One of the other women hid it for her.

Kathy was thoroughly surprised. Of course, she accused Judy of the leak.

"I didn't say a thing," Judy said.

"My sister's boyfriend works with Mark." One of the women jumped to Judy's defense.

"Sorry," Kathy said. "I've just been so nervous lately."

"Wedding jitters," said one of the other women.

They had a fun time. Kathy got several other skimpy outfits. Some nameless person even gave her a package of condoms.

"You don't want to get pregnant right away."

"That I don't have to worry about." Kathy grinned.

"Lucky you," one of the young secretaries said.

They all took a very long lunch that day. Kathy and Judy made arrangements to leave early. They went up to the new place to get dressed. Joe was to pick them up and bring them to the church. Mark would be waiting for them there.

While Judy was happy Kathy found someone to spend the rest of her life with, she hoped her sister would be as happy as she was with Steve. Her wedding seemed so long ago. And, she was so much younger.

The wedding itself was short and sweet and to the point. After Joe paid the minister, they left, Kathy and Mark in one car and Joe and Judy in Joe's truck.

The restaurant was located in an historic hotel. Crystal and silver sparkled from everywhere.

"We can eat hearty," Mark said. "Joe's picking up the tab."

Judy noticed that neither Mark nor Kathy were interested in food. They did drink a toast.

"We're going to leave now." Joe got up. "I don't want to keep Mom up too late waiting for us."

Judy stood. Then Mark and Kathy stood up also.

"Thanks for everything." There were hugs and kisses all around.

"I want to bring your car to the condo and get what I need for the weekend," Judy said.

Kathy pulled a key ring from her purse. "You need these." Judy had forgotten her set of keys at the condo.

"If you want, I can lead you back again," Joe said as they left the restaurant.

"That'll be fine. I think I know my way, but I hate getting all turned around, especially since we have a drive ahead of us."

XIV

Traffic was light and Joe was an easy person to follow. Judy remembered how Brad would have people follow him and then try to lose them.

Judy pulled the car into the garage. "I'll just be a minute. Do you want to come in?"

Joe shut off the engine and followed her into the house.

"Let me get out of this first," Judy said about her dress. "Otherwise, I'm all packed." She went into her room and put on a good pair of slacks and a cotton sweater. She slipped into a pair of sandals as she picked up her suitcase and walked into the living room. Joe was perched on the edge of a chair. He sprang up as she came into the room.

"Here, let me take that." He took her suitcase. "Is this all?"

"That's it."

"Most women take enough along for a month."

Judy didn't say anything, but took this comment as a compliment.

Within minutes, they were speeding along the freeway heading northwest, according to the truck's compass.

Away from the city lights, the stars twinkled, even with the light of an almost full moon. Neither of them spoke for the first hour.

"We have another hour's drive. Would you like to stop for a cup of coffee? There's a diner at the next exit," Joe said.

Judy didn't need coffee as much as she needed a bathroom. "That would be fine."

"I need to find a men's room. All the champagne and coffee has caught up with me."

"And I need to find the ladies' room,"

They had a cup of coffee in the diner. Joe called his mother on his cell phone before they went to the car. "Mom is so excited. She has the guest room all made up for you."

At least he didn't say us, she thought. "I don't want to put her out."

"She loves company. Says I never come often enough...especially bringing a friend."

"Joe, I hope she doesn't get the idea that we're more than friends."

"She won't. I told her you were widowed recently and are here visiting your sister."

"Thanks." Judy didn't want to have to go through the whole explanation.

In the darkness, Judy couldn't see much scenery, though she did make out the dark outlines of trees and mountains. The headlights of oncoming traffic and the headlights of Joe's truck didn't show much of their surroundings.

Joe took the off ramp into what appeared to be a black hole. He made a right onto a gravel road. "We'll have to go over that way."

It didn't seem like they slowed down one bit. She gripped the armrest to keep from sliding off her seat.

Joe barely slowed down as he made a sharp left turn onto a narrow drive. There was some sort of arch over it, but Judy couldn't see if anything was written on it. She could see a light in the distance.

"That's where we want to go." He pointed toward the light. He slowed down now as they bumped along what was probably a road, or maybe just an open field.

Joe braked suddenly as a steer ambled across the path. "Sorry about that," he said as Judy jerked forward. She would have smashed against the dashboard if it hadn't been for her seatbelt. "This happens all the time. During the daylight, you can see them sooner."

"Is this open range?"

"Naw, just sometimes the fence needs fixin' and some of the cattle get out. The sheep roam all over the place at their will. As long as the border fences are closed, there usually isn't a problem."

A light on a tall pole illuminated a large area. Now this was what she'd always imagined a ranch to look like. There were outbuildings, rail fences and a low house with a porch all across the front.

Joe stopped his truck at a rail and turned off the engine. "Wait a second. Just let the cloud of dust settle first. It seems to filter in no matter how well the cab is sealed up."

Judy choked as dust enveloped them. Joe used the windshield wipers to clear it off. Then, Judy saw a figure in bright colors coming off the porch.

"That's Mom." Joe grinned

Joe's mother was nothing like Judy imagined. She was a big woman dressed in a teal jumpsuit and wearing a white cowboy hat. Judy pictured her as small, plump and wearing a dark house dress with an apron.

"Come on. Or Mom will jerk the doors off to get to us." Joe laughed.

Joe and his mother hugged each other and he spun her around, even though she probably was only a few inches shorter.

"Mom, this is Judy Evans," Joe said.

"Pleased to meet you, Judy," The woman stuck out a big hand.

Judy took it. It was warm and calloused.

"Just call me 'Toots'," Joe's mother said.

"Toots?" Judy repeated it without meaning to.

"It's a long story. My grandfather gave me that name when I was born. Couldn't stand what my mother named me."

"Do I dare ask?"

"Theda, like Theda Bara. My mother loved going to the picture shows. Thought I'd be just like that little vamp. Actually, my whole name was Theda Ophelia O'Toole, hence Toots." Her laugh sounded like little bells. "Well, let's not waste time out here. Joe, you bring in the bags."

Judy felt like a dwarf walking beside Joe's mother. They walked up the steps to the porch. There were benches and an assortment of chairs. Along one end was a clothesline with what was probably a dish towel waving in the little breeze. Behind the screen door, lights glowed.

Toots reached forward and opened the door for Judy. "Come on in. I made a little snack for you kids. Thought you might be hungry after the drive."

"I would like to use your bathroom first." The coffee from the diner and the rough ride had taken their toll.

"First door on the left. I'll see if Joey needs help."

Joey? This was more bizarre than she expected. She grinned and went into a small powder room. She half expected an outhouse. This room was lovely. There were even little fingertip towels and fancy soap.

"You put Judy's things in there," Toots told Joe. "You can sleep in the loft or the bunk house, whichever you prefer." She turned to Judy, "I'm in the process of having Joe's room painting and the floor refinished."

"Your home is lovely," Judy said.

"Why, thank you." Toots headed toward an open door and Judy followed. "I try to keep this as refined as possible with all these men around."

"Refined" wasn't a word Judy would have used. "Elegant" would be more appropriate. The floors were plank but there were oriental rugs under the Queen Anne's dining room set. Wedgewood china was displayed in a cabinet.

"Big Joe never wanted me to feel like I married beneath me."

This was more intriguing than Judy ever imagined. Bordering on the weird. What had she gotten herself into? She followed Toots through a set of bat-wing doors into the kitchen.

The kitchen looked like a relic from the past until Judy recognized it only seemed that way. Everything was reproductions.

"I just had my kitchen remodeled," Toots said. "I wanted it to look as old as possible with the newest materials. Sit down. Make yourself at home."

Judy sat on a plank chair at the big oak pedestal table.

"So what kind of a career did you have?"

"I was a school teacher. Taught first grade."

"What made you quit? You look too young for social security." Toots filled a large teakettle with water.

"The state offered us such a good retirement package, we couldn't refuse."

"Was your husband a teacher too?" Toots set the kettle on the stove that was styled like those during the era of the First World War.

"Yes, he taught math in high school."

"I taught high school, too. Did Joey tell you?" She took three mugs out of the cupboard.

"No, he didn't." Joey hadn't told her much of anything.

"I taught music. I studied to be a concert pianist when I was in college. Oberlin. Not much of a need for that out here when I was first married. So I taught choir. I also did some private lessons."

That might explain Joe's appreciation of classical music.

"Mom telling you all the family secrets?" Joe came in and thumped down on a chair.

"I haven't had enough time yet." Toots grinned. "Would you rather have tea or coffee?"

"I like tea," Judy said.

"Fine with me," Joe said.

Toots opened a canister and took out several packets. "Say, son, when you go to England next week, bring me home some of that good tea."

"Just write down the name." Joe pulled his chair around.

"Did you know that Joey..."

"Mom, you can just call me Joe, not Joey."

Toots sighed. "I keep forgetting. Anyway, he could have been a concert violinist except that he broke his hand playing football in high school."

"No, he never told me."

"What did you tell this young woman?" Toots joined them at the table.

"Not much. We've only known each other a few weeks. Am I supposed to march out all the family skeletons on the first date?" He reached over and tweaked his mother's nose.

"Well, no, but how do you expect to know someone if you don't talk?"

The teakettle started to whistle and Toots got up to fix the tea. "Do you take anything in it? Sugar? Milk? Lemon?"

"No, I like it plain."

She set the mugs on the table. Next to each cup she put a ceramic tea bag holder shaped like a leaf.

Joe spooned two heaping teaspoons of sugar into his cup and then proceeded to stir it. Toots took out several bags of cookies and put some on a plate. "As you can tell, my mother is a gourmet baker."

Toots winked at Judy. "I also have a cleaning lady." She sat down.

"Now that you know all of the family secrets, what do ya think?" Joe looked at Judy.

"Scandalous!" She took a bite of a windmill cookie.

"What do you plan on doing tomorrow?" Toots asked.

"I was going to take a ride over to the canyon. Thought Judy would enjoy the view."

Ride? Panic seized Judy. Did he mean ride a horse? She was afraid of horses.

"The jeep is in the shed."

"Then we're not taking horses?" Judy asked.

Joe and Toots both started to laugh.

"We haven't had a horse around here for years. Hands use ATVs and jeeps," Toots said.

"But if you want to ride a horse, I can borrow a couple from a neighbor," Joe said.

"No, that's okay. I'm not a horse person anyway."

"High school's putting on a musical this weekend. I think there's some tickets still available. Their musicals are pretty good," she added.

Joe gave Judy a questioning look.

"That sounds good" What else could she say? Anyway, it was only one night.

"We're going to have to leave early Sunday. I have to get ready for the trip," Joe said.

Judy stifled a yawn.

Toots must have seen it. "Come on. I'll show you to your room." She got up and waited for Judy to follow her out of the room.

"If there's anything you need, I'll just be down the hall." Toots switched on an overhead light. "There's a bathroom across from your room. I have my own bath, so you won't be bothering me at all. There are towels ready for you."

"Thanks, Toots," Judy said. It was hard for her to call the older woman by such a ridiculous name.

When she was alone, Judy looked around. A four-poster stood against one wall, but the room was huge. Bookcases lined another wall. She went over to read the titles. You can tell a lot about a person by the books they read.

These books were all over the scale. There was everything from Dr. Seuss to Stephen King. There were family photos hanging on the walls. She wondered who they all were. There was one of a young woman. It looked to be the latest. Judy wondered if it was Joe's-Joey's- daughter. She was too tired to speculate further.

Her suitcase was on a chair. She opened it up and took out her makeup case. She went to the bathroom, brushed her teeth and washed her face. She didn't have much makeup in the case. She decided to take a shower in the morning.

In her room, she got ready for bed and had to step up on a stool to get into bed. She hoped she didn't forget where she was and fall out.

The sheets smelled of sunshine. Judy snuggled down and was asleep in no time. It was unusual for her to sleep so well the first night in a strange bed.

Judy woke to the smell of coffee mixed with the sound of voices. She opened one eye. It was still dark out. She could have slept for another hour or so. Not good for a house guest. She let herself drop off the side of the bed onto her feet. She took a shower and dressed. Wearing jeans and a T-shirt, she followed her nose to the kitchen.

"Did we wake you?" Toots asked as she hopped up from a chair.

"The smell of coffee woke me." Judy was going to pour herself some, but Toots motioned for her to take a seat.

Joe sat there, wearing faded jeans and a plaid shirt. He stirred his coffee. Clink. Clink. He nodded at her.

Judy accepted a steaming mug from Toots.

"Sleep well?" Toots asked as she poured more coffee into her own mug.

"I sure did," Judy answered She took a sip of coffee, but it was too hot and burned her lips.

"We'll take lunch with us. There aren't any restaurants where we're going and it's too far to come back to eat." Joe clinked his spoon again.

"That'll be fine." Judy thought poorly of eating with dust flying everywhere, but she wasn't going to look bad in front of her hosts.

"Wanna go along, Mom?" Joe said.

Toots didn't look surprised. "No, I have plenty of chores that need doing. Thanks for thinking of your dear old mother." It must have been a family joke as Toots and Joe burst into laughter.

"When do you want to leave?" Judy glanced up at the clock. It was barely after six.

"How soon can you be ready?"

"Now don't you rush her. I have some breakfast ready and I'll make your picnic. You go and gas up the jeep and take care of yourself." Toots popped a couple of pieces of toast onto a plate and covered them with a gooey mixture. "Hope you like creamed chipped beef." She plopped the plate in front of Judy. "We had this for breakfast when I was growing up. It would be in a chafing dish on the dining room sideboard. My dad thought it was wonderful. So do I."

"In the army, we used to call it something else," Joe called over his shoulder.

Judy knew it was also called shit on a shingle. "I haven't had this in years. I loved it as a kid. My mom used to make this for Saturday lunch."

"You eat what you can. I have a habit of dishing up too much for folks."

It was okay, but heavier than Judy usually ate. She was able to finish one piece and a few bites of the other. "I'm going to finish getting ready,"

"You just take your time. That man has got to learn patience one of these days."

It didn't take Judy long to brush her teeth and put some liquid makeup on. Just a touch of lipstick. Tiny hoop earrings and a watch finished her preparations. Quickly, she made the bed.Joe was sitting on a kitchen chair when she was ready. There was a large cooler on the table and next to one of those gallon thermos jugs.

He nodded. "Ready to go? Don't forget sunglasses." He grabbed the cooler. She slung her purse over her shoulder and carried the jug. "Put on your seat belt. We might hit a few bumps and you'll fly out. Can't lose you or your sister will have my hide." He gave her a lopsided grin.

The road was bumpy. She clenched her teeth so they wouldn't bang together. A cloud of dust followed them. Ahead, it was beautiful. Sunlight filtered through a haze, giving the scene a surrealistic look, an aura. Much more vegetation than she had imagined. Grassy clumps and shrubs lined the roadside.

Joe maneuvered onto a half-hidden lane and stopped the jeep at a gate. He got out and opened it. Then he got in. When they were through, he stopped the jeep again and closed the gate. "Just one little crack in the fence and we have to find half the herd." He drove along a sort of road. There were cattle here and there, grazing on nearly invisible blades of grass.

Every once in a while, Joe would take a clipboard off the

dash and write something down. "I'm noting what condition the fence is in and anything else of interest. That way, the foreman doesn't have to send anyone to check it out. Saves time and effort."

The sun was getting hot. It was still a couple of hours till noon. Joe pulled to the side of the hill. "Let's go and have something cold to drink and get out of the sun for a while." He pulled over and stopped. He took out two plastic glasses and the jug. They walked up and sat down under the trees.

"It's amazing how much cooler it is under the shade," Judy said. The remark sounded stupid to her.

They sat down and leaned against the tree. "That sun can be brutal." He handed her a glass of cold water. Just what she needed. "So what do you think so far?"

"I've never been to a place like this before."

"I thought you spent winters in Arizona."

"Only a couple. But it's different than this." She paused. "It's difficult to compare the two."

"Sometime, you'll have to show me Arizona." Joe drained his glass and stood up. He gave Judy a hand and pulled her to her feet and into his arms. Before she could even think, he was kissing her gently. "Sorry, I couldn't resist," he said, before she had a chance to respond.

"There's a place up ahead where we can have our picnic lunch."

Without another word, they went to the jeep. Judy's thoughts were scrambled. Was she safe out here alone with Joe? She hadn't given it a second thought. What had she gotten herself into? She would have to be more alert.

Judging from the sun, it was just before noon when Joe took a wagon path off the road. It wound up and around a couple of curves. There was a cabin sitting amongst a small grove of trees.

"This is it." He smiled proudly to Judy. "This is where a herder would live during the summer." He got out. "Come on."

Judy was reluctant, but got out anyway. She was having second thoughts, remembering the kiss earlier in the morning. She took the penknife out of her purse and slipped it into her pocket when Joe wasn't looking.

"There's an outhouse over behind the tree. This place doesn't have running water." Joe pointed off to the other side of the cabin.

All that jostling about in the jeep made Judy eager to find a place to relieve herself.

"I'll grab the stuff out of the jeep while you're gone."

Except for a few cobwebs, the outhouse was surprisingly clean. There was even a full roll of toilet paper. She listened carefully to the noises outside. Nothing more than the rustling of branches. She could hear Joe stomping around by the jeep. She felt much better when she rejoined him.

"Mom packed some of those wrapped towelette things." He tossed Judy one. "Don't want to waste any water in washing up."

It felt good to wipe off her hands.

"Go on into the cabin. We'll leave the food in there, but we can eat out here." Joe walked off toward the outhouse. Judy went inside the cabin.

It took a few moments for her eyes to adjust to the dimness. It was clean and furnished. Judy wondered why. She went over and opened the cooler. A Tupperware box was full of sandwiches. There was a bag of carrots and one of cookies.

"Almost all the comforts of home."

Judy jumped. She hadn't heard Joe come back. "I thought

this was deserted, but it's too neat for that," Judy said.

"Some of the boys stay here if they have to work on fixing the fences for several days. It's also used in case someone gets stranded in a storm. There are many of these little line cabins all over the area."

They helped themselves to some food and went outside. Joe spread a blanket underneath a couple of trees. Judy was hungry. The ham sandwich tasted better than any she remembered. She drank a cup of water.

"I have some lemonade in the cooler. I'll be right back." He got up and took her glass and disappeared into the cabin.

All the sun and fresh air made Judy very sleepy. She would have liked to lay down and take a nap.

"Here you go." Joe handed her a glass. He sat next to her. "There is a wonderful view from just above the cabin. Would you like to see it?"

"I'd love to. If I sit here much longer, I'll nod off." Joe held out his hand and helped her to her feet, but didn't let go of her hand. They walked hand in hand to a rocky outcrop of stone.

The view was spectacular. Across the valley below, there was a ring of mountains all around. Everything looked lush and green, not dry and dusty the way it was.

"Well, was I right?" Joe slung his arm about her shoulders.

"Yes, but there are no words to describe it." Judy felt him tense.

"Look over there." He pointed to where dark clouds were forming, casting shadows across the valley. "These storms come up so fast. Let's get back to the cabin."

By the time they got down, Joe had just enough time to throw a tarp over the jeep when the first clap of thunder sounded. Judy stacked the glasses in one hand and snatched up the blanket in the other. She ran into the cabin just as a bolt of lightning flashed.

Now what was she going to do? She and Joe would be stuck here together. She was nervous of him and the weather. Another a crash of thunder sounded. There was more lightening and a steady rumble of thunder. Joe came running in just as the rain started.

"I'm glad I got that done." He stood by the screen door and looked out. "Storms in the mountains are magnificent." He motioned for her to come to him. He put his arm around her and they stood, watching the light show.

"How long do they last?" How would anyone know how long a storm lasts?

"Usually when it blows up this way, it blows over soon. If it doesn't, we'll have to spend the night here. I don't want to take a chance on the roads in the dark."

Spend the night? Judy was on the verge of panic. Just then a loud clap of thunder made her jump.

Joe just tightened his grip around her shoulder. "Sometimes it sounds like we're in the clouds."

"Storms can seem that way at home too."

"Come on. Let's see what we have for provisions." Joe went over to the drawer in a cabinet. "Flashlight. Good. Candles. Good." He took out a few more things and laid them on the counter. "I better call my mother and tell her we're safe. And not to expect us to go to the play tonight."

"Call your mother?" Judy looked around to see where there was a phone.

Joe reached into his shirt pocket and took out a tiny phone. "I never go anywhere around here without one of these." He held it up so she could get a better look.

"I didn't think a cell phone worked out here."

"If we were out further, it wouldn't, but we're really only two miles from town, the way the crow flies." He pointed off in a direction. "The road snakes around." He punched a few buttons and put the phone to his ear. "Hey, Mom, we're up at the cabin. Go to the play without us. If the storm doesn't let up soon, we'll be back in the morning. Yes, I know the road might be washed out. Don't worry. I'll be a gentleman." He snapped the phone closed and returned it to his pocket.

He grinned. "Mom says I have to act like a gentleman." He wiggled his eyebrows.

Judy got a sinking feeling in her stomach. She was alone with him and at his mercy. She casually felt her pocket. The knife was still there. "I don't expect for you to behave in any other way," she said bravely. Maybe if she pretended to be cool and confident, it might keep him away.

"Well, my mother worries too much." He went over and emptied the picnic basket.

Judy went and looked out the back door. The storm sounded like it was moving away though the rain was still pouring. She hugged herself.

"Cold?" Joe asked. "I can build a fire to take the chill off."

"Maybe later." She knew the night air would be cool. "Can I do anything?"

"There isn't much to do. I hope you don't mind having room temperature water to drink. We always keep a few gallons of bottled water, but there's no way to cool it off."

"No problem." Judy felt restless and penned in. She wasn't used to not having something to do. She walked around. There wasn't much to the cabin except one big room. There was a large bed, a table with four chairs, a couple of rockers and a glassed-in bookcase. She went over to see what was there.

"If we didn't keep those in a case, the mice would have eaten them long ago." He came over to stand by her.

"It helps keep the dust off too." She took out one by Louis L'Amour.

"I think we have all his books here."

There were a couple of books that looked interesting. She took one and went to sit in a rocker near a window for light.

"I think the storm is over. But it's too dark to leave. I'll light a lantern for you to read by." He opened a cupboard and took out a Coleman lantern. Instant coziness. He also started a fire in the cast iron cook stove "That'll take the dampness out. I'm going to go out and look around to see if there was any damage." Joe took a flashlight and went outside. She could hear his footsteps as he walked across the porch and down the steps. She saw the beam of his flashlight bob along as he walked around the cabin.

Joe was gone for about half an hour. She was still sitting in the rocker when she heard his footfalls come toward the cabin and then onto the porch. At least, she hoped it was him.

"Joe?" She spoke with caution.

"Yeah, it's me. Sorry to be gone so long. I went down the road a bit." He went around and lit a few candles. "There. That's better."

"Is the road washed out?"

"No, it looks fine. We can get going right after sunrise. The storm didn't seem to do much damage at all." He sat down in the other rocker.

"Except to my ears."

He grinned. "It was pretty loud. How about finishing off our picnic? I think there may even be a bottle of wine around here."

"Food, yes. Wine, no." Judy got up and went over to the

cupboard. She wasn't about to let anything cloud her senses.

"I'll put some more wood on the fire. We can heat some water. I know there's instant coffee and tea here."

"Either sounds much better than wine." She took out a picnic cloth and put it on the table. There were plenty of paper plates and napkins. Judy couldn't help but wonder how many other women Joe lured up to the cabin. She was still a bit wary of him, but that feeling was shrinking. What she did fear was her reaction to him. It was pure animal magnetism. This morning, his abrupt kiss startled her, but it also aroused some dormant senses. And the cabin was intimate.

"You can take the flashlight to the outhouse. No, better take the lantern. It'll make you feel more secure."

She took the handle of the lantern and went out the door. She remembered the outhouse was just to the right of the path at the edge of the trees. She paused just before she went in. She didn't hear anything. Still, she didn't waste any time and was back in the cabin quickly. "Give me my modern conveniences any day." She sat the lantern on the counter.

"So much for the good ol' days." He produced a container of wash and dry towels. "This is one good invention."

Judy helped herself. Joe tossed the used towelette into the fire. Then they sat down to the remainder of the lunch.

"Good thing it was packed in ice," Judy said as she bit into a piece of chicken.

"We don't need food poisoning, along with everything else's that's happened today."

Dinner talk was relaxed and nondescript. After they finished, Joe threw the plates and food scraps into the fire. "I don't want the bears to think we have something for them."

"Bears?" Judy hadn't thought of anything bigger than a

raccoon.

"They can be pesky if they think there's food around. I'm going to put the rest in the cooler and stick it outside. No use tempting fate."

That wasn't very reassuring. She wanted to use the outhouse before they went to sleep, but she was damned if she would if there was any chance there was a bear out in the vicinity.

Joe must have read her mind. "I think we should go down to the outhouse together. One of us can stand guard for the other."

Judy looked at him. She couldn't tell if he was kidding or not. She didn't care. She was glad for his company. "Do you have a gun?" she asked.

"No. Most of the time, bears are more afraid of us than we them."

"Most of the time?"

He reached over and caught her around the shoulders with one arm. "I'll protect you," he whispered in her ear. His warm breath on her neck was more startling than the thought of a bear. So was her reaction. Her stomach did a little flip.

They went into the cabin. Joe closed and pulled the slide bolt in place. "No use taking any chances."

Judy knew he must be serious. He went around and secured the windows.

"I'll fix a bed on the chairs. You can have the bed."

"No, I'll do the chair thing. I'm smaller and this is your place."

"But you're my guest."

"Don't worry about it." Judy went over and started to fix the chairs.

"Or, we could share the bed," Joe said.

Judy shot him a look. "Excuse me?"

"I'll sleep on top of the covers."

Judy knew she might be playing with fire, but she really didn't want to sleep on those chairs. "I guess that would be okay." Her stomach did another flip.

"I'll be a good boy. I promise."

Judy laughed. "You better be or I'll tell Toots."

Joe threw back his head and roared with laughter. "That is quite a threat." He checked the stove. "I'm going to let the fire die. With the windows closed, it should stay comfortable," he said.

Judy was exhausted. She took off her shoes and crawled into bed, fully clothed. She barely felt Joe when he lay down.

There was a loud screech that woke her. She sat upright. She couldn't remember where she was for an instant.

"Screech owl," Joe mumbled.

"Oh." She flopped down. The sound came again. She shivered. She heard owls before, but none like this. It made the hooting of the owls back home sound wimpy.

Joe put out his arm and drew her close. True to his word, he was on top of the covers. She hesitated, but curled up with her head on his shoulder. She felt so much safer. Even so, she felt the outside of her pocket. The knife was still there.

In no time, she was asleep. She awoke with Joe's lips on hers. She didn't fight him. She didn't want to. It felt so good. His tongue slipped into her mouth. A thrill ran through her insides. She moved closer to him. They were wrapped in each other's arms with their bodies pressed close, only the blankets and their clothing separating them.

The cell phone began to ring, restoring sanity. Joe groaned and got up and retrieved it from the table. "Hullo," he mumbled. "No, we were awake....We just woke up...Sure, Mom, we'll be there for breakfast....About an hour...Bye."

While Joe was talking, Judy hurried to the outhouse. What had she been thinking? Would she have gone any further than a kiss, a hot kiss? She had mixed feelings about the interruption. She knew it was too soon to even think that way, yet she wanted to feel the pleasures of intimacy. Was it Joe or the circumstances? This was going too fast.

When she got back, Joe had already made the bed.

"What can I do?" she asked.

"You can pack up the food. No sense leaving it around for wildlife." He smiled at her.

"I can do that." She went to empty the water out of the cooler.

"Here let me take that." Joe came over and took it from her. Their hands touched. Judy felt a shiver run through her.

Easy, girl, she thought. Don't blow it now.

Joe set the cooler on the table and went outside. Judy quickly packed it up. She was just wondering what to do with the extra bottle of water.

"We'll just leave the water here. It won't freeze for the next few months and someone might need it."

She turned, bumping into him. He caught her up in his arms.

"I didn't mean to rush you." He looked her in the eyes. "You need time."

Judy didn't know what to say.

He bent over and gave her a kiss, one that made her heart start to race again.

"I really like you and don't want to scare you away."

"I like you and you only scare me a little." She managed a weak smile.

"You can take the penknife out of your pocket." He winked.

Judy felt her face get hot.

"Listen, I don't blame you. A strange guy who comes on to you like I did." He kissed her again. "I'll behave myself. Just stop being so appealing."

"Appealing?"

"You have no idea." Joe picked up the cooler and headed for the door. Judy ran ahead to open the door for him.

She looked around the cabin. They had taken everything. She picked up her purse and followed Joe.

"I'll be right back. I want to make sure everything is closed up. No use asking for trouble." On the way she lay her head against the seat and closed her eyes. The sun felt so good as it came in through the open roof of the jeep. The air was so clean and pure. She hated the thought of going to town. Kathy would be with Mark and Joe would be gone too. She had one more week of work. By this time next week, she would be on her way home and this would be just a memory.

"Penny for your thoughts." Joe reached over and squeezed her hand.

She sighed. "I was just thinking about the next week. Kathy will be living in town with Mark. I leave on Saturday. You'll be gone all week."

"Miss me already?" He squeezed her hand again and then put his back on the steering wheel.

"After the whirlwind of this past week, it's going to be downright lonely." She sighed again.

"I could call you."

Judy's heart did a little leap. She tried to keep the eagerness out of her voice. "Sure. You could tell me how things are going."

"It's been a long time since anyone cared about how things

were going for me." He stared straight ahead.

Joe took a shortcut to his mother's. They were there in what seemed no time. Judy was surprised that she felt no awkwardness with Joe, even after what might have been their romantic interlude.

Toots met them at the door. Joe was carrying the cooler, so Judy stepped aside and let him go in first.

"You two don't look any the worse for wear." She went over and adjusted the dial on the griddle.

"I would like to at least wash my face," Judy said.

"Go right ahead. It'll be a few minutes before breakfast is ready. Didn't want to burn breakfast waiting on you two."

Judy went into the bathroom and washed her face and brushed her teeth. She felt much better. The luxury of hot water...

Toots had pancakes with Canadian bacon on the table. Joe was pouring orange juice.

"Did you see any deer or fox?" Toots asked. She motioned for Judy to sit down.

"No, but we did hear a screech owl. Scared me for a moment."

"They can sound menacing, especially when you've never heard one before."

"I was more worried about the bears."

"What bears?" Toots looked over to Joe.

"Well, um, I... "

"Joseph, did you tell this poor girl there were bears up there?"

"Yes, ma'am." Joe hung his head, but his shoulders shook.

Waving her fork in the air, Toots said to Judy, "He used to do that to all the girls. They'd cuddle up to him for protection."

"Now, that was when I was just a kid."

"Some people never grow up." Judy put a piece of pancake into her mouth.

"Guilty as charged. Now let's change the subject. Judy's leaving on Saturday."

"Well, I hope you've enjoyed your stay."

"I've had a wonderful time, though I do miss my kids and my other sister. They can get on my nerves sometimes, but I'm ready to go home."

They made small talk for the rest of the meal.

Shortly after breakfast, Joe packed up the truck.

"Judy, when you get this way again, make sure you come and see me." Toots gave her a hug.

"I'll do that."

Joe honked the horn as they drove off. "You made a hit with my mother."

"She's quite a woman."

"Well, she doesn't like just anyone. She can be rather standoffish." Joe stopped to let some sheep cross in front of them.

"She didn't seem that way to me."

"She told me that you are special," He paused. "And I think so, too."

Judy swung her head around to look at him.

"Don't you think so?" He slowly drove after the last lamb crossed.

"I never thought of it." That was the truth. She was just been herself.

"Well, think about it. You are a very special person." He reached over and took her hand until he had to shift again.

When they got to the open road, Joe turned on the CD

player. The soft music and the warm sun caused Judy to doze off.

"I'd like to stop for some coffee," Joe said, awakening her.

Judy blinked a few times. "I'm sorry. I usually don't sleep in the car."

Joe pulled into a truck stop and they got out. Judy went into the ladies' room. Joe was waiting for her outside the door.

"It might be a good time to grab a sandwich or something," he said as they went over to the hostess.

"I'm not very hungry, but I could have a bowl of soup or a salad." She was just being polite. The breakfast was still with her.

"Have whatever you wish."

Judy felt groggy so she ordered some iced tea.

"What time does your plane leave on Saturday?" Joe asked.

"I think about eleven." Judy was having trouble peeling the paper off her straw. Joe reached across and took it from her. He took the paper off and stuck the straw in her glass. They grinned at each other.

"Damn, I don't get back until about six that night."

"What are you going to Europe for?"

"I have to check on one of the machines. They were having some problems with it. While I was there, I was going to make a few follow-up calls with some other firms. I wish now I hadn't made those plans."

Judy didn't say anything.

"I'd like to spend more time with you."

The waitress took their orders. Judy was going to have a cup of soup. That would be more than enough.

"What are you going to do when you get home?"

"I have some business to take care of. My married son, Andy, called last week. He and his wife are planning a trip, so I'll stay with my grandchildren."

"You're lucky to be able to do that. My daughter will never get married and have children."

Judy wanted to know why he felt that way, but she didn't want to pry. "I might do some volunteer work."

"What about your place in Arizona?"

"I haven't made up my mind about that yet. It holds a lot of memories...good and bad."

Joe nodded, but didn't say anything.

It seemed so normal to be sitting there with him. She was so comfortable. She wondered how far they would have gone that morning if Toots hadn't called.

"Earth to Judy..." Joe said.

It took Judy a second to think of what to say. She certainly wasn't going to tell him the truth. "I was just thinking of how great this visit has been. I'm so much closer to Kathy now. Even working was a vacation."

"Paid vacation," Joe said.

"Now it'll be back to reality." She sighed.

Judy stayed awake the rest of the way. The closer they got to town, the more traffic picked up.

"Everyone must have been gone this weekend," Joe said as he tried to change lanes.

"Wonder if Mark and Kathy are back yet?"

"If I know Mark, they won't get home until the last minute," Joe said.

"I really don't know him very well, but as long as he keeps my sister happy."

They took the next exit. Judy felt a little blue. She was going to miss this new part of her life. Still, she needed the familiar.

Joe walked her to the door and set down her duffle bag. He cupped her face and brought his lips to hers. The kiss was gentle, but intensified. He put his arms around her, holding her close.

Judy could feel his hardness against her stomach. She was amazed to think she could still arouse a man. Oh, of course, Steve always reacted that way, but that was because they had been married so long. This was different. It gave her an odd sense of power.

"I better go. I have to pack," he whispered.

Judy watched him walk to his truck and get in. She gave him a little wave and unlocked the door. He hadn't backed out yet. She opened the door and picked up her bag and started to go in. Joe honked his horn.

From the open door, she watched him drive away. A sudden loneliness hit her and she burst into tears. She cried as she carried her bag into her room, changed her clothes, and sat down on the edge of the bed.

XV

Judy had never been so lonely and isolated in all her life, even after Steve died. But then she had her family clamoring around her.

Joe had asked her what she planned on doing when she got home. What was she going to do? Her future looked like a blank sheet of pap1er. She had no future. She went to the bathroom and splashed cold water on her face. It helped...some.

She went out to check the mailbox. Nothing but ads and junk mail. She threw it into the wastebasket. Next, she checked the answering machine. The light was blinking. Six messages. She groaned. "Here we go!"

Sandra. Grace. Two hang ups...Sandra again. And Kathy called.

"What did Kathy want?" She dialed the number Kathy gave her.

"Mark here," came his voice.

"Hi, Mark. This is Judy. Kathy left a message for me to call."

"Yeah, I'll let you talk to her."

Judy could hear him say, "Hey, Kath, its Judy."

"Hi, Jude, must have got my message." Kathy paused. "How was your weekend?"

"Fine, and how was yours?" Judy tried to keep the smile out of her voice.

"Ohhh, is all I'm going to say." Kathy giggled.

"Is that what you called me about?"

"No, I really called to tell you there's a real estate person coming by tomorrow with a client."

`"Anything special you want me to do?"

"No. She'll be there when you're at work."

"Thanks for letting me know. I'll throw those beer cans out and take the lingerie off the shower rod."

Kathy got into the banter. "And take that picture of Mr. July off my bedroom wall."

"Who's Mr. July?" Judy heard from the background.

"Well, I gotta go," Kathy said.

Judy decided not to call Sandra. Sandra would call again soon enough. Grace said she didn't need to call her.

She went in and unpacked her bag. Then she gave the place a once over. Everything looked good. She would check it again in the morning.

The phone rang. Judy knew it would be Sandra. "Hello," she snapped.

There was a pause on the other end. "Is everything okay?" It was Joe.

"I'm sorry. I thought you were my sister, Sandra. She left two messages while I was gone."

"I just wanted to call and let you know again that I was glad we had a chance to spend the weekend together."

Judy was still trying to recover from her embarrassment. "I had a great time too."

"Do you mind if I call you when I get back?"

"I'd love for you to call, and I'll try not to bite your head off."

He laughed. "I'm glad you told me about your sister so I can understand."

After Joe's call, Judy felt lonely again. What was it about him? She knew it was too soon after Steve's death to be interested in anyone else. It was just loneliness and the feeling of excitement, she told herself.

Sure enough, Sandra called a short time later. Judy was more cautious answering the phone.

"Where have you been?" Sandra asked.

"I went with a friend and spent the weekend at the family ranch." Judy didn't want it to come out that she had been with a male friend.

"Where's Kathy?"

"I think she spent the weekend in town with friends. I'll tell her to call you."

"Fine thing. You go out to visit her and she deserts you on your last weekend there."

"Sandra, for Pete's sake, cool it. What did you want?"

"What time are you coming back?"

"My flight is due in about six Saturday night."

"So you want Brad and me to come in and meet you?"

"No, Grace is going to do that."

"Oh, well, just thought I'd ask."

There was something in Sandra's voice that caught Judy's attention. "What's going on?"

"Oh, nothing." That was a sure sign there was something going on.

"Spill."

"Andy's staying at your place."

"What?"

"I said Andy's..."

"I heard what you said. He called me last week to see if I'd watch the kids so he and Tammie could go on vacation. Why is he doing that?"

"He and Tammie had a fight and he moved out."

"Okay. I'll give him a call." Judy sighed.

"Don't tell him I told you."

"I'll try not to. Talk to you later." Judy hung up.

She buried her face in her hands. "What was going on with my family? Steve, you jerk, you just had to leave me cope with all this by myself!" She got up and went to the fridge. She found the bottle of wine and poured herself a tumbler full. Then she dialed her number.

"Hullo?" A male voice answered.

"Is Andy there?"

"Hey, Andy, there's some old lady on the phone," the voice said without taking his mouth away from the receiver.

"Hello, this is Andy."

"And this is your mother."

There was silence. "Hi, Mom! Everything okay? How's the trip going?"

She recognized Andy's attempt to be nonchalant. "More to the point, what are you doing?"

"I'm staying here for a couple of days." She heard him swallow hard.

"Andy, why are you staying at my home? And who was it who answered the phone?"

She could barely hear him when he answered, "We had a fight. I just needed some place to cool off." Then in a normal voice, he added, "That was Tom, an old friend."

"All I can say is that the place better not be messed up in any way and that your friend needs to be gone when I get home." She didn't wait for an answer, just hung up.

Judy realized she was shaking all over. She took a big gulp of the wine. It was horrid tasting. She rinsed the rest down the drain. So much for drinking her problems away.

How did she get herself into such a mess? None of this was her problem. Yet, she felt helpless to fix everything for everybody else. Kathy still hadn't told Sandra about her wedding. Andy was separated from his wife. Ellyn was Lord knows where. Grace was in the process of a divorce and starting a new life for herself. For a fleeting moment, she thought about staying in Colorado or maybe going to Arizona. Damn! She took a shower and went to bed.

Sleep didn't come easily, though she was bone-tired. She wished for someone to bounce her thoughts off of. She and Steve solved the problems of the world that way. What would he tell her to do? Talk it out with those involved. First, she'd talk to Kathy. That was her last thought before she fell asleep.

The buzzing of the alarm clock woke her up. At least the drive in to work would keep her from thinking too much about her problems. Work would help too. She planned on meeting Kathy for lunch. They had made those arrangements the week before.

She stuck her head into Kathy's office before going to the file room. "How was your weekend?"

Kathy sighed. "It was won-der-ful. How was yours?

"I'll tell you all about it at lunch."

"Well, I'm not going to tell you everything about mine." Kathy gave her a wink.

"And I don't want to hear it either."

The morning went quickly as usual. Judy slipped out a few minutes before twelve. She wanted to make sure she got them a table at the café.

"Hey, wait up," Kathy called just as Judy was going to cross the street.

Judy waited for her sister to catch up and together, they went to the café.

"I thought I'd leave just a few minutes early to get us a table."

"That was my thought, too." Kathy smiled.

They found a table by the window so they could watch as people went by. While Judy stayed at their table, Kathy went to the counter and put in their orders.

"How was Joe's ranch?" Kathy asked.

"Haven't you ever been there?"

"I really don't know Joe that well. Though I have met his mother, Toots."

"You were right; Toots is fun."

Their number was called and Judy went up to retrieve their lunch.

"I enjoyed myself. We went all over the ranch and got stranded for the night in a hunting cabin."

"So, what happened?"

Judy told her about the storm, but she didn't tell her about her almost interlude with Joe.

"Sounds romantic." Kathy dabbed at her mouth with her napkin.

"In a way, it was."

"Hmmm," Kathy looked at her. "Are you interested?"

"Come on, Kath, let me get on with my life before I think

about a man."

"You protest too much. Are you going to see him again?"

"Okay." Judy lowered her voice to almost a whisper. "I find him attractive and fun to be with. And he said he would call me."

"Good. And I agree with you that you need time to get things together."

"Now that we have that settled, let's change the subject."

"Do you need a ride to the airport?"

"Yes, I do. On Saturday, my plane leaves right after lunch, I think. I'll have to look at my ticket again."

"Great. Why don't you plan on coming in early and having brunch with Mark and me?"

"Sounds okay."

"Wanna have lunch again tomorrow?" Kathy pushed her plate away.

"Sure, that way I won't have to fix anything for supper." Judy pushed her plate away and stacked it on top of her sister's. "Sandra called."

"For joy."

"She wanted to know where you were."

"I'll call her tonight and tell her the news."

"Andy's living at my place."

Kathy choked and sputtered. "How come?"

"They've separated." It was out in the open now, but she didn't want to talk any more about it. She was still in shock. She also wanted to hear Andy's story first.

"Oh, honey," Kathy reached over and laid her hand over Judy's. "I'm so sorry."

Judy managed a weak, "Thanks."

They sat for a few minutes, just sipping their tea.

"Well, we better get back," Judy said abruptly. "I don't want to get fired."

They laughed, breaking the tension. The sun was hot and they were sweating by the time they walked the few blocks to the office.

"I might not see you until tomorrow lunch," Kathy gave her a hug.

"Give me a call after you talk to Sandra tonight."

"Okay." They parted ways.

The rest of the day passed quickly. The ride to Kathy's was a bit frantic, but easier than usual. When she got there, Judy changed into her robe and slippers. After making some iced tea and a sandwich, she took both into the living room. She ate as she read the newspaper and worked the crossword puzzle from Sunday's paper.She felt so comfy here. Just for a moment she thought it might be fun to buy Kathy's condo and work as a file clerk. Oh, it might be fun for a while. But, maybe too peaceful.

The ringing of the phone startled her. She got up and answered the phone in the hall.

"Hi, remember me?" the voice greeted her.

"Hi, Joe, where are you?" She felt herself smile.

"I'm somewhere over the Atlantic. We should be touching down in an hour or so."

"You sound like you're in the next room."

"Ain't technology wonderful?"

"It sure is."

"How's everything going?"

"Fine." She wasn't going to tell him about her son.

"And how are the honeymooners?"

"Kathy seems happy. I haven't seen Mark yet."

"That's good." He paused. "Just thought I'd call. I sure had a good time this weekend. We'll have to do it again someday."

"Without nature's fireworks."

He chuckled. "That can get pretty scary." Then he said, "Well, I better go."

They said goodbye and hung up.

Judy went to the living room and switched on the TV. After a couple of minutes of channel surfing, she turned it off. She picked up the puzzle again and started to fill it in.

Again, the phone rang. Now who? She was pretty sure it wouldn't be Joe again. She was right; it was Kathy.

"I just got off the phone with Sandra and is she hot!" Kathy hadn't even said hello.

"What did you expect?" Judy could have predicted Sandra's reaction.

"I know. It was unfair of me, but she's really torqued at you for not snitching."

"I figured as much." Just then, the beep of call waiting went off. "Just a second. I got another call coming in."

"I'll wait," Kathy said.

Judy switched over to see who else was calling.

"How could you?" Sandra screamed in her ear.

"Lower your voice or I'll hang up on you."

"Kathy just called and told me they got married and you were her matron of honor." Sandra paused for a breath and then went on. "You knew and didn't tell me."

"Kathy asked me not to," Judy said. It took all her willpower not to return the scream.

Sandra started to say something else and Judy cut her short. "I'll call you back. I'm on the other line."

She didn't wait for Sandra's answer, but clicked back to Kathy. "It was Sandra."

"I might have guessed. Sorry to put you in the middle of this," Kathy said.

"Don't worry. She'll get over it and when she meets Mark, she'll be just fine."

"I sure hope so."

"Believe me. She can't stay angry for long."

When they ended their call, Judy called Sandra like she promised.

"Are you over your shock?" Judy asked.

"Oh, I guess so. What's he like?"

"Who?"

"Kathy's husband. Who did you think I meant?"

Joe flitted through Judy's mind. "He's nice. Moreover, he seems to adore Kathy."

"Has he been married before? Did you get to meet any of his family? Where are they living?"

"Whoa! Kathy said he was widowed, but no children. None of his family was at the wedding, just me and a friend of Mark's. They just bought a new condo right downtown, about six blocks or so from where Kathy works."

"What about--"

Judy cut her short. "If you want the answers, call Kathy and give her the third degree." Judy smiled as she said that.

"You're right." Sandra must have heard the smile in her voice.

The two sisters talked for a few more minutes and then hung up.

Judy gave up on the crossword puzzle. She was afraid the phone would ring again, but it didn't.

The rest of the week was routine. She and Kathy met for lunch and had a good time. Kathy certainly seemed happy.

On Friday, it was difficult to say goodbye to her new coworkers. Judy hugged many of them after they had a surprise lunch for her in the employees' lounge. They gave her a Colorado T-shirt and a company coffee mug. Then they made her promise to stop by and say hello the next time she was in town.

The drive to Kathy's was easier than usual. Judy had gotten used to the traffic. The one thing different was the large lump in her throat. She hadn't planned on this being so gut- wrenching. She had become attached to this place.

She heated up some leftover Chinese for supper, though she wasn't particularly hungry. She ate in the living room while watching the Weather Channel. She wanted to know as close as possible what the flying weather was going to be the next day. To her relief, it looked like it would be clear all the way home.

She'd do most of the packing tonight. No reason to leave it until the morning. She wrapped the coffee mug in her new T-shirt to protect it and tucked it in a corner of her suitcase. She left out clothes to wear in the morning.

The phone rang and she went into the kitchen to answer it. It was Sandra just checking to make sure she had all the flight information correct. Call waiting buzzed and Judy was able to cut Sandra off quickly.

The next call was from Kathy. She just had some last minute instructions for Judy regarding the condo.

"Don't bother and do any cleaning. Mark and I are going over after we take you to the airport. We want to see what to bring over here."

"Well, I did run the vacuum and dust a little."

"That's fine. I think I'll get a cleaning service to come in even though it's already on the market."

They chatted for a few more minutes and then hung up.

The phone rang again and this time it was Joe.

"Still in Europe?" she asked.

"Yup, I have to stay a few extra days. I was hoping to get back before you left, but no such luck."

"It doesn't seem possible that I've been here for over a month."

"Time has a way of flying."

"It sure does. I've really enjoyed myself here. I don't even mind the drive into the city every day."

There was a pause. Then Joe said, "How about staying longer?"

It was her turn to pause. "It's a tempting idea, but I have things to take care of at home."

"Well, darlin', anytime you want to come here, you'll be welcomed."

"I'll remember that. Besides I don't have a place to stay. Kathy's anxious to sell this place."

"You can always stay with me." He chuckled.

"You can stop and visit me the next time you're in my neighborhood."

"Can I stay with you?" He asked suggestively.

"I don't think so, but I can find a place for you to stay."

"I might just do that. Say, I got to go. I was in the middle of a meeting."

After she hung up, she felt the tears slide down her cheeks. She was more confused than ever. It had been a mistake to come here. She didn't want to leave. Maybe she could buy Mark's loft and move out here...a tantalizing thought.

Judy took a shower and got ready for bed. She found the morning paper and started to work the crossword. The phone rang again.

"Now who?" she asked herself. She was sick of talking on the phone. "Hello?" She tried to keep the irritation out of her voice.

"Judy. I'm so glad I caught you." It was Toots.

"I was wondering who would be calling. Everyone else has called." Judy laughed.

"I talked to Joe earlier today and he reminded me that you were leaving tomorrow. I wanted you to know how much I enjoyed your visit."

"Thank you and I enjoyed it too."

"You have a safe trip home and come back and see us."

"Thanks, maybe I will."

Judy felt herself smiling. She had been welcomed into the community. She would have to come back.

Sleep came quicker than she expected. Before she knew it her alarm was going off. She hopped out of bed and stripped off the linens. Quickly, she gathered the towels and shoved them all into the washing machine. It was the least she could do.

While the washer was running, she made herself some breakfast and coffee. Then it was time to get dressed and pack the last few things. With clothes in the dryer, she packed the car and washed up the few dishes. When the linens were dry, Judy hung the clean towels back in the bathroom and put the folded sheets in a pile on the bed. If she made the bed, Kathy might not know the sheets were clean and rewash them.

Finally, she was ready to leave.

"Goodbye and thanks for the wonderful visit." she said to the condo as she closed and locked the door.

The traffic was light and she took her time driving to town. She wanted to remember this day with the mountains off in the distance and the clear blue sky.

There was a parking space on the street in front of Kathy's building. Judy left her suitcase in the car and went into the lobby. She pressed a security button and was buzzed in.

Kathy greeted her at the door. "I'll get a light jacket and we'll go to the deli for lunch."

"I left my suitcase in the car. It looks like you've settled in pretty good." The place looked great.

"It won't look like this when I start bringing my things over. I'm not sure where it's all going to go. Mark and I've been having this discussion the past few days." Kathy picked up her purse.

"I think I left the place in good shape," Judy said as they headed for the elevator.

"Ah, don't worry about it."

They walked the few blocks to the deli. The place looked different on the weekend. The counter person took their orders. They sat down to wait for their number to be called.

"Where's Mark?" Judy asked.

"He went golfing with some client."

Judy took a sip of the Coke they brought to the table. She was going to miss this. She knew the minute she got home, she would be bombarded with all the cares of her family.

Their number was called and Kathy got up to retrieve the tray.

"So what about Joe?"

Judy had just taken a large bite of her sandwich. She had to finish it before she could answer. How much did she want to tell Kathy? Kathy would tell Mark and so on and so forth. "We had a very nice time at the ranch."

"Nice? Come on, you can do better than that. How did you

like Toots? Was the house grand or plain? What did you do while you were there?"

Judy held up her hand. "Whoa! His mother is wonderful. I liked her right away. The house is just like the ranch houses you see in the old westerns." She took another bite. She needed time for her to think of what to tell Kathy about what they did.

"Sounds good so far."

"Well, Joe took me on a tour of the ranch."

"On horseback?" Kathy interrupted.

Judy gave her a scowl. "You know better than that."

Kathy shrugged. "Just thought I'd ask."

"He has a jeep. His mom packed a lunch for us. He has this great spot with the view of the mountains."

"Sounds romantic. Did he kiss you?" Kathy gave her a wink.

"Kath-y!" She felt her face flush. "Yes, he kissed me. Now, don't interrupt. He showed me a hunting cabin. A storm came up and we spent the rest of the time waiting it out in the cabin."

"How long did the storm last?"

"For a couple of hours. It was something! I thought the lightning was going to hit the cabin."

"Did Joe hold you tight to protect you from the big bad storm? Is that when he kissed you?"

Judy was saved when the door opened and Mark and another man came in.

He walked over to them. "I thought you might be here." He kissed the top of Kathy's head. "Mind if we join you?"

"Be our guest," Judy said and pointed to a couple of vacant chairs.

"I want you to meet John. He works with me. We just got done with our round of golf and I thought I'd try to catch you before you left."

"That's sweet of you," Judy said.

"We'll go over and order. John lost, so he's buying lunch."

With Mark and John showing up, Judy was off the hook. She couldn't tell about her time with Joe with the guys there.

The four of them sat and ate and made small talk. Mark told some humorous golf stories which Judy didn't understand.

The two women waited while the men ate. Then the four of them left together. John left in one direction and the rest of them headed to Mark and Kathy's.

"I'll come with you, if it's okay," Mark said.

"That would be nice," Judy said quickly. With Mark there, Kathy surely wouldn't ask anything more about Joe.

Mark unloaded Judy's luggage onto a cart. "I'm so glad you came out so I could get to know you," Mark said as he gave Judy a hug and a big wet kiss on the cheek. "Please come out again and stay longer."

Kathy gave her sister a hug and kiss. "Yes, please come out again, soon. I'm going to miss you."

By this time both women were in tears. "I'm going to miss you, too, but ..." Judy couldn't finish the sentence. She just gave Kathy another squeeze. A skycap offered to wheel her luggage in. She waved goodbye to Kathy and Mark as she went into the terminal.

The plane took off on schedule and landed on time. She napped a bit and looked out the window. She didn't even bother to take out her book.

XVI

Grace and Sandra met her in the terminal. After hugs and kisses, they all went to get her luggage.

"You look rested," Sandra said as they made their way to the parking garage.

"I feel rested. I could get used to that way of life. How's everything going, Grace?"

Grace smiled. "Everything is going great. The job. The apartment."

"How's Kathy and her husband? You'll have to tell me all about him." Sandra put her arm around Judy's shoulders. "I've really missed you."

Judy didn't say anything. She didn't want to tell her that she hadn't missed all the commotion.

Grace suggested they stop for dinner.

"Great. I don't feel much like cooking tonight," Judy and Sandra said together.

At dinner, Judy told them about Kathy and how she was doing. Then she told about what she thought of Mark and the job."

"Sounds like you settled in pretty good," Grace said.

"Don't give her any ideas," Sandra said to her niece

When they got to her condo, the three women put her luggage in the foyer. "Thanks for picking me up. I'll see you in a day or two. We'll get together as soon as I settle back in."

The house was dark except for the hall light. She switched on another light. The place looked clean and neat. After looking closer, she was satisfied it was. She wondered if Andy was still there.

There was a note on the kitchen table. Andy said he had gone out with some friends and would be back the next day.

Judy was relieved. She wouldn't have to face that problem right away. She found a stack of mail on the counter. She went through it. Mostly credit card applications and other junk mail. There was a letter from the manager of the park in Arizona. She had a buyer for her unit, if she was interested. Maybe that wouldn't be such a bad idea. She had no desire to go for another season, not without Steve. It had been difficult enough with her sisters as company.

She found some Coke in the fridge. She took it into the bedroom and unpacked her suitcase. She stacked what she bought for the kids on the bed. The rest she put in drawers and the bathroom cabinets. The phone rang. Instead of taking the call in her room, she picked up her Coke and the stack of souvenirs and went into the kitchen.

It was Grace. "I forgot to ask you if you'd like to go for lunch on Monday. I have the day off. That way you could see my place."

"Why, I'd love that." Judy said, smiling to herself.

"Great. You know where it is?"

"Yes."

"See you then." Click.

She sorted the souvenirs according to family. She'd give the things for the kids to Andy when he got back. He'd be able to make sure the kids got them. Ellyn's she'd just mail. Same with Clark's and Tina's. Great. She hadn't forgotten anyone.

She had better call Kathy and Mark to let them know she was at home. The phone rang several times and the answering machine picked up. Kathy's voice told her to leave a message, so she did.

Now she was at loose ends. She was still on Mountain Time, but she was so tired, she decided to go to bed. She left her door open so she could hear when Andy got in.

The phone rang. She had just fallen asleep according to the clock. It was only ten-thirty.

"Mom?" the voice said.

For a second, the voice sounded strange. "Andy?"

"Yeah, it's me." Pause. "Were you asleep?"

"I just dozed off. When will you be home?"

"That's what I'm calling about. Tammie and I are going to try and work things out. I've been here for the past three nights."

"That's wonderful, dear." One less thing to worry about. Thank you, God.

"I was wondering if we could stop by and see you tomorrow. The kids want to see you."

"Why don't you come for an early supper? That'll give me a chance to go to the grocery store."

She heard the sound of muffled voices. Then Andy's voice came again. "I just asked Tammie and she said that would be fine. We'll see you then."

Hmmm, situations fixed themselves without her help-just God's. Maybe her children were growing up. She would love to talk to Steve about this turn of events. She got out of bed, took his picture off the dresser, and brought it to bed. She switched on the bedside lamp.

"Steve," she began. "I think I'm going to make it, but damn, I miss you." She couldn't say anything more. It was already six months since he died, yet it seemed like yesterday. She burst into tears. She slid the picture under his pillow. Her tears soaked into the pillow as she cried herself to sleep.

The next morning, she awoke with a fierce headache. A couple of Motrin seemed to help. Her face was swollen and her eyes were red from crying. But she was surprised at how well she felt like she was making progress. She washed her face with cold water. Then out to the kitchen to make coffee.

The sunlight sparkled and cast colored patterns as it shone through the sun catchers on the French doors. There were eggs in the fridge. The date was still good. The bread seemed fresh, too. An egg sandwich would hit the spot. She started her breakfast and stepped outside to pick up the Sunday paper from the front steps.

After breakfast, Judy took a shower and made her bed. She put Steve's picture back on the dresser.

She put on jeans and a sweatshirt. She walked to the French doors by the deck. Andy must have found the lawn furniture. The rattan loveseat and rocker were in the usual place. Her chaise lounge was further away next to the picnic table. He always did rush the seasons. It might be another month before it would be comfortable to sit outside. But then again, Wisconsin weather was fickle.

Maybe it wouldn't be that cool outside. Putting on her sunglasses, she took a wastebasket and her mail outside. The sun felt so good as Judy sorted through the mail. Most of it went into the wastebasket. She found the grocery ads in the newspaper and checked what was on sale for that week. She needed to go out and get something at least for today. She felt so lazy. She had to force herself to go to the store.

The meal was going to be simple. Steak, salad and rolls. Maybe ice cream for dessert. She'd buy a few hot dogs for the kids.

Before she left, Judy looked at herself in the mirror. Hopefully I won't run into anyone I know, she said to herself. She grabbed her purse and keys and went to the garage.

Her car felt strange since she had been driving Kathy's SUV. Maybe she should get an SUV. She had Steve's car to get rid of anyway. Tomorrow, she'd make a few phone calls.

There were only a few cars in the parking lot. Great, I'll be in and out quickly. She dashed inside and grabbed a cart. Within minutes, she was waiting in the checkout lane. She gazed out the window. A steady stream of cars were pulling into the lot. Got here just at the right time, she thought. As people began to come in, she realized church just got over and most of them were from her church. She pretended not to notice anyone.

"Hi, Judy," a voice from behind her spoke.

She turned. It was her neighbor, Sue, with her husband in tow.

"We're glad you're home, aren't we, Cal?" Cal nodded his head.

I'll bet you are, Judy thought, but she said, "I got back last evening. The kids are coming for dinner and I needed to get some supplies."

Just then, she had to put her items on the conveyer belt. She busied herself with the business at hand, ignoring the couple behind her.

As she walked out the doors, a church member stopped her. They chatted for a few minutes when the woman said, "How do you like your condo?"

"Its fine, but I think it's too big for one person."

"I know what you mean. My mother went into a smaller place after my dad died."

Judy remembered her mother. The woman must have been eighty when she was widowed. Suddenly Judy felt very old. She smiled and said, "I'll see you next Sunday in church. I have to get going. Andy and Tammie are bring the kids over and I'm fixing dinner."

She had been told not to make any big decisions until Steve was gone a year. She knew she had some changes to make. Could she wait a year? Already six months had gone by. Well, selling their Arizona place was a major decision. Still, she was certain about selling it. Even though everyone was so friendly and the desert was beautiful, she didn't enjoy it that much when Steve was alive.

It was wonderful to see the grandkids again. Judy couldn't believe how much they had grown and changed. At first there was tension between Judy and Tammie, but it lasted only for an hour or so. Soon things were normal. Judy could see that both Andy and Tammie were trying to be considerate and get along.

"I think I'll see about selling the Arizona place," she said. They were sitting outside. Andy did the grilling.

"Make sure you get a good price," Tammie said. "I heard that some people really get taken with selling in a hurry."

"There's been an inquiry about ours...mine. I'm going to check it out tomorrow."

"Are you planning on staying here?" Andy made a large circle in the air with his hand holding the long fork.

"If you mean this condo, I'm not sure. I'll have to give it more thought. I certainly don't need all this room, but some smaller places would cost just as much. I'm in no hurry."

"Tell us about your visit with Aunt Kathy," Tammie said.

"Just a second," Judy said, hopping up from her chair. "I'll be right back." She had forgotten the souvenirs and went to get them.

She sat down. "This is for Drew and this one is for Katie." She handed Tammie some T-shirts.

Tammie held one up in front of Drew. "This is so cute."

"And this is for you and Andy." She handed her a white box. She took both grandchildren onto her lap.

Tammie slid her fingernail under the tape and opened the flap. "Oh, Andy, look at this."

Andy came over and peered into the box. Tammie lifted two mugs out. They said Colorado and had the state motto emblazoned in bright colors. He read aloud, "Nil Sine Numine."

"What's the translation?" Tammie asked.

"Nothing without the Deity," Judy answered.

"Thanks, Mom," Andy dropped a kiss on his mother's head.

"We need some new mugs. Drew grabbed one out of my hand the other day and the handle broke off." Tammie put the mugs in the box.

"Good, I'm glad you like them. I got a set like that for Clark and Tina, too." Buying souvenirs was not Judy's favorite pastime. She was always afraid the person wouldn't like it or that she would find something more suitable later.

Andy and Tammie left not long after dinner. They had to go to work the next day and the kids were getting cranky.

Out of curiosity, Judy spent the evening going through the real estate section of the paper. First, she checked to see what condos were going for in her town. There were a few listings and the prices didn't seem too bad. There were two units for sale in her development. The prices had gone up considerably. She would stand to make a tidy profit, especially since hers was paid for.

Next, she scanned the listings under the out-of-state and vacation property headings. There were only a few prices included and they were for lake properties in the area. She wished she had a computer so she could do some checking on the internet. Well, there was really no rush.

In the morning, she lay in bed long after the sun was up. There was no urgent reason to get out of bed. She certainly didn't have much to do. She and Steve always had something to do...together. Now she missed the routine of a job. For a moment, she wondered what Joe was doing and how she missed Colorado.

Finally, she dragged herself out of bed and into the shower. Next came breakfast and the morning paper. She remembered longing for a day like today when the children were small. Ironic. Now she longed for those hectic times.

Judy tucked the portable phone in her pocket and the morning newspaper under her arm. She poured another cup of coffee and went out to the patio to catch up on what was going on in her small town. Most of news was of Milwaukee. The sun was warm, as long as she stayed out of the wind, she would be comfortable. It seemed like she had been gone years instead of just a few weeks.

There was an ad for a new computer with free internet access for a year. Maybe she should check it out. She vowed that someday she would do the family tree for her children and grandchildren. She now had the time. She wished Steve was around with his advice. She had to stop thinking about what it would be like with Steve around. He was gone forever and she had the life expectancy of another twenty years.

Judy got up and took the phone into the house. It was time to call Arizona. She hated making these types of calls.

The manager told her about the prospect.

"It's rather an odd time for someone to want to buy a place, don't you think?"

"Oh, the interested party is moving here to help with the grandchildren. I think there was some mention of a divorce."

"I guess I would consider it, if the price is fair."

"Give me a call back in a couple of days," the manager said before hanging up.

Judy had always liked the manager and thought she was a fair person. Nice to deal with, but Judy needed to do her own research. She couldn't rely on intuition alone.

It was only eleven so she decided to go to the library and use one of their computers. At least it was something to do. By noon, she had found out the going prices of units similar to hers in Arizona.

The next couple of days crept by. She was bored out of her mind. She spent most of her time out on the patio reading and napping. Maybe she should get a job. In Colorado she hadn't been bored. That made her think of Joe. She could always go back.

It was Thursday before the manager called. She had an offer she thought was fair. Was there some place she could fax a copy to Judy?

"Let me do some checking and I'll call you right back." Judy remembered the convenience of the fax machine at school. She called the school's main office. Sure, she could have something faxed there. Thank heavens for old friends, Judy thought as she called the manager to make arrangements. Then she hurried over to get the fax.

Judy wondered if she should get a lawyer to look over the contract. Instead, she went home and compared it with the one they signed when they bought the place three years ago. The contract was almost identical. The price offered was more than she expected.

She called the manager. "I'll take the offer."

"I'll get it in the mail right away. Just have it signed, notarized, then I'll return it."

"When do they want to move in?" Judy asked.

"As soon as possible."

"Would they be interested in moving in before closing?"

"I don't recommend it. Something can always go wrong at the last minute."

"Would you find someone to pack up my personal belongings and ship them here?"

"No problem. We do that frequently."

After the phone call, Judy felt energized. She would make arrangements to drive down if she needed to. She had removed most of what she wanted when she was there with her sisters. As good as security was in these places, there were still at least three or four break-ins during the off season. So they never left much. Maybe the new owner would be interested in buying some of the larger pieces of furniture.

Judy hesitated for a moment. This had been their dream,

hers and Steve's. But Steve was no longer around to share. It was time for her to move on with this part of her life. Piece by piece.

She made an appointment with her lawyer to finish the rest of the details regarding Steve's death. Some papers needed to be signed. The new will was ready also. Another piece of her new life.Judy went to Grace's for lunch. Her apartment was tiny, but cute.

"How are things going?" Judy sat at the kitchen table watching her daughter tear up lettuce for a salad.

"Not too bad. I like my job. The divorce is moving right along. I'm making new friends."

"Sounds like you're on the right track."

Grace sat the bowl of salad on the table. "I feel much better. I've been going to group therapy for battered women. Man, am I ever glad I got out when I did."

"So am I. The support groups they have nowadays are supposed to be very helpful."

"I've learned a lot."

"I'm going to sell the place in Arizona." Judy said.

"Too many memories?" Grace set a basket of dinner rolls on the table and reached into the refrigerator.

"That's part of it. It's not much fun to go down there by myself."

"I can understand that."

Judy enjoyed the time with Grace. The tension was gone between them. It was a good idea for Grace to have a place of her own.

It was still early when Judy got home. She went into the

kitchen and poured herself some iced tea. She sat at the table and read her mail.

The news would be on in a few minutes so she topped off her drink and went into the living room.

She was watching a segment on identity theft. The phone rang and she absently reached over and answered it. "Hello?"

"I didn't wake you up, did I?" the voice at the other end said.

"No." The voice was familiar but she just couldn't place it. "Who is this?"

"Me. Joe." He laughed. "How quickly you forget."

Judy was embarrassed. "I'm sorry. I had the TV on and was watching the news." She hit the mute button on the remote.

"How are you doing?" he asked.

"Fine. Where are you?"

"I'm in Colorado. I have to leave again tomorrow. That's why I called."

"Oh?" Now she was curious.

"I was wondering if you would mind if I spend a few hours with you tomorrow?"

"No, sounds like fun."

"How about a late lunch or an early dinner?"

She thought for a moment. As far as she knew she didn't have any plans, but her calendar was in the kitchen. So what... She'd just reschedule whatever it might be. "Sure. Where?"

"Would you mind coming to the airport? I have a three-hour layover. There's supposed to be a great upscale restaurant there."

"Can't remember the name but, I've eaten there a couple of times. It is good." She and Steve had eaten there for their anniversary just before they flew to Hawaii.

"I'll call you from the air."

Judy's hands were all sweaty when she hung up the phone. She was eager to see Joe. She felt like a sixteen-year-old going on her first date.

The nice sleepy feeling vanished. She went to bed, but couldn't sleep. All she could do was replay their brief conversation, think about what she was going to wear and what they might possibly talk about.

When Joe called, he said his plane was getting in later than he thought, but he still wanted to see her.

"I'll be there waiting," Judy said. Then she got dressed and drove to the airport.

The traffic was heavy. There had been an accident and part of the freeway was closed so she got off and took some surface streets.

Joe was already in the restaurant when she got there. He got up and gave her a kiss. "It's good to see you. I thought maybe you changed your mind about coming."

"No, the traffic was terrible."

He held out a chair for her and she sat down. Then he motioned to the waiter. "What do you want to drink?"

"I'll just have a diet Coke, but I'd like a double vodka martini after that drive."

He looked surprised.

She laughed. "Don't mind me. One of those things would put me out for hours. I can't even stand the taste of a martini."

They chatted while they waited for the waiter to bring her drink. Then they placed their order. Joe looked at his watch.

"I wish we had more time."

"Where are you off to this time?"

"New York. Wanna join me?"

She wasn't sure if he was kidding or not. "Not this time."

She knew she was treading on dangerous ground, but didn't care. It felt good to flirt.

Joe's eyebrow went up. "Is there a possibility of that happening?"

"Who knows?" She couldn't look him in the eyes.

The waiter brought them their food and they concentrated on that for a few minutes.

"My mom wants you to visit again real soon. She took a liking to you."

"I like her too, but I don't know when I'll get the chance." She told him about selling the Arizona place and taking care of the loose ends.

"You know you could just come north afterwards and spend a few weeks with us? You could just fly out after you get things settled."

He wasn't giving up. "I'll see. Just one thing at a time."

"Fair enough. I won't bug you for a while." He looked at his watch again. "I better get to my plane. I wouldn't mind missing it to be with you but it's a real bitch to get another flight."

They stood up and he placed his hand on the small of her back as they made their way out.

In the middle of the concourse, he put both arms around her. They were oblivious to the crowds around them. He gave her a long slow kiss that made her heart flutter and her bones begin to melt. "I'll be talking to you." He smiled at her. Then they went their separate ways.

XVII

Joe called her later that night to say he was safely in New York.

Judy felt lonely after his call. She couldn't help but wonder what it would be like to go off with him somewhere for a few days. What would he be like in bed? Now, cut that out, she told herself firmly, but it didn't work. Her mind kept replaying the embrace and kiss they shared earlier that day.

Sandra called the next morning before Judy was dressed. "How about going to the church dinner with us on Friday? The youth group is doing a fish fry as a fundraiser."

"That sounds fine. I don't have anything else going on."

Judy heard from the Arizona park manager later that day. The closing would be in three weeks. Would she be there in person or just have a lawyer there represent her?

"I'll let the lawyer handle it."

"Fine, I'll have her get in touch with you," the manager said and hung up.

Judy met Sandra and Brad at the church on Friday. Judy still went to the church where they had grown up, but Sandra found a more conservative church the past few years. They went back and forth for various social functions.

Long tables had been set up. The youth scurried around seating people, pouring coffee and water, and bringing plates of seconds around. The tables were only partially filled.

They got plates of food and went to find a place to sit down.

"Let's sit over there," Brad said as he pointed with a plastic fork.

"Okay," Sandra said and Judy followed them.

There were several men sitting there already.

"These guys are all widowed or divorced. And they're retired. Brad meets with them on Saturday mornings to do some of the maintenance on the building," Sandra whispered in Judy's ear.

Brad introduced them to Sandra and Judy. Then he said, "Judy's husband died recently. She's a retired schoolteacher."

Judy felt like crawling under the table and resisted the urge to slug Brad. Instead, she smiled her sweetest smile and attacked her food.

"Where did you teach?" a rather good-looking man asked. He sat right across from her.

"At Hamilton Elementary. First grade." Judy took a bite of fish.

"I had a son that went to that school. Jeff Smart."

Judy nodded. She had her mouth full. It was good because she had to think of something positive to say. "I remember him."

"Well, he's in the Marines now." There was pride in the man's voice.

Judy thought for a moment. What was it about Jeff? She couldn't remember offhand.

"I'm a retired plumber. Had to take early retirement because of a bum back."

"Hmm." Judy took another bite of food.

"What do you like to do for fun?"

Judy hadn't thought of what she did for fun. She and Steve had so many things they enjoyed doing together. "I read and do some sewing." Boy, did she sound boring.

"Do you bowl or play Sheepshead?"

She shook her head.

"I could teach you." The man grinned broadly. "I taught my ex-wives how to bowl."

Ex-wives? More than one? Judy didn't even want to know. "No, thanks. I've got some projects to finish up before I take anything else on."

"Well, if you change your mind, just let ol' Brad know. He knows how to get in touch with me."

Judy couldn't help but wonder if Sandra and Brad had planned this.

"Well, I'm going to be late for league if I don't get going." The man stood up. "Nice talking to you." He bowed his head slightly at Judy. She smiled, hoping it wouldn't encourage him.

"Nice, don't ya think?" Sandra nudged her.

"Nice," Judy said under her breath.

Brad had been talking to the guy across the table from him. "Hey, Judy, come on over after this. The night's still young."

"Yeah, come on over. I got a new dress I want you to see anyway," Sandra added.

"I guess I can come for a while."

Judy knew something was up when Brad was so jovial. There was another car parked at Sandra and Brad's house when Judy pulled up. She had stopped at the store for milk before going on to her sister's.

She should have known. There was the guy who sat by Brad at church.

"Sit down. This is Gordon. Sandra's making some coffee." Brad motioned for her to sit on the couch next to Gordon. Instead, she sat in a chair on the other side of the room.

"Coffee'll be ready in a few minutes." Sandra came in and looked around for a place to sit. The only place left was next to the man on the couch. Judy chuckled to herself.

Sandra sat for only a moment. "Let me show you that dress."

Judy followed her out of the room. How was she going to beat her sister to that chair so she wouldn't have to sit next to the guy?

Sandra tried on her new dress for Judy.

"I think if you take a tuck here," Judy pinched the dress at the waist an inch, "and take it up about an inch or so, it'll be great."

"I'll do it tomorrow. We have a party to go to next week. The neighbors are having a special birthday party for their mother."

The night went from bad to worse. Judy found herself cringing every time Gordon opened his mouth. He was so stupid. His grammar was the worst she'd ever heard. Besides, he could have used some deodorant and at least three teeth...

"Listen, I have an early appointment in the morning. I'll take a rain check on the coffee," Judy said. It was true. She was getting her hair cut. She stood up to leave.

"Are you busy on Saturday night?" Gordon asked.

"Yes, I already have plans." She planned on renting a movie.

"Well, then maybe some other time."

Judy just gave him one of her fake smiles.

One day, she was going to kill her sister or brother-in-law or both if they didn't leave her alone. Sandra had good intentions, but what about Brad? She needed her space.

A few nights later, a man called her up. "This is Leroy." When she hesitated, he said, "Leroy Smart, Jeff's dad. Would you like to go to a movie on Sunday afternoon? We could get a quick bite after."

Deal with it, she thought. Maybe it would get everyone off her back for a while. "I'd love to go to the movies. What did you have in mind?"

"There's a new James Bond movie opening. Do you like James Bond?"

"That would be fine." She didn't mind James Bond, just thought it sort of mindless.

"I'll pick you up about four."

Judy told him where she lived.

After she hung up, she started to think. Matinee prices. Probably with a senior citizen's discount. Oh, well. It was just for one time.

Saturday evening, Leroy called to cancel their date. "I have a terrible cold," he sniffled loudly. "I'll call when I feel better."

Judy felt relieved. Now she would have time to think of an excuse not to go out with him.

Grace stopped over right after Judy got the call from Arizona saying the papers were all signed and the check was in the mail. "I'm just glad to have that behind me. Come on in the kitchen. I made some tea."

"I got an email from Ellyn this morning and made a copy of it for you," Grace handed her mother a sheet of paper.

"Thanks," she said as she sat down to read it. "It's amazing how you can communicate with each other when there are so many miles between." She read more. "I see she's not going to be home until after the holidays. It sounds like she's seeing progress at the school."

"I keep her posted as to what's going on around here. I do miss seeing her. But email is sure great."

After she finished reading Ellyn's email, Judy moved a pile of papers around on the table to make room.

"Mom, what's all this stuff about?"

"I'm sorting out things. I'm thinking about selling my condo and finding something smaller." There, she finally told someone. Right then, she knew it was the right decision.

"You're what?" Grace sat down on the nearest chair.

"This place is just too big for me."

"Isn't this rather sudden? I thought a person should wait for a year before making any big changes."

Judy poured Grace a cup of tea and handed her the sugar bowl. "I sold the Arizona place this week."

Grace nodded. "I know, but this place too?"

Judy looked at her daughter. "It may not sell that fast. I can't stay here. This was never home to me. It was a place to stay for half the year. Same as the place in Arizona. Neither place holds any long, dear memories. I would probably feel different if we-I-were in the old house yet."

Grace was silent for a few minutes. Judy poured herself some more tea and sat down at the table, too.

"Well, Mom, I guess we all have to make up our own minds. You supported me with my divorce. It's only fair for me to support you in this."

There was the phrase again. Life isn't always fair, but Grace's support was wonderful.

"So, take what you want. I'm going to tell your brothers and sister to do the same."

"Where would Ellyn keep her things?"

"I don't know. I'll find a place for them. I know it sounds terrible, but it's time for you kids to rely less on me."

"You're right."

"Hey, would you like some cookies? They're just from the grocery store."

"You're not going to get rid of your cookie sheets, are you?" Grace sounded the way she did when she was nine.

Judy laughed. "I won't get rid of the cookie sheets. I promise." She raised her right hand as a sign of the oath.

They drank tea and munched on cookies. Grace told her mother about what was going on in her life.

"What are you going to do with all your furniture?" Grace asked.

"I'll keep some and probably sell the rest. I sold almost everything with the park unit."

Grace looked at her watch. "I better get going. I have a double shift tonight."

"I'm happy you stopped over. We haven't had much of a chance to do this."

"Have you told Aunt Sandra about selling this place?"

"Not yet. You're the first to know."

"She's going to have a bird."

Judy laughed. "Maybe a whole flock."

When Grace was gone, Judy went to the kitchen. She couldn't leave it like this. She started to carry boxes down to the family room. It would be a good place to put everything she wanted to get rid of. A central location.

After everything was taken down, she opened the cabinets again. They looked bare. Next she would tackle the china cabinet, but not today. She took the morning newspaper into the living room and took out the classified. There were a lot of apartments for rent. Some were even in the same complex she now lived in. Did she want to rent a place or just find a smaller condo? She'd have to think that one over.

Sandra called before Judy called her. "I'm at the hospital. Brad was having chest pains and he's up here in ER." She spoke in barely over a whisper.

"I'll be right up," Judy said.

"No, don't bother. I'll call you when I know something. They might not even keep him here. Who knows?"

"Just call and I'll be right there," Judy promised. "I'll give Kathy a call, just to forewarn her."

"Thanks."

An hour later, Sandra called saying Brad was going home. He just had indigestion.

Suddenly, resentment came over her. Brad who had neglected his health and abused his body was given another chance at life while Steve, who had been so careful about taking care of himself was gone. It just wasn't fair.

Tomorrow she would call each of her other children and tell them about the condo. She mentioned it to Kathy earlier that evening when she called about Brad. Late as it was, she called Kathy to let her know Brad was doing all right.

XVIII

Deciding to sell the condo took a great weight off her shoulders. Besides, getting ready to sell and finding a new place would keep her busy for a while at least. She'd worry about that issue later. She was beginning to understand Scarlett O'Hara.

She could have predicted how each of her family members would take the news. Grace and Kathy encouraged her. Clark whined that he would certainly have no place to call his own. Judy reminded him he was on his own and never lived in the condo anyway. Andy seemed miffed she had not asked his advice. Sandra just couldn't understand her sister's haste.

"Who talked you into selling the place and downsizing?" She asked.

"No one talked me into anything. You know me better than that."

"It was Kathy and that Joe guy."

"Oh, for crying out loud, they had nothing to do with it. Besides I haven't talked to Joe for over a week" They talked for a few more minutes. By the time the call ended, Sandra was offering to help with anything Judy might need, including the rummage sale.

Judy hung up with a smile on her face. Thank God for sisters.

She hadn't talked to Joe. What was he up to? She had a letter from Toots. Well, it was just as well. No use complicating her life at this time.

That week she talked to a realtor and the president of the condo association. Once again, she was in luck. The president told her of a couple of people who had approached him about units that might be for sale.

"I'll get back to you with their names." He promised.

Things were going too fast. But then it was a great opportunity. She started to look at apartments. A senior complex had just opened up and she looked there. "No," she thought, "the places just didn't suit her needs. They were for the elderly and she wasn't there yet."

A couple and then a single woman looked at her condo. They were the ones the condo president had sent over. Neither seemed very interested. Judy was disappointed. Still, she kept looking for apartments and packing up. She gave the kids and Sandra's kids all sorts of odds and ends.

"If you keep giving it all away, there won't be anything left for a rummage sale." Sandra said when she came over for coffee one evening.

"Rummage sales are such a hassle anyway. And don't worry, there's still plenty."

"Do you want to have Thanksgiving this year?" Sandra changed the subject.

"I'd rather have Thanksgiving instead of Christmas. I hope

by Christmas time I have this place sold."

Joe called late that night. "I'm sorry I didn't get a chance to call sooner but I've been out of the country in a rather remote area of Brazil. It's even farther from civilization than your daughter."

"I get emails from her. Well, I don't. She sends them to my other daughter and Grace prints them out." Then she told him about moving into a smaller place and selling the condo.

"What are you going to do then?" Joe asked.

"I haven't a clue and that frightens me." She hadn't expressed this to anyone. Why could she tell him?

"I know I would go bonkers if I wasn't working."

"I guess I'll worry about that when the time comes."

"You can always come out here and keep my mother and me company. She talks a lot about you. Matter of fact, she scolded me for not at least writing to you."

"I probably wouldn't have answered it anyway... I'm terrible at letter writing. I owe your mother a letter now."

They talked for a few more minutes and Joe promised he would call again soon.

What was she going to do? The question had nagged at her ever since Steve died. She liked to work, but she didn't want to come out of retirement. Did she even want a regular job? Part-time? She found the newspaper and skimmed the employment section. Nothing looked good.

The next day, the condo association president called Judy, wanting to know if she still wanted to sell.

"Yes. I just haven't gotten around to listing it."

"Great. Remember the couple who looked at it?"

"Sure."

"Well, they found out that yours is the best one around. They looked at dozens and yours is the best location and size for the price. The association realtor will be with them."

Judy felt a twinge of panic pass through her. "When do they want to see it again?"

"Tomorrow."

Judy was up half the night working and tidying up. She was worn out. She was asleep before her head hit the pillow.

She was awakened by a phone ringing. Who could be calling at this hour? It was only a little after seven. Everyone would be leaving for work before this. Maybe something was wrong with Brad. She grabbed the receiver. "Hello?"

"Good morning, Mrs. Evans, and how are you today?" the voice chirped.

Judy was just about to slam the phone down when she realized it was the real estate agent.

When Judy didn't answer, the agent said, "I didn't wake you up, did I?" Still the little chirpy voice.

"As a matter of fact, you did." Judy dragged herself to a sitting position. In another life, she would have politely said, "No, I was just getting up, "or something to that effect.

"I'm sorry," but she didn't sound very sorry.

"Why are you calling so early?"

"Oh, the people who want to see your house have to leave town at noon. We wanted to see how soon we could come over." Chirp! Chirp!

Judy groaned silently. "I'll need an hour to get the last minute things taken care of and get out of here."

"Oh, they want to talk to you, so please don't go." Chirp!

"Then I still need an hour to have some coffee and a shower." And probably in that order.

"See you then!" Chirp!

The bed felt so good, but Judy hauled herself out and made it quickly. Then she padded into the kitchen and started a pot of coffee. While that was brewing, she checked to make sure everything was in order. She found the stack of utility bills the realtor requested. They wouldn't show much because they hadn't spent a winter at home, so the heat was on a low setting.

By then, the coffee was ready and she went into the kitchen and poured herself a cup. She brought it to her lips, but it was too hot to drink. She took it into the bathroom with her.

The shower revived her and by the time she was dried off, the coffee cooled down enough to drink. After getting dressed, she still had enough time to maybe read the newspaper. A gust of cold air came through the open window, surprising her. She forgot how cold the fall could be. Maybe she was too hasty selling the place in Arizona. No, she knew she did the right thing.

She had just about finished reading an article when she heard a car pull into her drive. She folded the paper and set it on the coffee table. Her hands were sweaty. Until then, she hadn't realized she was the least bit tense. When the doorbell rang, she rushed to answer it.

After introductions, the couple wandered around the house while the realtor followed them around. Judy sat in the kitchen, having another cup of coffee, feeling like a nervous wreck.

***

Finally, the couple came to the kitchen.

"Do you have any questions for Mrs. Evans?" the agent asked.

"Do you have those utility bills?" the man asked.

Judy handed them to him. "My husband and I spent the winters in Arizona, so these bills might not reflect how it would be for a family."

He nodded as he glanced through the pack before handing it to Judy.

"Are the window treatments staying?" the woman asked.

Judy said they were.

They had a couple more questions and then they left.

"We'll be in touch," Chirp said as she wiggled her fingers at Judy as a sort of a wave.

Judy fixed herself some breakfast. She felt all shaky inside and didn't know if it was nerves or hunger. It was too early to go anyplace. She debated whether she should stick around to see if the realtor called or not. How many times would she have to endure this? She opened up the paper and started to look again at the apartment listings.

Judy was cleaning out the coffeepot when the phone rang. Chirp! Chirp! It was the realtor. "They made an offer. Could I bring it over right away?"

"You can bring it over for me to see, but I'll want my lawyer to see it before I sign anything."

"Fair enough. Toddles."

The offer was more than fair, as far as Judy could tell. It was a cash sale, so there wouldn't be any contingencies about selling another house or waiting for financing to go through. Still, she wanted an expert to look at it.

"They want an answer before they leave town."

"I'll see what I can do." Judy dialed her attorney's office. He wasn't available, but one of his associates would have time.

Taking separate cars, Judy and the agent drove to the attorney's office. The agent stayed in the waiting room while Judy took the contract and went in to see an associate.

The young attorney looked it over. "It looks fine to me." She handed it to Judy.

"I thought so too, but just needed an expert opinion." The two women shook hands.

In the waiting room, Judy was about to sign the document when she saw the closing date. In all the haste, she hadn't noticed it before. Two weeks? "I will need more than two weeks to be out of there. I don't have any place to go yet." Now panic really seized Judy.

"They're relocating and will be starting their new jobs in three weeks. They want to be settled before they go back to work." No chirp.

This had all been too good to be true. It was what she wanted. Besides, things always had a way of working out.

As she signed, the agent said, "I have a couple of nice apartments if you'd like to look at them. They're in the same complex you're in."

"Right now?"

The realtor looked at her watch. "I have to get this to my office. Say, in an hour. I'll even spring for lunch."

"Great. Where do you want me to meet you?"

She dug around in her purse for a few minutes and took out a piece of paper. Then she seemed to change her mind. "I'll pick you up." The chirp was back.

"I'll be ready." Judy waved goodbye to the receptionist and went home.

It was just about an hour when Judy's phone rang.

Chirp! Chirp! "I'm coming around the corner by your house. Are you ready?"

What did we ever do before cell phones? "I'll put my coat on right now."

They drove a few blocks from Judy's and pulled into the parking lot of a new building in her complex. "There are all sorts of options here." The realtor got out of her car and took a ring of keys out of her pocket. "What are you looking for?"

"I'd like two bedrooms and a balcony. And if possible, two baths. Other than that, I'm not really sure."

"Then we'll look at as many as you wish till we find one. And if we don't find one here, I represent another complex on the other side of town. This will give you an idea of what a two bedroom looks like."

Judy liked what she saw, but these apartments wouldn't be ready for over a month yet.

"I'd like to see what else is available." So they drove across town, which wasn't really that far. The complex was smaller and older, but well maintained on the outside.

"Apartment eight is empty. We just had it painted and new carpeting put in." The realtor got out of the car.

"Is this the one that I could take?"

"No, this one is rented, but they won't be moving in until the weekend." She jangled the keys while they walked. "The one you can have is in another building. The people just moved out. They left quite a mess. I want you to see this one first."

The realtor opened the front door and went through another door and down the hall. "This has a security system with a buzzer. And underground parking and an elevator."

She opened the door and the smell of fresh paint and new

carpeting enveloped them.

"This is nice. Very bright." Judy liked it. It was roomy and clean.

"Do you have a pet?"

"No, are they allowed here?"

The realtor nodded. "It's an extra fifteen dollars a month though."

Judy walked through the apartment. She liked almost everything about it. Lots of storage space, a bath and a half. Plenty of room for guests.

"I'd like to see the other unit."

"So you like this?"

"Yes, I do."

"Well, just be prepared to use your imagination with this one. Don't worry, we'll have it done for you before closing."

The realtor led Judy down to the basement. "I'd like you to see this before I show the place to you." She opened the door to the garage. It, too, was clean with only a few cars parked.

"Most people are at work."

"I figured that," Judy said, taking notice of the layout of the basement garage.

They walked down the one side and through another door. They walked up another flight of stairs.

"The elevator is over in a corner. We'll come back that way. You can get to the other buildings through the garage, but you have to have a key to do so,"

They walked down the hall to the last door on the right. The realtor unlocked the door and went in first.

***

The place was a mess but paint and new carpeting would fix it up. Judy remembered the first house she and Steve had. It was even worse than this.

She walked from room to room. The balcony overlooked a wooded area. She noticed there were bird feeders out. When she went in, she found the realtor looking in the refrigerator. "This will be replaced and so will the stove. Maybe even the countertops." She grimaced.

Judy realized the other woman hadn't been chirping since they got there. "How much is the rent and do I have to sign a lease?"

She was told the fee and no, there would not have to be a lease.

"Great, I'll take it."

"Why don't we get out of here before we talk anymore?" The agent wrinkled her nose.

"Fine with me." They went out into the hall.

"I'm sorry that is such a mess. If you decide to take this unit, I'm not going to have you pay the first month's rent. My gift to you." She smiled. "Just a security deposit of one month."

"Fair enough." Judy took out her checkbook.

The realtor held up her hand. "You can do that when we get to the restaurant. I don't know about you, but I'm famished." The chirp was back.

Lunch was at a Chinese restaurant that had a buffet. Judy had been there for dinner many times, but this was the first time at noon. It was wonderful.

She wrote out the check for the deposit and the realtor tucked it in her bag.

***

It wasn't until Judy got home that the enormity of what she had done hit her. She hadn't discussed her decision with anyone. Once again, she was reminded of how she and Steve would talk over all the pros and cons before deciding on something this tremendous. Who could she talk to anyway? It was her life and that was that.

Now she would have to pack in earnest. Two weeks! This weekend, she would have to call the kids to come over and pick through what she didn't want. No time for a rummage sale. And what about Thanksgiving?

XIX

In the evening, she wasn't hungry for dinner, so she microwaved a bag of popcorn.

Joe called. "What's going on?"

"I sold my place," Judy blurted out.

"Well, congratulations. I didn't know you had even put it on the market." He did sound pleased.

Joe was someone she could talk over with Judy told him the whole story, ending with having rented a new place and closing in two weeks.

"Need a hand?"

"You're kidding, right?"

"No, I'm serious. I finished the other job and have taken the rest of the year off."

Judy hesitated. "I can't put you up here. It wouldn't look good to the neighbors, or my family."

"Don't worry about that. I'm sure there's a motel not too far away."

"But that will cost."

He cut her off. "I wouldn't have offered if I hadn't meant it.

Besides, it will give me something to do."

"I'd love to have the help. My sister, Sandra, will be helping some, too."

"Can my mother come?"

"Toots?"

"She's the only mother I have." They both laughed.

"Sure, and I can have her stay here. With her as a chaperone, you could stay here, except I have already emptied out the other bedrooms."

"No matter. She'd love to stay with you."

They talked over arrangements.

"I'll call you as soon as everything is set."

After they hung up, Judy found herself grinning. She hadn't wanted to do this alone and now she wouldn't have to. Her heart pounded at the thought of seeing Joe again. Thank heavens Toots would be there to chaperone.

Of course, Sandra was all upset Judy sold her condo so fast and was moving into an apartment without consulting her. She was even more upset to learn Joe and his mother were coming to help Judy with the packing.

"You'll be sorry. I've had friends who have moved into apartments that weren't only for seniors. It was a mistake. Kids clamoring around all the time. Loud parties."

"If I've made a mistake, then it's my mistake." Judy's nerves were raw with the move. And if she would have admitted it to herself, the prospect of seeing Joe wasn't making them any calmer.

Joe and Toots showed up on her doorstep a couple of days later. There were hugs and polite kisses. Even a polite kiss from Joe made Judy's blood race.

"You can put your mother's bags in my room." Judy led the

way.

"Oh, my dear, I can't take your room," Toots said.

"I have a spare room downstairs and it'll be just fine."

"It doesn't look like you're going to be out of here in just a bit over a week." Joe poked his head into the living room.

"Oh, but I will." Judy grinned as she opened the closet door to reveal box upon box stacked neatly.

"And then again, maybe you will." Joe gave her a wink.

"Now you just tell us what you need help with." Toots rubbed her hands together.

"Why don't we have a cup of tea while we discuss it?" Judy said. She had a list and they could go over it. There was plenty of time to start to work.

Judy started the coffee maker. "I have tea in my coffee maker. It works very well." Judy motioned for them to sit down at the table.

"I've heard of people doing that. Now I can see for myself." Toots sat down.

They talked about the trip and the weather. The coffee pot gurgled away. Judy set out the milk and sugar and a plate of cookies. When the tea was ready, she poured them each a mug full.

Joe looked skeptical as he took his first sip. "Not bad."

Toots took a sip. "I'm going to have to fix it this way. It's sure a lot easier."

Now that they were all settled, Judy went over the list with them.

"It sounds like you have most of it done," Toots said.

"The kids are coming this weekend to get whatever they want. Even though the furniture is fairly new, I've decided to replace most of it. I don't think it'll fit right in the new place."

Judy really did have everything taken care of. Having moved into the condo just a few years ago, she and Steve had gotten rid of many of the extras.

"When can you move into your new apartment?" Joe asked.

"I have the key, but I don't think I want to move anything until after the painting is done and the carpeting is laid."

Joe nodded approvingly.

"I'll take you over for a tour tomorrow. It'll give me a chance to see the progress," Judy said.

They loaded up the car for a Goodwill run. That would help get some things out of their way. Joe took out the backseat in the minivan to make room for boxes and garbage bags.

"I didn't think we could get it all in one load," Judy said.

"Aren't cha glad I came?" he drawled. He brushed his lips on her cheek as he walked past her.

Shivers ran through her and she followed him into the condo.

"I think I'll just stay here while you two bring the load over. I could stand a few minutes by myself." Toots flopped down on the couch.

Joe drove the van. The air was charged. It was the first time they were alone since he and Toots had arrived. He put his hand on her knee.

She wanted to push it off, but yet she didn't. He oozed sexuality. Did he really care for her? Or was she just going to be a conquest? She knew she had lost her fight already.

"I'm sorry about having you stay in a motel," she said, sounding lame to herself.

He took his hand back. "Don't worry about it."

"It's just that my family would think the worst."

"And what is the worst?" he said softly.

She felt her face get hot. "Never mind."

He laughed.

She tried to change the subject by pointing out various landmarks, like the art museum or one of the mansions along Lake Michigan's shore. "If we have time, I'd like to show some of them to you and Toots."

Joe helped one of the workers unload the items while she did some paperwork. She might as well get a donation receipt for taxes. They stopped by the apartment, but the painters were there, so Judy told Joe they'd come later.

"Just go one block to the left and we'll be right back on the main drag." Judy pointed.

"I can find the way from there," Joe assured her.

On the way, Judy leaned her head against the headrest. She dozed off and didn't wake until Joe pulled into the drive.

"Have you been getting enough sleep?" Joe's voice was full of concern.

"Yes, actually, I have. It must have been the warm sun that put me out."

"Now I remember you did that when you came to visit us."

They went into the house. Toots was glued to some soap opera.

"So you wanted some time to yourself, eh?" Joe teased her.

"You know I never miss my story unless I can't help it." She didn't get defensive.

Judy went in and made a plate of sandwiches for their lunch. Then they sat at the table and ate.

"Did you rent a car?" Judy didn't remember seeing any car parked on the street. But then she hadn't see them arrive.

"No, we took a shuttle from the airport. I didn't think I would need a car."

"No, if you need to go someplace, you can use mine."

"That's what I thought. I think I'll borrow it right after lunch to go check into my motel."

"Fine." Just don't ask me to take you there, she thought.

"When I get back, I'll treat you two ladies to dinner."

"Oooo, you're so gallant." Judy swooned and fluttered her eyelashes at him.

"I try to be, ma'am." He bowed to each of them.

Judy cleaned up the kitchen. "Why don't you go and take a nap? I imagine you're tired," Judy said to Toots.

"I don't know about taking a nap, but I think I'd like to lie down and read."

Judy busied herself around the kitchen, then went downstairs to make her bed up. She threw a load of laundry in and sat down to look at a magazine.

The words didn't register. All she could think of was that Joe was here. Stop being so stupid, she told herself. You're acting worse than a sixteen-year-old in heat. She didn't even remember that she felt this way about Steve, though she was sure she did. How was she going to handle this?

Judy was checking to see if the mail was there, when Joe came. "Toots is laying down, so come on downstairs. I'm finishing up some laundry."

Quietly, they went down to the family room. Before she had time to think, Joe was kissing her. "I've wanted to do that all day."

"Wow," was Judy's reply.

He led her to the sofa and sat down, pulling her onto his lap. She could feel his hardness. It felt so good. His tongue slipped into her mouth. A thrill ran through her. She shifted and he gave a small groan.

Joe's hand slid up her back under her shirt and unfastened her bra. She let him. His hand moved around her ribs and cupped one breast. Her nipple automatically hardened. Another thrill ran through her. He moved her shirt up and gently licked at her nipple. "She couldn't breathe. "I think I hear someone walking around," she whispered.

Joe put his head up, "Yeah, I think Mom's up."

Judy slid so she was sitting next to him. He reached over and rehooked her bra, but not before giving her nipples one last rub.

"Stop that," She gently pushed his hand away. He kissed her ear. "I have to see if the clothes are finished drying. You go up by your mother."

"I better wait a minute or so." He looked down at his crotch where a large bulge was apparent. He grinned at Judy.

A few minutes later, Judy went upstairs, and overheard Toots say, "I told Judy I would lie down, but I was going to read. I didn't hear you come back."

"I just did," Joe said.

They went out for an early dinner. Later, they had cheesecake and tea.

It was time for Joe to go to his motel room. He was using Judy's van and she walked outside with him. They were in the garage on the way to the car when Joe stopped and pulled her to him. More fiery kisses. His hands wandered over her body. Then he broke away. "I'm going back and take a cold shower." He kissed her nose and went out the door. She thought about taking one too.

Sandra called just before Judy went to bed.

"Did that friend of yours and his mother show up today?" There was an edge to Sandra's voice that Judy hated.

"Joe and his mother arrived this morning and we really got a lot done. Took a bunch of stuff to Goodwill. The kids are coming over tomorrow to go through what's left." Judy fought to keep her voice even.

"I suppose you put them up at your house."

Judy had already told her the arrangements. "No, Toots is staying here and Joe is at a motel."

"Did he rent a car or do you have to drive him back and forth?"

"He's using my car."

"You're letting a stranger use your car?"

Sandra must have been spoiling for a fight, but Judy wasn't going to let her get the best of her. "Well, I don't think of him as a stranger. Besides, it's really nobody's business."

Sandra humphed. "I guess not."

Judy decided to change the subject. "How is Brad doing?"

"Fine."

They talked for a few more minutes. Judy tried to end the call. She was so tired.

"Could you come over for lunch tomorrow and bring Joe and T...his mother?"

Judy smiled to herself. Sandra couldn't bring herself to call Joe's mother Toots. "I don't think we have any plans. What time are you looking at?"

"About one."

"Unless there's a change, we'll be there."

Judy went in and washed her face and brushed her teeth. Then she snuggled under the covers. The mattress was unfamiliar to her. It took her some time to get comfortable. She woke up every few hours. It stayed dark so late in the morning, she was surprised when she woke up and the clock read almost nine.

She lay in bed, listening for noises coming from the upstairs. Was Toots awake yet? She crawled out of bed and went in and took a shower. After she got dressed, she went upstairs.

Joe and Toots were in the living room, reading the morning paper.

"Well, it's about time you got up." Joe grinned.

"Did we wake you?" Toots asked.

"I didn't hear any noise. I just am not used to the bed." She could have bitten off her tongue. She didn't want to have Toots feel she was putting her to any inconvenience.

"I understand. I woke up several times myself. Then I just decided to get up and make coffee." Toots got up. "Would you like some?"

Toots amazed Judy. Here she was a guest in her house and she was waiting on her. "You bet and if you want to come in the kitchen, I'll make us some breakfast."

Judy poured herself the last cup of coffee in the pot. How long had Toots been up? And how long had Joe been there? "I'll fix us some waffles." She took out the waffle iron and plugged it in. Then she mixed the batter and made another pot of coffee.

"I haven't had waffles in years," Toots said as she blotted the corners of her mouth with a napkin. "They were wonderful."

"Certainly were. You can cook me breakfast anytime," Joe said.

Judy felt her face get warm. She dropped a spoon into the sink with a clatter. She hoped no one would see how flustered she got. "Glad you liked them. By the way, my sister wants us to come over for lunch at one today."

"Kathy?" Toots said.

"No, I have a sister, Sandra, living not too far from here."

"I'd like to meet her," said Toots. Joe just gave a slight nod.

***

Lunch went better than Judy had expected. Joe and Brad had some interests in common. As usual, Sandra made a great meal.

"Toots is a gem," Sandra whispered to Judy when they were in the kitchen alone.

"I thought you'd think so. You're going to have to believe me someday that my judgement can be trusted."

Sandra gave her a hug. "I just don't want to see you taken advantage of. You are so vulnerable at this time."

Judy returned her a hug. Sandra did mean well.

They left Sandra and Brad's before the schools got out. The traffic could be horrendous at that time. Judy drove to the new apartment.

"Let's see how much is done. I'd like to start moving in." Judy used her key to get into the building. "It's right down this way."

The apartment door stood open and she could hear a radio playing. Paint fumes greeted them as they stepped into the apartment.

"Anyone here?" Judy called.

"We're in the bathroom."

Judy, Joe and Toots all looked at each other. Were they painting it or using it for the purpose intended?

A workman came out, wiping paint off his hands with a shop rag. "That was the last room to be painted."

"What else needs to be done?"

"I'm just putting on the finishing touches. Are you the new tenant?"

"Oh, I'm sorry. Yes, I'm Judy Evans." She stuck out her hand, but then she pulled it back.

"Better not. I still have paint on my hands." He laughed.

"Mind if we look around?"

"Be my guest," the workman said.

Judy gave them the grand tour. The place looked so much better than the first time she was there.

"I've thought about moving into a smaller place, but I'd miss my view of the mountains," Toots said.

"I can understand that, but I do have a view." Judy opened the drapes to show the patio and the view of the wooded glen.

"You have a nice view."

"Well you know we don't have any mountains around here."

The painter said, "I think you can probably start moving things in this weekend."

"That would be wonderful. I have to get some different furniture and I'll have that delivered sometime next week unless I have to do a special order."

Grace came over before she went to work. Judy introduced her and then she took Grace to the pile. "You get first choice. Clark and Andy will come after dinner." Then she added, "Also, choose some things you think Ellyn would like. You know her tastes."

Grace pulled Judy's arm and pulled her into the hall. "Who's this guy anyway? He seems nice enough but what about Dad? Aunt Sandra-"

Judy put up her hand to halt Grace. "Joe is a guy I met in Colorado. He's a friend. I'm not ready to get into a relationship so soon. And as far as my sister is concerned, she's just speculating."

"Okay, Mom. You don't have to get all bent out of shape. Just thought I'd ask."

"What are you going to do with Ellyn's?" Grace said as she put a quilt to the side.

"Sandra said she can keep them until Ellyn gets home, as long as it's not too much."

"Would you like to stay for dinner?" Judy asked

"No, I have to go to work early." Grace picked up her things and left.

Toots made them supper. "Just show me where you keep the soup and can opener. I'll do the rest."

Andy came over by himself. "The kids aren't feeling very good. Tammie thinks they're coming down with colds." Judy was disappointed. She wanted to show off her grandkids.

Clark came just as Andy was leaving.

"Where's Tina?" Judy asked.

"She has an early morning class," he said. "She told me to pick her out something, too, if it's okay with you."

"Whatever you kids don't take goes to Goodwill. We took one load over there yesterday."

Both sons gave Judy the third degree like Grace had. Judy reassured them that Joe was a friend, and that's all.

"You have some fine looking youngsters," Toots said after Clark left. "Too bad the rest couldn't make it."

"Maybe we'll get a chance to stop by and see my grandchildren before you leave. We seem to be getting a lot done." Judy looked at what was left, now that the children took what they wanted. "There isn't much here."

"I have some business calls to make before it gets too late. All of my things are in my room," Joe put on his jacket and kissed his mother. "Come and walk me out," he said to Judy.

Another steamy goodbye scene occurred before Judy gently shoved him toward the door. "Remember, you have calls to make."

"See you in the morning."

Sandra came over the next morning. "You really have the situation under control," she said as she helped herself to coffee. "What about all the big stuff?"

Judy explained she was leaving some of it. She had hired movers to bring whatever furniture she was taking.

"I wouldn't even want to imagine moving. Brad is such a packrat. The kids have their things stored at home."

"I was thinking the same thing," Toots got up and started clearing the table. "Not only have I lived there since shortly after I was married, but my husband's family lived there, too. You can imagine just how much has accumulated. There are just so many memories."

"Will you need help cleaning after things are moved out?" Sandra asked.

"No, I hired a cleaning service." Judy paused, "Unless you want to come and dust and clean the bathrooms."

Sandra shot her an angry glance.

Judy just laughed. "I've always hated those two jobs, so when we were kids, I'd foist them on Sandra and Kathy. The advantage of being the oldest."

"I remember you and Kathy talking about that when you were visiting." Joe chuckled.

When Sandra left, Judy offered to show Joe and Toots around the town.

"I'll make sure I put on my walking shoes," Toots said as she went to change her clothes.

***

They went to the library, saw where the new civic theater was, and where Judy had taught school. "We can go to the museum after we get something to eat," Judy said. "It's too cool for a picnic, but there's a restaurant with an atrium."

Toots and Joe agreed.

"You have a lovely town, Judy," Toots said as they waited for their order to come.

"But not as lovely as our home in Colorado." Joe winked at his mother.

"I didn't think that way until I'd lived there for many years. Chicago was the only place to be."

"I've never lived any other place, except for the recent winters spent in Arizona," Judy said.

"I would find it difficult to move to a different part of the country," Toots said.

"Mom, don't tell Judy that. I was hoping I could persuade Judy to move out to Colorado."

"We'd certainly love to have you closer, but the choice is entirely yours." Toots reached over and patted Judy's hand.

"Well, I'm not giving up so easily." Joe unwrapped his silverware as the waiter brought their food.

"What are you going to do after you move?" Toots asked.

Judy shrugged. "I don't know yet. I thought about getting a job of some sort, but I really don't want to be tied down." She paused. "Maybe I'll do some volunteer work."

"I've done lots, but not so much any longer." Toots took a sip of coffee. "Joe's hobby is making money, just like his dad."

"Mom, I don't have any other interests and I love my work. I get to travel to all parts of the world, meet new people, and not be bored."

"At least your father didn't travel without me."

"I think part of the fun of traveling is sharing it with another person who enjoys the same things or the adventure," Judy said as she remembered the fun she and Steve had on their travels. They would take a week or two every summer to go someplace different. When the kids were younger, they'd go camping or to a relative's in another state.

"You could go with me," Joe said, not looking at her.

"Joe!" Toots said indignantly. "That isn't a good idea. Don't you take advantage of her vulnerability."

"I'm not, but I really like Judy." He reached over and gave Judy a kiss on the cheek. "I'd never do anything to cause her discomfort."

Yeah, right. Judy thought about the passion they shared. Joe was the one in more discomfort, she remembered his hardness pressed against her.

"I'll pick up the tab," Joe said as he grabbed the check and got up from the table.

When he was out of earshot, Toots said, "He likes you a lot. I've never seen him put himself out for anybody except his daughter and me."

Before Judy could reply, Joe was back. "Now, let's see your museum."

"Let's go to the movies tonight," Toots suggested. "If we get there before six we can get matinee prices, or at least, that's the way it is in Colorado."

"Here too. What would you like to see?"

"Any of these." Toots dug around in her purse and handed the newspaper clipping to Judy.

There were a couple of adventure movies, several cartoon types, and there were several R-rated. Judy didn't need anything erotic. "Why don't we wait until we get to the cinema?"

"Fine, and it'll be my treat." Toots got up and went put on a sweater.

"That was simple," Joe said as he got up and put on his coat.

The adventure movie was good, or at least the parts Judy could remember. Joe sat between Judy and his mother. He held Judy's hand through most of the film, gently stroking her fingers and tickling her palm.

When the movie was over, Joe insisted they get something to eat.

"Nothing much for me. I'm still full from lunch," Toots said.

"Me too, but I could probably eat a bowl of soup."

"Boy, you're a couple of cheap dates." Joe grinned. They went to a Denny's and ate.

Joe didn't even get out of the van when they got to Judy's. "I'll see you in the morning. I'll even go with you furniture shopping, if you'd like."

Neither Judy nor Toots took very long before they were in bed. This night, Judy slept well except for the erotic dreams she had about Joe. She wondered if she was just reading more into him than was really there or did he really care for her? Time would tell. Hopefully, she would let her mind overrule her body.

This morning they were running later than the previous morning. It was cold cereal and tea for breakfast. No one seemed to care.

"Anytime you're ready to go, we can leave," Joe said to Judy.

"I'll just stay here. I'll make dinner for us. It'll give me a chance to read," Toots said.

"Are you sure? I could stand some advice," Judy said. She was disappointed and a bit scared. She had never really bought furniture on her own. Steve had always been with her.

"No, it's your place and it should reflect your taste."

"Okay. There's a variety of food in the freezer. You can use anything you want." Impulsively, Judy gave Toots a hug and a kiss on the cheek. "I'm going to miss you when you go back to Colorado."

"This is a bad time to buy furniture. Everyone wants it for the holidays," one clerk at a furniture store told them.

"I don't always have good timing. I can get by with what I'm keeping for a while."

Judy found a bedroom suite that could be delivered the day she moved. She opted for a queen-sized bed. A king-sized was just too lonely without Steve... She was going to keep her kitchen table and chairs. They would fit perfectly. The guest room furniture would fit in the second bedroom. All she needed for the living room was a couple of matching love seats. Those would take a couple of months.

"You could just use lawn furniture," Joe said.

The clerk gave her a funny look, but Joe just laughed.

"Your husband has a strange sense of humor," the clerk said.

Before Judy could correct her, Joe put his arm around Judy possessively. "No, she's just a pioneer at heart."

"This ought to take care of most of what I need," Judy said when she wrote out a check for her purchases.

Soon the paperwork was completed and Joe and Judy were in the car.

Joe took out his cell phone, "Hello?"

"I didn't hear it ring," Judy whispered.

"Vibrate," Joe mouthed.

Judy didn't pay any attention to what Joe was saying on his call. She tried to picture how best to arrange the new furniture.

She would think of the other things later, like window treatments and such.

"I need to go to my room," Joe said. "I have to fax some papers to a client."

Little red flags popped up in Judy's mind.

"Don't worry, it'll just take a few minutes. I know just where they are."

Time wasn't what Judy was nervous about. She didn't know if she could trust herself in a room with a bed and Joe.

As if reading her mind, Joe said, "I won't take advantage of you." Then he added with a wicked smile, "Unless you want me to."

"I don't think it would be a good idea," she said, but thought it would be fun to try. Now stop that, she told herself sternly.

He did give Judy a long, lingering kiss just as they were about to walk out of his room. "Change your mind?"

"No," she said, hiding the regret.

Joe took the papers to the desk clerk for faxing.

"What do you say we have a drink before we go to your place? We've hardly had any time by ourselves." Joe started up the engine.

"A glass of wine would taste good."

"What do you suggest?"

"Go up to the light and hang a right. Two blocks down is a microbrewery."

"Sounds good to me, but do they have wine?"

"It's a microbrewery and a winery."

There were only a few people at the place. The waitress showed them to a cozy booth by a fireplace.

Joe looked around. "Very nice."

"Glad you like it. I've had lunch here with some girlfriends."

"I'm a bit hungry. Why don't we get an appetizer or two?"

They ordered a sampler of appetizers and Joe had a beer while Judy ordered a glass of the featured wine.

When the waitress left, Joe reached over and took Judy's hand. "I admire how you're handling all of this."

"Pardon?" Judy wasn't sure she heard what he said. So he repeated it. "Why do you say that?"

"You aren't whimpering or whining about having to give up your condo."

"I'm not having to give up my condo. I'm choosing to do so. I just don't want to be tied to such a big place."

"I didn't mean it that way." He stroked her hand. "I meant you are being so proactive. You're quite a woman." He might have said more, but their drinks arrived.

"Speaking of quite a woman, what about your mother?" Judy steered the conversation away from herself.

Joe grinned. "She is, isn't she? You know, she could have outlasted either of us with the shopping business this afternoon?"

"I know."

He took her hand and brought it to his lips. His warm breath made her shiver. "Are you cold?"

She lied. "Just a little." She was really burning up inside.

He got up and stripped off his jacket and hung it around her shoulders. "Better?"

"Much." She snuggled into its warmth. She was enveloped in his scent.

"When you get settled, why don't you come out and spend some time with Toots and me?"

She hesitated.

"It would give you a chance to be with Kathy, too." He knew

her weakness was her family.

"I'll give it some thought." And she would.

"You should see the mountains covered with snow. Do you ski?"

Judy shook her head. "Remember, I'm not much for any athletic activity."

"Want to go to the movies again tonight?"

"I have never gone to the movies two nights in a row. Is there anything special you'd like to see?"

"No, but it would give me a chance to hold your hand in the dark." There was a glint in his eyes Judy found just a bit dangerous and very tempting.

"That would be fun." She meant the movie and realized what she had said as soon as it was out of her mouth. She put a hand over her mouth.

Joe just laughed. "I better call Toots and ask when she's planning on serving dinner."

"Maybe she'd like to come with us?" Judy suggested.

"Good idea." Joe punch in some number on his cell phone. Judy excused herself and went to the ladies' room.

When she came to the booth, Joe said, "Mom will have dinner ready in two hours. She wants to watch something on TV tonight, so she passed on the invitation. So, I guess it's just you and me." He wiggled his eyebrows.

Judy got a little quiver in her belly.

Toots made pork chops with stuffing and a green salad. "Hope you enjoy this."

Judy swallowed the bite she had in her mouth. "It's wonderful. I usually don't bother to cook a meal like this for myself."

"I don't either. That's why I offered to do it." Toots twirled her fork in the air.

Judy never remembered much about the movie. Joe had his arm around her all during it. His other hand held hers and he kept bringing it to his lips. The spell was broken as soon as they got in the brightly lit lobby and walked out into the cold.

"Where are we going?" Judy asked when he went in the opposite direction from the house.

"How about a mocha or cappuccino?"

"That sounds good."

The next few days were busy with moving into the apartment. Even though Toots moved into the motel with Joe, Judy and Joe didn't have any time alone. Kisses were stolen, but that was it. Box by box, dishes and other things were moved into the new apartment and put away.

The movers came early in the morning. It didn't take long for them to load the large items Judy was keeping. Joe, Toots, and Judy met them at the apartment. In no time, the spare bed was set up and the rest were in place. The furniture store delivered her order right after the movers left.

Joe set up the lawn furniture in the living room. Toots and Judy made the beds.

"We are flying out in the morning. We'll have a celebration dinner at a good restaurant. We all need some time to relax," Joe said as they surveyed the rooms. "Mom and I will go to the motel, change and pick you up about six. Is that okay?"

It was more than okay with Judy. She longed to shower and just unwind.

***

"You have no idea how much I appreciate all your help. Both of you." Judy said as they sat over cups of tea at a restaurant. "I don't know how I can ever repay your kindness."

Joe reached over and held her hand, giving it a little squeeze.

"It has been our pleasure. I haven't had so much activity for months. There isn't much to do in the mountains during the winter. I have the rest of fall and all of winter to rest up," Toots said.

"Activity is putting it mildly. More like a three-ring circus," Judy said.

"I heard your sister saying you were to host Thanksgiving. What are you going to do?" Toots asked.

Judy smiled. "Make reservations."

"Good girl." Toots gave her a wink. "I like your style."

"And if anyone objects, they don't have to come."

"I can't see how you would get everyone in your apartment, anyway," Toots went on.

"We usually don't have as many for Thanksgiving. Some of the nephews go hunting and Ellyn won't be back. I think Grace said she had to work." Judy shrugged. "I suppose I could have them over." She thought for a moment. "No, I can't, as I gave my extra set of dishes to Grace."

"I thought you'd come to your senses." Joe gave her hand another squeeze.

Toots excused herself and headed for the restroom.

"My mother thinks you're great," Joe said as Toots disappeared around a corner.

"I think she's pretty great too." A lump formed in Judy's throat. "I'm going to miss having you two around." She tried to hold back the tears.

"Any time you want, you know our doors are open to you."

Joe brought her hand to his lips. "I'm getting pretty attached to you too." He kissed her fingers again.

Judy withdrew her hand and searched in her purse for a Kleenex.

Toots came out and Judy noticed how tired she looked. "Joe, you better take Toots back to your room before she collapses."

"It would be nice if you'd drop me off at the motel before you took Judy home. It would give me a chance to take a bath and get ready for bed before you get back. You can just leave her car there and take a taxi to the motel." With a knowing look, she said, "It would give you a chance to say goodbye."

Joe paid the bill and they drove over to the motel. Joe stopped in the circular drive in the front.

"Take your time. I want to take a long soak," Toots said as she got out. She opened Judy's door and gave her a hug. Judy hugged her back while Toots kissed her cheek. Judy could feel tears on Toots's face.

"Thanks for everything, and I promise to come out and visit soon."

They watched Toots go into the lobby and walk down the hall before they drove off.

Joe went in with Judy. He took off his coat and laid it across one of the chairs.

"The place looks pretty good for just moving in," Judy said as they walked in the door. "And it will stay that way by not fixing Thanksgiving dinner."

Judy took off her coat and hung it up in the closet. "I think I can find my electric teakettle if you would like a cup of tea. Or there might be something cold to drink."

Joe came over to her and put his arms around her, drawing her so close, she could feel his heart beat.

"I was thinking of more along the lines of hot and passionate." He didn't give her a chance to answer by crushing her mouth under a hungry kiss.

Her knees went to jello and she clung to him for support. "I'm going to miss you," he breathed into her ear. "You're quite a woman."

All Judy could think of to say was, "Thanks."

"I don't want to leave you. I've fallen in love with you." Joe whispered. "I know you need more time," he continued. "I don't want to rush you into anything. Just know my door and my arms are open for you."

She kissed him, wrapping her arms around his waist.

"Does that mean you'll consider it?" Joe smiled at her.

The lump in her throat was back, so she nodded against his shoulder.

"I better get out of here before my mother sends out the militia for me." He took out his phone and called the taxi company. "There's a cab in the neighborhood. It'll be right here."

She walked him to the door. This kiss was short. He walked out the door and she closed it behind him. If her apartment had faced the front, she could have watched him leave.

Joe called the next morning just before the plane took off. "Good morning, beautiful, I miss you already." In the background Judy heard Toots say, "Me, too." Their call ended with Judy wishing them a safe flight. "We'll call when we land," Joe promised.

XX

Judy felt so lonely. She'd been so busy with the move and having Joe and Toots to keep her company. Now it was like a vacuum cleaner had emptied everything. She wanted to cry, but couldn't. Even the apartment was in good order; only a few boxes needed to be sorted through.

Later that afternoon, Toots called to say they'd gotten home safely. Joe had already left on a business trip. "I thought he was done for the year," Judy said.

"Some kind of emergency," Toots answered. "And it's in one of the remote places where it's hard to get messages back and forth."

Judy thanked her again for all her help.

Judy felt a bit disappointed that Joe didn't call her himself, but she shrugged it off for the time being. After all, they had no strings attached.

Every few days, either Judy called Toots or vice versa. Toots told her Joe was still out of town. She didn't expect him for Thanksgiving.

"If I would have known he wasn't going to be around for the

holiday, I would have had you stay. I hate the thought of you being alone."

"Don't worry about me. I have plenty to keep me busy. One of my friends talked me into getting a computer so I can go online-whatever that means."

"That'll keep you busy."

"Maybe I'll hear from my granddaughter once in a while."

"I hope so," Judy said.

After she hung up, she thought about Joe's daughter. He never said much about her. He didn't mention much about his ex-wife, either. Come to think about it, she didn't know much about Joe at all. For all she knew, he was a jewel thief. That thought made her smile. He had stolen her heart.

Time flew. Between settling into her new digs and getting ready for Christmas, Judy didn't give much thought to Joe, except when she went to bed at night. Why didn't Joe call? Was he still in that remote area? She didn't have the handkerchief with Steve's aftershave any longer. She stopped using it when she moved. Steve was in the old place. Now she was starting a new life.

For Thanksgiving, she took the family out for dinner. Andy and his family went to his in-laws. Ellyn was still in Africa. Grace had to work. Sandra's children were busy elsewhere. So, it was only Sandra and Brad, Clark and Tina, and Judy. I could have had everyone at my place after all, Judy thought, but I'm not going to bring the subject up.

Judy missed Steve. This would be the first holiday season in over forty years he wouldn't be with her. It seemed like he'd been gone for years, yet it wasn't even one year. Every now and then she would want to share an incident or thought with him. Then, sadly realize he was gone. Her heart ached and tears came.

A few days before Christmas, Joe called to see what she had been doing. "I'll be going home for the holidays," he told her. "My daughter will be home! I haven't seen her for a few months."

"Toots said she got a computer so she can communicate with her."

Joe laughed. "I know. I think that's pretty cool. Toots is quite a girl. And you're such a woman.'

Judy's breath caught. "Thanks." She felt so dumb.

"No, thank YOU. When are you coming out?"

"I can't even think of that right now with Christmas just around the corner."

"I'll ask again," he said. "Oh, they're calling my flight. Talk to you later." The phone went dead.

What a strange call! What a strange man!

Ellyn came home two days before Christmas. She brought a young man with her. Steve would have liked him.

"Don't worry, Mom, he's going to stay with Andy. I think I'm going to stay with Grace."

Judy felt a twinge of something she couldn't name. She looked forward to spending time with her daughter. Disappointed was probably what it was. Her kids didn't need her anymore.

Not that it was bad. She and Steve raised them to be independent. They called it giving the children roots and wings. She missed Steve right then. He might understand her feelings. He would probably have the same reaction.

Christmas time was hectic. Judy found herself entertaining

her grandchildren while Andy and his wife did last minute shopping. Ellyn spent long hours at Judy's with her boyfriend. Grace worked double shifts for others so she could have Christmas Eve and Christmas Day off.

Judy made cookies and several other baked goods to bring to Sandra's for Christmas. She was too tired to think about Joe. At night, she fell into bed, exhausted. She didn't want to think about the letdown she always had after the holidays were over and her life calmed down. This year there would be no winter months in Arizona.

Christmas Day was dazzling. A couple of days before, it snowed a few inches. While the roads were clear, the grassy areas were sparking white in the sunlight.

Judy half expected a call from Joe or Toots that morning before she left for Sandra's, but there was no call. She tried calling Toots, but there was no answer. She left a "Merry Christmas on the answering machine and hung up. Once at Sandra's, there was no time to think about anyone else. Her grandchildren and Sandra's grandchildren raced around. All the cousins laughed and talked while Sandra and Judy set up the brunch. Brad grumbled in a corner. Last year, he had Steve to keep him company.

Kathy called while they were opening gifts. Everyone took a turn talking to her. Judy was last. Mark talked to her first for a few minutes, then handed it over to Kathy.

"All settled?" Kathy asked.

"Pretty much so. Joe and Toots were so much help. I can't ever repay them."

"Joe will find a way," Kathy said with a hint of secrecy.

Judy just laughed...nervously.

"Isn't his mother a stitch?"

"They were both great. Toots is one of my favorite people."

"When are you coming out for a visit?"

"I don't know. I have some things to do."

"Well, Joe asked me to twist your arm a bit."

"We'll see," was all the answer Judy would give.

"You're all he talks about. It's Judy this and Judy that. I think the man is in love with you."

Judy felt her face get hot. "I don't know about that."

"You could do a lot worse," Kathy said.

"I don't even know him very well. I know what he does for a living, but I don't know anything much about his past. I don't-"

Kathy interrupted. "Okay. Okay. I was only saying what I think. Anyway, don't write him off."

"I promise I won't."

For the rest of the day, Judy kept thinking about the conversation. What about Joe? The miles were too many between them for her to know him.

Ellyn and her boyfriend announced their engagement.

"Mom, I hope you won't be mad at me, but we want to fly to Jamaica and get married," Ellyn told her when Judy asked when they planned on being married.

"Do you want a reception when you get back for family and friends?" Judy's mind was already making a list of details.

"No, we'll have a picnic or something this summer. Neither of us wants to spend the money."

"I'd pay for it." She and Steve had an account setting aside money for each of the children's weddings.

Ellyn kissed her mother's cheek. "No, we just want it to be no fuss or bother. Besides, we have to find jobs. No telling where we'll end up."

Judy felt disappointed. She looked forward to each of her

children's weddings. The preparations were fun, even though the brides got a bit touchy. But this was Ellyn's choice.

Ellyn and her boyfriend left the day after Christmas to visit his family someplace out East.

Joe called just as Judy was getting into bed.

"I was going to call earlier but knew you were going to gone," he explained.

"I've been home for a while. Remember we're an hour later than you." Judy crawled into bed and cradled the phone with her pillow. "Tell me what kind of a day you had?"

They talked for an hour or so. They talked about how the day had been. Joe told her about his job.

"I have to leave in the morning. Lord only knows how long I'll be gone. The communications system is sketchy to say the least. There are only a few places where I can make a call. I'd like to hear your voice more often."

The call last for a few more minutes. Judy fell asleep still holding the receiver.

XXI

Sandra planned a New Year's Eve party. Her parties were always fun. She had some of the most eclectic friends anyone could have. There would be people from church, former co-workers, old neighbors. The food was always good. Everyone tried to outdo the others with what they brought. Judy arrived early to help with the set up. Even Brad would be on his best behavior that night.

Judy was introduced to a former co-worker of Brad's. She knew who he was, but hadn't seen him for several years.

"David's wife left him last year," Sandra whispered to Judy when they were alone in the kitchen.

"Why?"

"She found someone else."

"Oh." Little red flags went up. Her sister was matchmaking, but what the heck.

"So, David, what have you been up to?" Judy sat down next to him at a table.

"I got a new computer for Christmas as a gift to myself." He moved his chair so that it angled to face her.

"I've been thinking about getting one. My kids think I should."

They talked to each other for the rest of the evening. Judy found out they had much in common. So when he asked her for a date the following weekend, she said yes. They seem to have a great time. They went to a movie and then out for dessert. He gave her a kiss at her front door.

The week after, David took her to a store and she bought a computer. He spent several hours at her apartment setting it up for her.

"Just play around with it. Get the feel. You can't break it easily."

Judy didn't find that comment very reassuring, but would give it a try. "How can I get on the..inter...whatever?"

"You have to be connected over the phone lines or a cable to do that." He looked at his watch. "I have to get going, but if you want to get connected, I can come over one evening and do that for you."

."And I'll make you dinner."

"It's a deal."

Judy fooled around with the computer. She used the word processor to write a couple of letters. She found out where the solitaire game was. She made herself a spreadsheet for her accounting. But what she really wanted to do was to go onto the internet.

Wednesday evening, David came over and got her connected and she made him a roast beef dinner.

"I don't know if I can sit close enough to your computer to see after that wonderful meal." He leaned back and rubbed his stomach. Then he got up and went to Judy's computer. She cleared the table and cleaned up the dishes.

"I need you to tell me what you want for an email address."

"Any suggestions?" Judy asked.

"Some people use their first name and the year they were born. Some use a hobby, like knitting or skiing. I guess it's really up to you, as long as no one else has taken it."

Judy decided on her first name and the old house number. "It should be easy for me to remember."

"You'll need a password, too. Better write it down in case you forget it."

David registered the address and showed her how to log on. "I could use a router so you can be online and still receive phone calls."

"I like that idea."

"I'll pick one up for you and install it on Saturday."

"That would be great. Can I use the word processor without using the phone line?"

"Your phone will be busy only when you're online"

This was all very confusing, but she couldn't change her mind now. She spent a lot of money and she was determined.

David was easy to be with. He didn't talk much, but he was very bright. She liked his company. He was like a pair of comfortable shoes. However, he never tried to kiss her again. She didn't have any romantic feelings for David, but she wondered if there was something wrong with him.

One day, she and Sandra went shopping and stopped for lunch.

"How are things going with David?" Sandra stripped the paper off a straw.

"He's very nice and has helped me a lot with my computer. I can't believe how dumb I was."

"David is the best friend anyone could have."

"Is there something wrong with him?"

"What do you mean?"

"He kissed me the night we had a date, but hasn't since then." Judy thought she sounded pretty vain.

"He's trying to get back with his wife. They have a legal separation but they've talked about reconciliation."

That explained it all.

Before David had a chance to install the router, she got a call when she was in bed.

"Who have you been talking to all evening?" It was Joe.

Judy told him about getting a computer and going online.

"So you decided to join the modern world." There was teasing in his voice.

"Well, they had computers and the internet at school, but I never did much with it."

"You know there's router you can put on your phone line so you use the phone even when you're online?"

"I know. David hasn't had a chance to do that yet."

"David? Who's David?"

Judy's heart stopped for a moment. She hadn't given David a thought other than as a good friend. "He's a friend who's been helping me with all this computer stuff."

Joe's voice got cool and remote. "Well, I hope David can help you then."

After a frosty goodbye, they hung up.

Tears came to Judy's eyes and overflowed. Joe didn't own her and, besides, she had told him the truth about David. She lay awake most of the night, weighing Joe's words, remembering his touch and all the fun they had. Could he really be jealous? That was ridiculous! The next time he called, she would tell him she was coming out for a visit.

But Joe didn't call. Judy told herself he had to be out of town again or busy with some deal he'd been working on. Or maybe he found another woman? That thought always made her stomach clench in fear...

She got a letter from Toots. None of the scenarios she thought of were mentioned by Toots. Joe had been out to see her often. He wasn't as busy as he had been. And when was Judy coming out for another visit?

Judy answered, saying that she didn't know when she would be out for the promised visit. She subtly told Toots about going online and how David, a friend, had been so much help. She stressed that David was just someone she knew. She asked for Toots's email address and sent hers. Judy hoped Toots would relay the message to Joe or maybe even let him read her letter.

Weeks passed. It was getting close to the anniversary of Steve's death. The apartment was in order and Judy felt restless. Her finances were in good shape. She thought of taking a cruise. No, that didn't have any appeal, especially by herself. Maybe a tour and a week at an Elderhostel? With either of those, she wouldn't feel like she was a fifth wheel or a man hungry widow.

She sent a letter, then decided to call Toots. "I answered your letter, but wanted to hear your voice, too," Judy explained.

"I'm so glad you called. I imagine you're rather blue with the anniversary of your husband's death coming up. I get that way, even now when it gets near Bart's, Big Joe's, death," Toots soothed.

"I'm so glad to have someone who understands." Maybe Steve's death was bothering her. Well, that was a good possibility, but it was also not hearing from Joe.

As if reading her mind, Toots said, "Joe is in the jungle again. We had a big snow the day after he left."

They talked for a few more minutes. "I'll see about coming out when spring comes," Judy said. She didn't want to be driving on those narrow roads in the snow.

"I'll look forward to that."

XXII

Judy borrowed an Elderhostel catalogue from a friend and paged through. There were several near where Joe and Toots lived. Very tempting. There were some close by. There was one in Lake Geneva on historic clothing. Another was in Door County and basket weaving. Finally, she decided on one in Chicago about architecture less than a hundred miles from home. It would give her a chance to meet others without having to travel far. The only problem was that it was short notice and there might not be any openings.

She dialed the number before she could change her mind. There were still a couple of slots available. After answering several questions, Judy gave the secretary her credit card number and received a confirmation number. She would receive the information in the mail.

When she told Sandra, she was surprised at Sandra's reaction.

"I'd love to go on one of those," Sandra said wistfully. "I've heard they are so much fun and the learning is great. Most of the people are from distant parts of the world."

"We could do that someday, just the two of us." Judy never thought Sandra would be interested.

"Brad wouldn't go for it," Sandra said.

"I wasn't going to invite him." Judy laughed, but she was serious. Brad would really be a bummer to have along-a real wet blanket.

"We'll see," Sandra said in the vague way someone tells you that the situation is hopeless.

Judy had a wonderful time at the Elderhostel. She was amazed at the variety of people. There were college professors and retired janitors along with CEOs from big companies. There were singles and couples and married people. Judy hated to see the week come to an end. Many of the people knew each other from previous seasons.

Back home, she felt invigorated. However, she was disappointed not to have a message from Joe or even Toots. She'd have to get over Joe and get on with her life.

She and Sandra had lunch a couple of days after Judy's return.

"I had a blast. Just the neatest people," Judy said when she told Sandra about all the activities.

"That does sound like fun." Sandra had a faraway look in her eyes.

"There were several family groups. They came together like a family reunion."

"I have an idea. Kathy, you and I will go to one."

"That is a good idea. We'll have to see about the arrangements." Judy had never thought of it.

"Have you heard from Joe Whatsitsname lately?" Sandra's question was so off the subject that Judy was caught off guard.

"No, I haven't and I haven't heard from his mother either."

"It's just as well. His mother seems like a flake and he is rather snooty."

"You sound more like Brad talking," She went on before Sandra could respond, "I think his mother is fun and he's not at all snooty."

"Well, don't get your undies in a bundle." Sandra leaned forward. "Hey, did you fall for the guy?"

Judy hesitated.

"You did, didn't you?"

Shades of adolescence leaped into Judy's mind. Sometimes she thought Sandra could read her mind. "I guess so."

Sandra got very close, and in a low voice, asked, "Did you go all the way with him? Or, at least wanted to?"

"Don't even go there." Judy cut her off. "And don't breathe a word to Brad or I'll have your hide."

"Okay," Sandra answered meekly

Judy knew that her sister would keep her promise. She was better at that than Judy was. Judy used to tell Steve everything. The only difference, Steve would never let on that he knew. Brad would blab it to the world.

The anniversary of Steve's death came. Andy and Grace called to reminisce about their father. Ellyn and her husband sent flowers with a little note. Kathy and Sandra both called to see how their sister was doing. There was no acknowledgment from Clark. Judy had a hollow feeling in her soul. So many memories. Her life had changed dramatically, but not at all. The biggest thing was that she was lonely.

Maybe it was time for another Elderhostel. She could become addicted to those.

One night just before Easter, she got a call after she was in bed. "Who can be calling at this hour?" she thought as she reached for the phone.

It was a collect call from a hospital in Colorado. All Judy could think of was something happened to Kathy or Mark."I'll take the call." She propped herself up on an elbow.

The woman introduced herself, but Judy didn't hear the name. All she could think of was her sister.

"I have someone who would like to speak with you. My grandmother, Toots."

"Toots?" It took Judy's mind a second to shift gears.

"Judy?" came the frail voice.

"Toots, is that you? What's going on?"

"I had a fall. Joe is out of town. I can go home, but I can't be alone. My granddaughter is here with me at the hospital, but she can't get time off. You're the only person I could think of to call."

"Of course, but what do you want me to do?" Judy's mind wasn't functioning yet.

"They will release me, if you could stay with me until I get back to normal."

There was no hesitation with Judy. "I'll make arrangements and let you know when I'll be there."

"Oh, I knew I could count on you."

Judy got the number where she could call when all her plans were set. That's probably why she hadn't heard from Toots for a while. She dreaded seeing Joe again, but maybe she would be gone before he showed up.

She got out of bed and went to her computer. Within an hour, she had made all the arrangements for her flight and paid for her ticket. This was great. No hassles with an agent and she felt proud of the price she got. She would be flying out later the next day.

With renewed energy, she stayed up for several hours, getting everything packed and making one of her famous lists. Judy fell right to sleep and got up early the next morning without a trace of fatigue.

She called Sandra to tell her about where she was going and the circumstances. She expected Sandra to get all upset with her leaving.

But Sandra surprised her. "Of course you have to go. They were so gracious when you were moving." She paused for a breath. "I suppose Joe will be there."

"I don't know. She said he was out of town. My real concern is for Toots. She is such a dear."

"Well, just keep me posted. I'll go over and water your plants."

"Sandra, I don't have any plants."

"Good."

Next, Judy called her children and was relieved to get their answering machines. She left messages as to where she was going and why. She added that she would keep them informed. She also left a message on Kathy's phone.

A couple of hours before her plane was to leave, the airport shuttle picked her up. She packed light. Staying at the ranch would mean mostly jeans, tees, and sweatshirts. If she needed anything else, she could either send for it or go and buy whatever she needed. Her main focus was Toots.

XXIII

Once in Colorado, Judy took a taxi to the hospital Toots was in.

From her hospital bed, Toots held out her arms to Judy. "Oh, my dear, it is so good to see you." Judy bent over and received the hug like a benediction. "How are you doing?" Judy asked as she straightened up.

"Much better, now that you're here." Toots smiled weakly.

Judy pulled up a chair and sat close to the bed. She took Toots's hand in hers.

"I fell, but was able to crawl over to the phone to get help. I fractured my arm." She held up an arm encased in a cast. "I also hit my head and needed stitches. She brushed her hair from her forehead. There were stitches along a three-inch gash.

"How long have you been here?"

"Five days. They ran some other tests while I was here. They talked about rehab but I just want to go back to my home."

There had to be more to it than that, Judy thought. No one stayed in the hospital with those kinds of injuries for more than overnight. "Where's your granddaughter? I'd like to meet her."

"She had to leave. She could only get a few days off."

"Where's Joe?" Judy tried to sound nonchalant.

"He's still in that remote place. Of course this happened after he left."

"I understand. Well, how soon before they can spring you?" Judy wanted to sound as light as possible.

"You go talk to the nurse. She can help you."

Judy went down to the nurses' station. She waited at the counter while a woman typed something into a computer. She finally looked up. "Yes, may I help you?"

Judy introduced herself. Then asked, "Why was she kept here for five days with just a broken arm and head stitches?"

"She also had a minor stroke. Her doctor wanted her to go to rehab for a week or two, but she wouldn't hear of it."

Judy understood. "Can she go home?"

The woman looked over some papers on a clipboard. "Are you Judy Evans?"

"Yes, I am."

"We've tried to reach her son but he's out of the country. According to this, she can go home any time after you arrived." She set down the clipboard and started to type on the computer keyboard. "Everything is in order. I'll get someone to explain her meds."

"How can I get her home? I didn't rent a car yet."

"We have a medical van to take her home, if you wish."

Judy knew she could use Toots's car when she got to the ranch. "Do you have any taxi service to take me out to the ranch?"

The woman glanced at her watch. "Well, our cabs aren't real reliable around here, plus they cost a fortune. I'm getting off in an hour. I'll wait around and give you a lift. I live not too far from where you're going. Sort of neighbors."

"That would be great, but I don't want to put you out."

"Oh, don't worry about that. I'll get things rolling right away."

Judy went in to Toots and waited. There was a flurry of activity. A nurse came in to help Toots get dressed. An aide put her plants and flowers on a cart. Another nurse came in to give Judy instructions on the medications. Still another came in to tell Judy about the routine to follow with rehab.

By the time Toots was all packed up and heading for the van, Judy's head was spinning. How was she going to do all this? What a responsibility. She could only do her best.

On the way to the ranch, the nurse chatted, but Judy didn't listen. Her mind was elsewhere.

"Someone did tell you that once a week, the van will come and pick up your mother and take her for rehab? That will give you time to yourself," the nurse said. Judy was about to correct her by saying Toots was not her mother but it wasn't worth the effort.

"Do you have any food in the house?"

"I don't know," Judy hadn't thought about that.

"There's a little store just before we turn off the main road. You can get some milk, eggs and bread to tie you over."

Judy just grabbed the few things at the store and hurried out. Then they drove into the long drive. The van was waiting for them.

"I'll help you with getting Toots settled," The nurse shut off the car engine and hopped out,

"I'm grateful for all the help, but I don't want to keep you from your own family."

"They're used to my erratic routine."

Soon, Toots was snug in her own bed. Judy only had the

plants and flowers to put around. "I can't thank you enough," Judy said to the nurse.

"Oh, pooh, if you need anything, just give me a call." She wrote her phone number on a piece of paper by the phone. "It's always good to have backup."

When the nurse left, Judy went in to check on Toots. She looked like she was sleeping, so Judy tiptoed out and went about checking over the house.

The house was as silent as a tomb. What an awful thought, Judy thought. The place needed dusting. Toots was gone for two weeks and if Joe had been around, he didn't do anything. Doesn't Toots have a cleaning lady?

After checking on Toots again, Judy went after the mail. The box was at the end of the driveway. It was quite a hike, but it felt good to get out and move around. The mailbox was stuffed. Toots's granddaughter hadn't thought to have the mail stopped. She took off her jacket and used it to carry the mail to the house. Once again she checked on Toots who was still sleeping.

Judy spread the mail out on the table and sorted through it. A lot of junk, but she wouldn't throw it away. She remembered Toots liked to check it out, just in case. There were bills and many cards.

Judy took the time to call Sandra. "I'm here safe and sound," she said.

"Are you at the hospital?" Sandra asked.

"No, I'm at Toots's. She's sleeping. I'll give you the number." She gave the number and had Sandra repeat it back. "Right. Would you give the kids each a call? I don't want to run up the phone bill here."

"No problem."

"Thanks. I'm going to leave a message on Kathy's phone.

She'll call me when she gets off work."

With that taken care of, Judy took a tour of the living room and dining room, looking into the bookcases and china cabinet. There was a small dinner bell on a shelf in the curio cabinet. Judy took it out and went in to check on Toots. This time, Toots had her eyes open.

"Did you have a nice snooze?" Judy went over by the bed.

"Getting dressed and riding out here was more tiring than I could ever imagine." Toots stifled a yawn. "But being in my own bed is heavenly."

"I found this bell in the other room. If you need me, just give it a shake. I don't want you to worry about my not hearing you." Judy set the bell on the bedside table.

Toots gave the bell a trial run.

"I went down and got your mail. The box was jammed full. I thought someone might have put a hold on delivery."

"My granddaughter wouldn't think of that, and Joe may not even know I've been in the hospital. I tried a couple of times to reach him, but he was out in the field. Whatever that means. They were supposed to give him a message. His cell phone doesn't always work"

"Well, that explains a lot. I'll bring in some mail, a little at a time. Whenever you're up to it, you can look at a few pieces. In the meantime, I'll give the place a little clean up."

"No need to do that. I have a young woman come and clean for me every week. I was able to get a hold of her so she wouldn't worry about me. I told her I'd call her as soon as I got back home. I could probably have done the work myself, before this, but she needs the money."

Judy couldn't argue with that. "Is there anything you would like me to do for you?" She felt rather useless.

"You could call Maria and set a time for her to come, but nothing else right now. I think I'll go to sleep for a while." Toots closed her eyes.

Judy went to the kitchen phone. There was a list of names and numbers taped to the wall. Maria's name was halfway down. Judy punched in the number and listened to the ringing on the other end. When someone picked up, Judy asked to speak to Maria.

"This is Maria." The voice sounded like that of a ten-year-old.

"I'm calling for Toots. She's home now and would like you to come over and clean her house."

"Is she all right now?"

"She's still weak, but she's coming along."

"I can come tomorrow, about eight?"

"Wonderful. I'll see you then." Judy wrote down the time so she wouldn't forget.

She sorted the mail. She was getting hungry. It dawned on her that there was probably little or no food in the house. She had put the groceries on the counter and forgot about them. When she put the milk and eggs into the refrigerator, she found only a few condiments, a moldy loaf of bread and some very outdated eggs. The cupboards were a bit better. There was cereal, canned soup, tuna and crackers. In behind of the other cans and packages, Judy found a new jar of peanut butter. There was also a carton of soy milk. This was enough to get them through until she could do some shopping. In the freezer, she found a loaf of bread, some ice cream, and frozen fruit and vegetables.

When Toots rang the bell, Judy was just finishing heating up some soup. She fixed them both trays. After Toots used the bathroom, they ate in Toots's room. Toots sat at an old fashioned vanity table, while Judy sat on the floor.

"Tomorrow, I'd like to have breakfast in the kitchen. I need to get my strength back. I can't do that just lying around."

Judy noticed how much stronger Toots sounded just since this morning. Or maybe it was just her imagination.

"Would you like me to find you a book or would you like to go through some of your mail?" Judy stacked the dishes and trays together.

"Some of the mail. I want to go to bed. I have some extra pillows in my closet. I need to sit up."

Judy found several pillows and wedged them behind Toots.

"Much better." Toots smiled and adjusted her glasses.

"I'll be right back." Judy put the dishes in the kitchen and brought a stack of letters and what appeared to be cards to Toots. "I'll be in the kitchen cleaning up."

"Did you get a hold of Maria?"

"I did and she's coming over about eight in the morning."

"Judy, when you go into the kitchen, will you try and call Joe? I have his cell phone number on the same list with Maria's. I want him to know I'm home and you're here taking care of me. I'm afraid he'll be worried."

Judy groaned to herself. Of course he'd be worried. "Yes, I'll try and reach him." One of the last things Judy wanted to do was to talk to Joe. She hadn't heard from him in so long. Suddenly, she felt awkward. But she did owe it to Toots to see if she could reach him.

In the kitchen, Judy punched in the number for Joe. It took some time before the phone started to ring. The phone rang many times. Judy was about to hang up when a woman's soft voice came on the line. "Hello?"

"Oh, I'm sorry, I must have the wrong number." She was about to disconnect when the woman asked who she was calling.

"Joe."

"You have the right number. Let me see if he's out of the shower yet" The woman must have taken the receiver away from her mouth, but Judy could hear her call to Joe.

"Hello?"

"Joe? This is Judy Evans. I'm at your mother's. She's recovering from a fall. She asked me to call you to tell you she's okay." Judy talked fast so Joe wouldn't hang up on her.

"Judy?" He paused, "Slow down. I had a message from the hospital, but when I called, they had no one registered by that name. Tell me what happened."

"Toots said she had the hospital try and reach you." Judy explained about the fall and why Toots had called her.

"I've been out in the field and just got back to civilization." He paused, "Let me call you on a land line. The connection is bad on this end. Are you at my mother's now?"

"Yes. I'll wait by the phone."

A few minutes later, the phone rang and it was Joe. "Are you sure she's recovering?"

"Yes, I'm sure. The only reason she went to bed is that the trip home exhausted her. She called me so she could come home. The only other choice she had was to go into a rehab facility."

"She must have hated that thought."

"You're right about that."

"I'll see what kind of arrangements I can make to get back."

"There's no hurry. I have nothing pressing."

"I'll hurry anyway."

"Just let me know," Judy said. She wondered, "Who was the woman? Would she be coming, too?" Judy wanted to ask but was afraid of the answer. Of course Joe had moved on. She was just a passing flirtation.

When they were done talking, Judy went in to tell Toots she'd finally gotten a hold of Joe.

"Oh, I'm so glad. Did he say how long it would take him to get home?"

"No, and I told him I had nothing to hurry home for." She patted Toots's hand. "Do you need anything before I go to bed?"

"Not a thing, but if I do, there's that little bell. You can use the same room you slept in the other time you were here." Toots eyes regained their twinkle.

"You bet." Judy bent over and gave Toots a kiss on the forehead.

XXIV

Judy got ready for bed. It was only eight o'clock. This time difference was playing tricks on her inner clock. She padded out to the living room and searched the bookcase. There were a couple of books that looked interesting, so she brought them to her bed. She propped the pillows behind her and read. But her mind kept thinking about Joe's call and wondering who the woman was.

Just before she switched out her light, she checked on Toots. She was sleeping and soft sounds were coming from her bed. Not snores, but gurgles. Judy smiled. She remembered those sounds from when Toots stayed at her place. It was reassuring.

Judy was overtired by now. So much for one day. In the darkness, again, she wondered who the woman was who answered Joe's phone. She didn't have a foreign accent. And Joe was taking a shower. She was jealous. She must be the reason why Joe hadn't called her.

Then she remembered the last time they talked. She had told him David was working on her computer. Joe asked who he was. Now the shoe was on the other foot. David was a friend-just a very dear friend.

A knot formed in her stomach. Was this what had happened? Tears stung her eyes. She finally went into a fretful sleep, only to be awakened by the phone ringing. She jumped out of bed and rushed to the kitchen. Thank goodness she turned off the ringer on Toots's bedside phone. The moonlight showed her the way without her tripping over anything.

"Hello?"

"Did I wake you?" It was Joe. "I'm sorry, but I didn't realize you'd go to bed so early. I think we're in the same time zone."

"That's okay. I was having trouble sleeping."

"I have a flight out of here in a couple of hours. I'll call you when I get stateside."

"Fine. Is it okay if I tell Toots you're on your way?"

"Sure, but tell her that I don't know when I'll be home. It could be another day or two." Where was he?

Judy checked on Toots on her way to bed. Still sound asleep. The soft gurgles were audible.

There was no getting to sleep. Judy remembered the cleaning lady would be there at eight. She wanted to have Toots up and both of them through with breakfast before Maria got there.

Along about six, Judy heard the tinkle of the bell. She went in to see how Toots was.

"Did you sleep well?" Judy opened the blinds.

"Like a baby. What about you?"

"Not very well, but I'll get along."

"Sorry to hear that. Maybe you'll get a chance to rest later today."

Judy helped her on with a robe and slippers. "Do you feel like some breakfast or a shower?"

"Both!" Toots voice wasn't as frail as it had been the day before.

"What do you want first? The choice is yours."

"I guess food first." She took Judy's arm and they walked to the kitchen.

While Judy made them scrambled eggs and toast, she told Toots about Joe's call. "You won't be needing so much help when he gets home. I'll go down to my sister's for a few days, then home."

"I was hoping you'd stay on. Joe and I love your company. It would give him some time to show you more of the country. He's told me he wants to show you the ski country and all the canyons, like Zion and the north rim of the Grand Canyon since you were here the first time."

"We'll see," Judy said. He won't want me around to cramp his style with a new girlfriend.

There was nothing wrong with Toots's appetite. She ate more than Judy.

"Would you like me to make more coffee?" Judy asked as she drained the pot.

"No, but maybe later, we can have some tea when Maria gets here. I like to share a break with her... I think I still have some sweet rolls in the freezer." She winked.

"Come on and let's get you into the shower." Judy held out her hand to Toots.

They tied a plastic bag with a piece of string around the cast. Then Judy helped her into the shower. "I'll stay right here in case you need me."

"I'd like that. I'm beginning to sound like an old woman."

The spray of the shower was mixed with the humming of some song. The shower went off and the curtain was drawn back.

"I think I'd better dry off on the rug. I hate getting water all over things, but I'm afraid I might slip."

"No problem." Judy held firmly to Toots's arms as she stepped over the edge of the tub. Then she handed her a towel.

"Could you get my back? I hope I don't embarrass you. After being in the hospital, I'm not very modest." Toots laughed.

"No, I have sisters and none of us thought much about any stage of undress."

When she finished drying Toots's back, she handed her the towel. Toots finished the job. Judy hung up the wet towel, then helped Toots with her robe. "I'll leave you alone so you can brush your teeth and what not. I'll go and make up your bed."

Toots didn't get dressed right away. "I think I'll lay down for a short time. That was more exhausting than I thought." Judy put a light blanket over her and went out to clean up the kitchen.

She started to run the water when there was a knock on the back door. She dried her hands and went to see who was there. A young pregnant woman with blonde hair was standing there. "Yes?" Judy said cautiously.

"I'm Maria," the young woman replied.

"Oh, yes, come in." She stepped aside and let Maria pass into the kitchen. "I didn't know who to expect."

"How's Toots?" Maria asked in hushed tones.

"She's been up, ate breakfast and had a shower, but now she's lying down for a short nap. She actually doing quite well."

"I'm so glad to hear that. Where would you like me to start?"

Judy shrugged. "I don't know. Where do you usually start?"

"In her room."

"Okay. Why don't you start in the living room?"

"Will the vacuum disturb her?"

"I hadn't thought of that. Start with the bathroom."

Maria dug under the sink for supplies and left the room. Judy did the dishes.

When Toots got up, the three of them had tea and sweet rolls. Judy found out that Maria lived on a neighboring ranch where her husband worked. This would be their first baby. The extra money Maria made helped ends meet.

"I hope I can work after the baby comes," she said.

"You just bring the little one along. I'd love to see him."

"Her. I'm going to have a girl."

Toots laughed. "You modern young people. Not knowing the sex was always the fun part. We'd pick out both boys and girls names."

"That's what my mom says too."

"Where are you from?" Judy asked.

"Montana. I met my husband when we were in college."

They visited for a while longer and then Maria said she had to finish up.

Just before Maria left, Toots handed her an envelope. "There's a little extra for the baby." She patted Maria's arm.

"Thank you." She bent down and kissed Toots cheek.

As Maria's pickup drove away Toots said," I could do all the cleaning myself except for right now." She held up her arm in the cast. "But the couple needs the money and I've got more than suits my needs."

"I was going to ask her how much college she got in, but didn't get the chance."

"I think she has a year or so to go."

"It's a shame she can't finish. It would help her make more money."

"And I'd lose the best cleaning lady I've ever had."

"And how many have you had?"

"Just Maria." Toots grinned and winked.

Judy shook her head.

When Toots was resting again, there was a phone call from a woman, giving her the information as to when Joe would be there. It sounded like the same woman Judy had talked to the previous day.

Would this woman be with Joe? Would Judy be like a hired nurse? Thank goodness she already told Toots about her plans to go to Kathy's when Joe got home. A lump formed in her throat and she blinked away the tears.

Joe would be coming in the next day or two, depending on the flight schedules. Toots was gaining strength hourly. Judy wouldn't feel guilty about leaving. She did the wash and hung it out in the beautiful sunlight. Toots came out and sat under a tree.

"This is wonderful. I don't know if it's more wonderful than usual, but it feels that way." Toots closed her eyes and leaned back. "We have to take these early spring days as something special, a bonus."

Judy pulled another chair close to Toots and sat down. They were both enjoying the afternoon breeze when a pickup truck drove in. Judy opened one eye and recognized the truck. Her heart did a little leap. Joe was here.

Toots sat straight up. "I didn't think you were going to be here for at least another day!" She squealed like a teenager.

Joe came running up and grabbed his mother out of her chair and only started to whirl her around. "Oh, I'm sorry, Toots, did I hurt you?"

"No, only my arm is broke." She was laughing. "I didn't

think you'd be here so soon."

"I decided to charter a plane. We flew into where my truck was parked."

Judy tried to be inconspicuous. She had been dreading this moment, but she didn't know why.

Joe turned to her. "Thanks so much for helping out." There was a smile on his lips but there was no warmth in his eyes. He offered her his hand. She hesitated before she shook it.

What had she done to cause him to act this way? She wanted to run away and hide. "I'm happy to do it. Turnabout's fair play."

Joe put his arm around his mother's shoulders. "Let's go into the house."

Once inside, Toots sat down on a chair. "Sit down and tell me what you've been up to. Judy and I have been wondering." She patted the seat of the chair next to her. "Judy, please put on a kettle to make tea."

"Glad to." Judy was happy to have something to do.

Joe sat down next to Toots.

Judy filled the tea kettle and set it on the stove. Then she fussed around, getting ready to brew the tea.

"Come on, Judy, sit down," Toots said. "Now, Joe, where have you been?"

"I was in Brazil again, fixing some equipment," he said.

"Where did you stay? What was the weather like? Do you have any friends there? How did they finally reach you?" Toots sat forward and rested her encased arm on the table.

Joe answered all her questions. "I stayed with some friends. My cell phone didn't work until I got there. I had all these messages, but I hadn't had a chance to listen to all of them before Judy called."

Judy didn't look at him, but at a speck of something on the tablecloth.

They had tea and some cookies from a tin in the cupboard.

Toots said, "I think I'll go lie down for a while." She got up and left the room.

Judy started to clear the table.

"How does David like your being here?"

"David is a friend. Besides, I don't have anything to do with married men. He and his wife have a legal separation." Judy rinsed out the cups. Of course, the only way Joe would know about David being married was if Toots had told him.

Joe didn't say anything. He got up and put his arms around her from behind. Then he nuzzled her ear.

She shrugged him off. "I thought you'd bring your girlfriend with you."

"My what?"

"The woman who answered your phone when I called." Judy was humiliated. She sounded like a harpy.

"She's the wife of my friend where I stayed." He looked into her eyes. "This whole thing is just innocent misunderstandings." He pulled her into an embrace.

"I don't know what to think," Judy said as she slipped out of his arms.

"I was wrong not to ask more about David. I was just so shocked." Joe kept trying to explain himself.

There was the tinkle of a bell. "That's Toots. She needs something," Judy said. Joe frowned. "It was a way for her to get my attention."

"I'll go see what she wants," Joe said and he left the room.

As soon as she had the kitchen tidied up, she called Kathy.

"Mark and I'll drive up tomorrow and get you. I've always

wanted to see the ranch. Joe has told us about it."

Judy knew there would be no getting out of this. She'd just have to avoid Joe for the next twenty-four hours.

She checked in to see Toots sleeping. Then she went into her room and quietly locked the door. She knew if Joe came to her, she would lose all her resolve. Judy took out her suitcase and started to pack. Some things would have to be put in last minute. Then she stretched out on the bed and dozed off.

She awoke to the tinkling of the bell. She shot out of bed and shook her head to clear the cobwebs. She ran a hand through her hair and straightened her clothes before dashing out the door. It took her a moment to remember the door was locked.

When she got into Toots's room, she was sitting up, smiling. "I was just seeing if this worked. I really won't need it anymore. Unless I want to use it to summon Joe." There was a devilment in her eyes.

"What's all the commotion?" Joe came into the room. It was plain that he also had been sleeping.

Toots shook the bell to demonstrate. "I was just seeing if you would come, even though I don't need it anymore."

"Mom! You're terrible. I thought the house was on fire or something." Joe flopped down on the edge of the bed.

"I'll leave you two alone." Judy went toward the door. "Oh, I talked to Kathy. She and Mark are driving up tomorrow to get me. They want to see you." She looked at Toots, "And also the ranch."

"What about me?" Joe pretended to pout.

"And you, too." Judy said and left. Her feelings were hurt. He had accused her of being with David. Well, maybe not accused. Maybe it was because he was with another woman. What really hurt was realizing she was in love with Joe.

To take her mind off Joe, Judy wrote out in the minutest detail the routine to take care of Toots, like the schedule of meds and therapy.

After dinner, Joe said, "Let's take a walk. The night sky from up on that rise is spectacular."

Judy hesitated.

"Go on you two. I am perfectly capable of taking care of myself for an hour or two," Toots said. Then she looked down at her cast. "Well, I won't do anything foolish. I'll just go watch TV."

Joe laughed. "We won't be gone long. That little bell can't be heard outside. Come on, Judy. Better grab a jacket. It gets chilly up there."

"If you're sure you'll be okay?" Judy asked Toots.

"Just go and don't make me feel more like a little old lady than I already do."

"We'll be back soon." Joe planted a kiss on his mother's head. Joe took Judy's hand as they walked across the lighted yard into the darkness. "Your eyes will get accustomed to the darkness quickly."

XXV

Joe's hand was warm and reassuring. It felt natural for him to drop her hand and put his arm around her shoulders. She moved closer to him.

"That's better," he whispered.

There was a rustling in the grass near them. Judy jumped.

"That's just the bear."

Judy laughed remembering what Toots said about Joe and his bear story. She relaxed completely.

Joe stopped and pulled her close to him. He drew her into a long smoldering kiss. "I've wanted to do that all night."

"Me, too," she admitted. She crushed her mouth to his. Their tongues touched and took turns exploring. Judy's knees went weak, but Joe's arms held her up.

"You have no idea how wretched I've felt, thinking you found someone else," Joe said as they broke for air.

"I tried to tell you." She lay her head on his chest, listening to the steady beat of his heart.

"I know and I was a fool. I acted like a kid." He paused. "I am so in love with you. All the time I was in the jungle, I wanted to go and confront you. Actually, more like try and win you back."

"Oh, Joe, I missed you so. I was so hurt when you didn't call." She raised her head to look at his face. She could feel his hardness and she ground her stomach into it.

He groaned and cupped and massaged her breast. "Let's start over except for the part where I love you."

"Deal."

They walked on a bit further, stop and kiss and let their hands become familiar with each other's body. Judy's arousal was almost unbearable.

At the top of a knoll, Joe halted. "This is what I want you to see." He made a grand sweeping motion with his arm. "As a kid, I felt I could see China from here."

The moon was but a sliver. The stars were close enough to reach out and touch. "This is breathtaking."

"Just like you." He kissed the top of her head.

For a long time, they stood, side by side, just watching an occasional shooting star. Once in a while, a plane would fly over. Judy shivered.

"Getting cold?" Joe asked as he drew her closer to him.

"A little," she said. The night air was cutting through her jacket.

"Then let's go back."

The kitchen light was on, but the house was silent. There was a note on the table from Toots, saying she decided to go to bed.

"Maybe that's a good idea for us, too," Joe whispered in Judy's ear.

The soft breath on her ear only heightened her desire. "Let's make sure Toots is okay first."

They tiptoed down the hallway and peeked in the room.

They couldn't see Toots in the darkness, but they heard her rhythmic familiar gurgles.

Hand in hand, they went into Joe's room. The only light was the glow of the LED readout on his clock. They walked slowly to the bed and sat down. Took off his boots and then her shoes.

They lay wrapped in each other's arms enjoying, the kisses. Then they undressed each other, taking time to caress skin.

"I can't take this any longer. I need you," she groaned. Joe groaned, too. Then she heard the ripping of plastic.

"Condom. Safe sex."

For a moment, the spell was broken until Joe sucked on her breast and ran his fingers between her legs. She was beyond stopping. She opened her legs and wrapped them around his waist as she arched her back. There was blessed relief and then, she needed him again.

Judy was tucked under Joe's arm as they lay, spent and refreshed at the same time. She never wanted this to end.

"You're a little vixen," Joe said.

"You're not bad yourself." She reached up and kissed his chin.

"I love you and don't ever want us apart again. No more misunderstandings." Joe talked into her hair.

"That sounds wonderful to me, but I should go back to my room." She made an attempt to rise.

"Just spend the rest of the night with me."

"But what will Toots think?" The very thought embarrassed her.

"If I didn't know better, I'd think my mother engineered the whole thing just to get us together."

"What?" Judy propped herself onto an elbow.

"She's been trying to figure out a way to bring us together

ever since the thing with David."

"You gotta be kidding?" Judy couldn't believe her ears.

"Oh, yeah. She thinks we belong together." He pulled Judy on top of him.

"But, still." Judy couldn't finish her sentence as Joe's mouth closed over hers.

They awoke to the sounds of banging pots and pans coming from the kitchen. Joe pulled on his jeans and handed Judy one of his robes. "We better face the music."

"I'll just go to my room and get dressed," Judy said as they walked down the hall.

"No way. We're going to face Toots and get this whole thing out in the open." Joe tugged her along into the kitchen.

"Good morning, you two. The little bell didn't get your attention so I had to bring out the big guns." Toots was grinning from ear to ear.

"I'm sorry. I didn't hear the bell." Judy gasped. What if Toots had needed them during the night? Guilt washed over her.

"I was just teasing," Toots said. "I'm getting pretty good at making coffee with one arm..."

Joe sat down and pulled Judy onto his lap. "Mom, Judy and I are in love."

"Finally you two admit what's been evident from the first time you came here, Judy."

"We haven't talked about her staying on," Joe said. He nibbled on Judy's ear.

She slid off his lap. "Here, I'll make the rest of breakfast."

"All I want is a piece of toast for now," Toots said pushing down a piece of bread in the toaster.

"I'll have a bowl of cereal," Joe said.

"If that's all you want, I'm going to take a shower and get

dressed." Judy headed toward the hall.

Joe jumped up and caught her. "You can't go unless you give me a kiss."

She gave him a peck on the check

"Not like that." He drew her close and kissed her, his tongue probing her mouth. His hand slid down her back, resting just below her waist. "Now that's more like it." He let her go.

Judy didn't trust her self-control, even with Toots in the room. Even the shower couldn't erase Joe's touch. Not that she wanted it to.

Dressed, she went into the kitchen and poured herself a cup of coffee.

"What time did your sister say she was picking you up?" Joe put a spoonful of some wet, soggy-looking cereal into his mouth.

"Later this afternoon. She and Mark were going to leave about noon."

"Have them stay for dinner," Toots said. "I'll get something out of the freezer and Joe can barbecue it. Are there salad fixings?"

"I bought some and we haven't had a salad since." Judy got up to top off her coffee.

"Then, it's all set." Toots put her dishes in the dishwasher and left the room. "Remember I have a therapy session this morning. The van will be here in an hour. I better get going."

"I guess she told us," Joe laughed.

"I'll help you in the shower," Judy said as she followed Toots.

"I have a doctor's appointment before rehab," Toots said.

"That's right. You probably will get the cast off. Then you can do all this by yourself." Judy pointed at the shower.

"No offense, but it'll be grand not to have to depend on you.'

"No offense taken." Judy smiled. "I'm just glad I was available to help out."

"That's what friends are for. I'm getting pretty good at this one-handed thing."

Judy stripped Toots's bed and washed the sheets. She'd have the bed all made before Toots got back. She'd do the same to her bed.

After Toots left, Joe led Judy into his room for a late morning romp. "See. I told you Toots would be fine with our sleeping arrangements last night."

"I guess I shouldn't have doubted you," she said as she snuggled closer. "I'd have a fit if my kids tried this under my roof."

"Sort of old-fashioned, aren't you?" he teased.

Judy stretched and yawned. "I'm not going to answer that question. I better get up and finish the laundry and my packing."

When Toots got home, she was tired, but with a big smile. "Look! The cast is gone."

"That's great, Mom."

"It looks pretty bad. Dr. said the dry skin and bruising will be gone in a few more days. I have to go to physical therapy a few times a week for a month. It'll help to strengthen the muscles." She yawned. "I think I'll take a bit of a nap before your sister gets here."

"We could take a nap, too," Joe said only loud enough for Judy to hear.

"We've got dinner to make, remember?"

"Rats!"

"What was that, Joey?" Toots asked from down the hall.

"Nothing, Mom."

Joe stood behind Judy while she tried making the salad. Finally, she said, "If you don't keep your hands off me while I do this, I'm going to have to wake up Toots to chaperone."

"Okay. I'll go check over the grill so it'll be ready when Mark and Kathy get here."

Judy hummed to herself as she cut up tomatoes, lettuce and onions and put them in the bowl. She was happy she and Joe were on the right track. And to think Toots was thrilled made everything better. She was pretty sure Kathy and Mark would be happy for her. The rest of the family, she wasn't so sure of. She covered the bowl and put it in the fridge. She looked around for some potatoes for cooking on the grill, but couldn't find any. She mixed up some biscuits. She just popped them in the oven when Joe came in from outside and his mother from her room.

"I couldn't find potatoes, so I made the biscuits. I hope you don't mind." Judy dried her hands. All three sat down at the table.

"Anything you do is wonderful, right, Joe?" Toots said.

They heard a rumble of a vehicle driving up. "Must be my sister and Mark," Judy looked out to see the SUV.

"Right on time," Joe said as he got up. Judy and Toots followed

The passenger door opened and Kathy hopped out and went to Judy with her arms outstretched. Judy met her halfway. The sisters hugged. "It's so good to see you." Kathy almost strangled her with her hug.

"Likewise."

"It's my turn." Mark said as he gave Judy a hug.

Judy took a step backwards and bumped into Joe. She hadn't

heard him come up to them.

"Good to see you, Joe." Mark and Joe shook hands.

"You too. I've been out of the country. Judy has been a lifesaver."

"Come on into the house. You have to stay for dinner," Toots gave Kathy and Mark hugs.

"Mark, we'll go get the fire going. Got a couple of big steaks ready for dinner," Joe said. He and Mark walked across the yard to a garage.

"I don't know what I would have done without Judy's help." Toots went on to describe all that Judy did.

Judy felt uncomfortable. She wasn't used to someone singing her praises.

"Judy has always been the caretaker in the family. If she can't do it herself, she organizes the rest of us. I remember when Mother was sick. Judy was working fulltime with four youngsters. She would spend the nights with Mom and make sure there was a detailed schedule made out. And everyone," she looked at Judy, "did their job without a peep."

"All I did was to do the scheduling, but the rest carried it out." Judy was embarrassed with all the attention.

Kathy looked at her and then at Toots and shook her head.

"When do you want to go?" Judy asked.

"You are coming to our place at a good time. We have a dinner party at one of our friends who lives in our building. You're welcome to join us, Judy."

"Sounds good to me. Anyone I've met?"

"I don't know," Kathy said.

"I better get those biscuits out before they burn." Judy opened the oven door and took out golden biscuits.

"Something sure smells good," Mark said as he and Joe

came inside.

"Are you ready for the meat?" Toots asked.

"Yup. These gas grills don't waste any time." Joe took out a long fork and a plate with two large pieces of beef. As he walked by Judy, he planted a kiss on her neck. It sent shivers down her spine.

When the guys went out again, Kathy asked, "So what's going on?"

"I think they're in love," Toots whispered conspiratorially,

"Oh, yeah, and when did this happen? Joe told us you have another man on the line---"

"Wait a minute," Judy interrupted. "David was a guy who helped get my computer set up. Joe just got the wrong idea, but we're past that now."

"That's a relief." Toots said. "I don't want to have to break my arm again just to get you two to see how much you care for each other."

Judy set the table while they talked some more.

"I want Judy to spend at least a week or so with us. We've got a lot of catching up to do," Kathy folded some napkins.

"That would give Joe time to see her before she leaves."

"I would much rather have her move out here."

"That's an even better idea," Toots grinned.

"Come on, you two, I'm right here. Don't talk around me." But Judy giggled.

"Here we come, ready or not," Joe called just before he and Mark came into the house.

"We're ready," Toots said.

"I'm ready. How about you?" Joe whispered in Judy's ear. Her face felt on fire.

After dinner, Judy and Kathy cleaned up the kitchen. The phone rang and Joe answered it in the hallway. Judy went to get her things. She overheard Joe say very quietly, "But, I'm busy, honey. Of course I missed you, too. I just can't drop everything the moment you call...Of course I love you."

That was all Judy could take. She gathered up her suitcase and carried it to the SUV. "We better get going before it gets too late," she said to Kathy.

Kathy looked at her watch. "It is getting late. Come on, Mark, let's get going."

"Aren't you going to wait for Joe?" Toots asked as the three gave her hugs.

"He was on the phone, last I saw him," Judy said.

"That could be awhile. Some of those calls last for hours." She gave Judy one last hug. "Don't be a stranger."

All Judy could do was to nod. Tears slid down her cheeks. She hoped Toots would just think they were parting tears, not the tears from her broken heart. So, Joe did have someone else. She wanted to curl up in a ball and cry her eyes out. She turned off her phone, though there probably wasn't service out here anyway.

"You're awfully quiet back there," Kathy said from the front seat.

"I'm just tired," Judy lied. There was no point in saying anything, especially with Mark right there. "I'll be better after a good night's sleep."

Judy was glad she was in the back seat by herself. She wanted to burst into tears. She was going to miss Toots for sure, but the way Joe treated her was even more heartbreaking. He lied about another woman. The conversation she'd overheard was proof enough for her. Never again was she going to fall for a handsome face...and a terrific body. She put her head against the headrest and tried to block it all out.

XXVI

Kathy and Mark had fixed up their place so cute and so very comfortable.

"Remember, this your room," Kathy showed her a bedroom with a wall of windows overlooking the city with the mountains as a backdrop. Judy remembered it from before.

"This is wonderful! You've done a fantastic job with the place."

"Mark has been a great help. We did most of the shopping together. We have similar tastes."

"Did I hear my name?" Mark appeared, carrying Judy's suitcase.

"I was just saying how we chose most of our furniture together." Kathy gave him a big kiss.

"So you like it?" He asked Judy.

"I certainly do. Those mountains. They're the same ones you can see from Toots's place."

"I think so," Mark said.

Judy stretched. Her body ached from the way she sat in the SUV. "I think I'd just like to go to bed. I'm beat."

She may have been beat, but her mind raced. Why didn't she trust Joe? It was all of the heartache she'd witnessed over the years. Steve was faithful. It was the second marriages that seemed to go wrong. She'd seen co-workers, even her sister, especially her sister taken in by some smooth- talking guy. He would turn out to be abusive or unfaithful. She truly loved Joe. Still, she was afraid to take the risk, even if it meant a wonderful relationship. Judy finally fell asleep.

What sleep she did get was fitful with snatches of weird dreams. She dreamt she was making love with Joe who became David who became Steve who turned into Calvin. Then they all laughed at her. She woke with tears streaming down her face, tears of humiliation. Going back to sleep, she was shunned by everyone she loved, including Toots because she made love with Joe. The embarrassment was palpable. There would be no more sleep for now. It was still very early so she went in and took a shower.

In the morning light, Judy saw her room more clearly. The earth tones of the textiles blended with the hardwood floors. The furniture was a mix of modern and antique. The pictures were family groupings in ornate gold frames.

After getting dressed and making her bed, she went into the living room. She opened the drapes and stood admiring the view. She started a pot of coffee and went to gaze at the scenery which changed as the morning light reflected on the landscape.

Judy was sipping her first cup of coffee when Mark and Kathy stumbled out of their room. "Do I smell coffee?" Mark groaned.

"Our guardian angel must have paid a visit," Kathy rubbed her eyes.

"No, just your sister who doesn't want to miss a moment of the view," Judy said.

Mark went just outside the front door and retrieved the newspaper. "How'd ya sleep last night?" He asked.

"Like a baby," she said. A baby that woke up every few hours.

"Anything new going on in the world?" Kathy asked Mark who was already reading the paper.

"Just the usual murder and mayhem," he said.

"What are you planning to do today?" Kathy asked Judy. "Want to go to lunch? Everyone would love to see you."

"That would be fun. At the deli?"

"Great. But that leaves a lot more time."

"Maybe I'll stop by some of those shops I love. I don't know what to bring home as souvenirs. Didn't you say there was a party tonight?"

"Yes, at one of the neighbor's," Kathy poured them each a glass of orange juice.

"Then I could use a new outfit."

"Is that all you women ever think about?" Mark said from behind his paper.

"The same way you men think about sex." Kathy dropped a kiss on his head as she walked by him.

"It's good exercise and doesn't cost as much money." He put down the paper and winked at Judy.

"Four kids are pretty expensive," Judy laughed. "And what about the guys who use hookers?"

"Touche." He dipped his head in a bow.

Kathy applauded. "Great comeback. Wish I could think that

fast, Sis."

Judy didn't feel very clever. She needed to keep busy so she wouldn't think of Joe. He'd been stringing her along all the time. What if she hadn't overheard him on the phone? How many others did he tell "I love you"?

The rest of the morning, Judy shopped. She decided against souvenirs for the family, though she found a pair of earrings for Sandra and a book for Andy's children. At her favorite shop, she bought lavender silk pants and a matching top. Kathy would have some jewelry she could borrow. She tried to block thoughts of Joe, but he kept sneaking in when she least expected it.

It was good to see the old gang from work. Even though she'd only worked there a month she felt like she'd known them all her life.

"When are you coming back to work? The position is still open and our files are piling up," one of the women said.

Others nodded their heads in agreement.

"I could fix you up with my brother," another offered.

"She's taken," Kathy said. "A good-looking cowboy."

There was a chorus of moans. Judy wasn't sure if it was envy or disappointment. Everyone wanted to fix up single people.

After lunch, Judy went to Kathy's. There was a blinking light on the answering machine. She hit the button. There were three calls from Joe, asking her to call him. Toots had called, too. Best not to open up her wound any more than it was.

Judy managed to take a nap without any weird dreams. Several times, she thought she heard the phone ring, but ignored it.

Mark came home first. He punched the button on the answering machine and listened to more calls from Joe. "Judy, did you know Joe called?"

"Yes, but I don't want to talk to him."

"What's up? I thought you two had a thing going."

"So did I, but I really don't want to talk about it." She needed to talk about it, but not with Mark. He shrugged and went into his room.

He was still in there when Kathy came home. "I'm going up and get ready for the party," Kathy said.

"I better, too," Judy said. "I might need to borrow some earrings and a necklace to dress up my outfit."

"I'll bring my jewelry box to your room and you can pick out whatever you like."

Kathy came in, carrying a white plastic padded box. Judy recognized it from their childhood.

"Still have the same box?"

"It suits my purposes. You know I'm not one for much jewelry. My wedding ring, a watch and a couple of sets of earrings does me fine." Instead of leaving, Kathy sat down on the bed. "So what's with you and Joe?"

Judy burst into tears. She needed to talk. She poured out the whole story, including the misunderstanding and lovemaking, though no details. Then she said, "I overheard him telling someone he loved them. It was just as we were leaving. Remember, I said he was on the phone?" Kathy nodded. "It was then." Judy burst into tears again.

Kathy put her arms around Judy. "Are you sure? It doesn't sound like the Joe we know, but then again."

"I'm so humiliated," she sobbed. "And Toots knows we slept together." Judy pulled back and covered her face with her hands.

"I don't know what to tell you, except I'm here to listen if you need to vent." She got up. "I better finish getting ready. Are you going to be okay?"

Judy nodded.

When she was alone, Judy tried to push thoughts of Joe from her mind. She found pearl earrings and a necklace, setting off her outfit. She used just a bit of make-up and a generous spray of perfume. One last look in the mirror. Not too bad for a stupid old lady, she told her reflection.

"Would you like something to drink?" Mark asked Judy when she went into the living room...

"Maybe a glass of wine."

"I'll pour you some."

They sat down on the big leather sofa that faced another wall of windows. Judy took a sip of wine and let the alcohol sting her tongue.

"Who's David?" Mark asked suddenly.

"Who told you about David?"

"Joe mentioned him."

"He's a friend. Nothing more. Joe and I talked that out. I don't date married men. David is not divorced, but legally separated. Besides, there was no chemistry at all with David. Joe seemed to understand"

"He was pretty shook up about it all."

"Well, he shouldn't be." Judy took another sip. "That's pretty much water under the dam." She was beginning to talk in clichés.

"Ready to party?" Kathy said as she came into the room.

"You bet." Mark set down his glass and twirled his wife around the room. "All you single guys, eat your heart out." Kathy giggled. Judy smiled. It was good to see her sister so happy. "Come on, Judy. It's not every time I get to take two gorgeous women to a party."

The place was crowded, but not smoky. The hostess forbid anyone to smoke in her condo. The buffet would shame all but the best restaurants. There was a watermelon boat overflowing with exotic fruit, veggie trays, smoked salmon, shrimp and various sliced meats and cheeses. Judy helped herself to a plateful and found a bar stool to perch on. She watched the guests as she ate and sipped a glass of merlot. Judy recognized several people. A couple of them came over to talk and ask how things were going,

"You know, Mark's loft is still for sale," one said. "We'd love to have you living here."

Judy was flattered. But that was out of the question, even though she had money to pay cash.

She excused herself early and went to Kathy's. The answering machine's light was blinking. She listened for a moment, then hit the erase button. She did this two more times. Persistent, wasn't he?

The lack of good sleep the night before, combined with the wine, put Judy into a deep sleep. She didn't hear when Mark and Kathy came home.

They all slept late the next morning. Mark had coffee waiting for her when she came out of her room.

"Have a good time last night?" he asked, handing her a steaming mug.

"The food was fabulous," Judy said. "It was good to renew old acquaintances."

"You want to buy my loft?" Mark said. "It hasn't sold yet. I'll give you the family discount."

"Someone at the party told me it was still for sale. Even suggested I buy it."

"Then, it's unanimous," Kathy said as she came into the room.

"I don't know about that. What about Sandra and my kids?"

"They could always visit. Plus there's the phone and the internet." Mark was giving her the hard sell.

"Okay, I'll think about it." Judy threw her hands up. "Just don't mention it again for a while." She would think about it, or would have, if it had worked out with her and Joe.

"What's on the agenda for you ladies today?"

"We could do some sightseeing. There's a new art exhibit that just opened. I also want to go to the green market. There should be some asparagus and leeks and maybe even some peas." Mark made a face. "Good. Then I don't have to share them with you."

"Are you coming with us, Mark?"

"No, I have to work. You two can do the sister thing. I'll order pizza for supper and we can go to the movies tonight."

"Great idea. Now I know why I married you," Kathy put her arms around Mark's neck.

"And why is that?" He rubbed his stubbly chin on her nose.

"Because you're so thoughtful and," she reached up and kissed him, "so damn sexy."

"That's enough, you two," Judy laughed but inside she remembered the kidding she and Joe did and that memory hurt.

The sisters had a wonderful time at the exhibit. They lunched at the gallery's coffee shop. "Anything else you'd like to do?" Kathy asked.

"Not that I can think of," Judy said.

This time there were no flashing lights on the answering machine. She'd blinked back tears. Shed hoped Joe would have called while they were gone.

"You could work with me," Kathy punched the up button.

"I don't want to be tied down to a full-time job." This was true. She liked not having the routine of work.

"But you worked here before."

"Yes, but I knew it was only for a month."

The elevator door opened and they got in. "Would you be willing to work part-time?"

Judy was getting exasperated. "Kathy, I have a nice apartment at home. I don't want to own anything right now."

"Mark would rent it to you for as long as you wanted."

Kathy had an answer for everything. The elevator stopped and they got out.

"What are your plans when you get back?" Kathy unlocked the door.

"Nothing." The rest of her life spread out like a blank canvas. "Maybe I'll volunteer or work in a bookstore or as a shelver at the library."

"Oooo, be still my heart. That sounds like so much fun. I suppose you're going to see Sandra once in a while and maybe your kids will want to see you once in a while, too."

"Kathy, just stop with the hard sell. Mark tried it this morning. I'm..."but she didn't finish her sentence. "Oh, Kathy, I'm so torn. I don't know if I can transplant myself here."

"You lived in Arizona for several months each of the past few years."

"I know, but that was Steve and I."

"Maybe you'll find someone here."

"I've had it with people trying to fix me up."

"You can always try the internet. E Harmony." They both laughed at that thought.

"Just give me time."

"Okay, Mark will be home soon. We have to decide on which flick to see tonight," Kathy relocked the door and they went to her place.

After pizza, the three went to the new theater at the edge of town. Mark insisted they see a certain show. It seemed out of character for Mark to be so insistent, but the choice of movie was fine with Judy, especially when Mark bought their tickets. She was glad he didn't ask for a senior discount for her.

"You two go in and find some seats and I'll get us some popcorn," Mark said when they entered the lobby.

"Make it extra butter," Kathy said.

Mark didn't make it before the lights dimmed. Kathy waved a white tissue to catch his attention.

"Here, take this. I'll be right back." He handed Kathy a large container of buttery smelling popcorn.

"Good. I love extra butter! Makes your hands nice and greasy." Kathy sounded like she had when she was seven.

"Some people never change." Judy reached in and took a handful and several napkins.

Mark settled in. He had his arm around Kathy's shoulders and the popcorn bucket between them. Judy had to reach forward to get some.

"Is this seat taken, Ma'am?" It was Joe and Judy felt trapped.

She wanted to run, but now that he was here she knew she loved him and that was that. "No, you can sit here."

"I brought some popcorn for us. Figured ol' Mark wouldn't want to share his." In one movement, Joe sat down, put his arm around her and handed her the popcorn bucket.

She had no idea what the movie was about. All she could think about was Joe sitting next to her.

"If I kiss you here, we'll get thrown out. I won't be able to stop with just one kiss," he whispered in her ear. "Sugar, we gotta talk."

Judy nodded.

When their popcorn was finished, Joe kissed the butter off her fingers. She thought she would explode with desire. I wish he wasn't able to do that to me. Where is my resolve?

The credits rolled and they all got up and filed out into the brightly lit lobby.

"I have to wash my hands," Kathy said. Judy followed her into the ladies' room.

"Did you know Joe was going to be there?" Judy hissed as soon as they were by the sinks.

"No, it was something he and Mark concocted. "

"Did he tell you what was going on?" Judy figured he probably hadn't. There hadn't been time.

"He told Joe why you hadn't returned his calls. Joe was completely baffled. He wanted to explain the whole thing to you. Mark and I think you two are made for each other." Kathy turned on the hand dryer and rubbed her hands together under the nozzle. "At least listen to what he has to say."

It was not quite dark when the movie was over. "Well, where do we want to go now? The night's still young," Mark said.

"I don't know about you two, but Judy and I have a visit to make and a lot of talking to do. There is someone you need to meet," Joe said.

Might as well get this over with, though I don't want to, Judy thought. Joe held her hand as they walked to his truck.

"You overheard my side of the phone call just before you left?" It was more of a statement than a question.

"Yes, you told the person on the other end that you loved them and wanted to see them." Judy's indignation rose.

"If that's the part you heard, then I don't blame you for getting the wrong idea." Joe stared straight ahead. "It's time you met the other woman."

"But..." she began.

Joe held up his hand. "There are no buts about this. I love you and don't want to live without you."

Judy shut her mouth. This better be good. She didn't like to be a jealous harpy.

XXVII

Joe pulled the truck along a tree lined street. He came around and helped her out. "She's expecting us." He placed his hand on the small of her back.

The apartment building was of red brick and stood several stories high. They were buzzed in and took the elevator to the fourth floor. A petite blonde was waiting in the hall. She launched herself at Joe and he caught her up and twirled her around like he did to his mother.

"This is my daughter, Holly. Holly, this is Judy Evans, the woman I'm going to marry."

"Pleased to meet you, Judy." She put out her hand and Judy took it. "Toots and my dad have told me so much about you. Sorry we haven't met sooner." She took a breath. "Come on in." She led the way to her apartment and ushered them in.

By now, Judy was embarrassed for doubting Joe, but she was also irritated with Joe. They both had been acting like teenagers. They sat side by side on the couch, holding hands.

"What do you do?" Judy asked. "When I came out here, Toots said you had to leave. Was it for school or a job?"

Holly carried in a tray with a tea service and a plate of cookies. "Both. You see, I'm a nursing student, but I'm also a nun."

"A nun?" Why hadn't anyone said anything about this before?

"I'll bet Dad thought Toots told you and visa versa." She poured each of them tea in bone china cups. "Dad leaves the telling of the family to Toots. She must have figured he'd already told you." She passed around the cookies. "At least we finally got to meet. I hope we can see a lot more of each other."

They didn't stay long. Holly had duty the next morning. Joe promised they would have dinner together soon.

"Joe, I'd like to strangle you," Judy said when they were in the truck.

"You have a perfect right to feel that way. I'm sorry about all the misunderstandings we've had. I love you." He reached over and kissed her. "I hate bucket seats."

"Where are we going now?" Judy asked. "And are there any more skeletons in the closet.

I've been so open with you."

"We're going to my place. I don't know what else we need to talk about."

"I don't want to go to your place," Judy said. "I want to be on neutral ground. My head is spinning enough."

"There's a Denny's not too far from here. Would that be better?"

"Yes, I think so."

There were only a few people in the restaurant. Joe asked for a booth in a far corner. "We only want coffee." he told the waiter.

They sat opposite each other. Joe reached over and held her hand. "Let's start over," Joe said after a long silence. "Hi, my name is Joe Barton."

Judy looked into his eyes and smiled. "I'm Judy Evans."

"I love you and want to marry you."

She laughed until her sides hurt. "That's not starting over." He took her hand and kissed it. His lips made her stomach flip.

"Didn't you ever hear of love at first sight? I wanted to marry you from the first moment I saw you, but you were still raw from your husband's death." He brushed his fingers over her cheek. "You have no idea how appealing you are. At the cabin, I know I came on too strong. I was afraid of frightening you away."

She remembered the knife. But she also remembered her reaction to his touch.

"Every time I called you, your voice made me want you even more. Not only in my bed, but in my life."

She looked at the little laugh lines around his eyes. "I responded and didn't exactly push you away."

"True. And then when Toots and I helped you move, I knew I wanted you in my life forever, but I felt it was still too soon. I saw how you were with your family and my mother. You are the woman I have always dreamed of. Then when a strange man answered your phone, I thought I'd lost you. After all, he was there and I wasn't." Their coffee was served. Joe took a deep breath. "I should have trusted you, but my ex-wife had pulled a similar stunt on me. I thought I was over it, but I guess not."

"But I told you the truth."

Joe shrugged. "So I can be a jerk once in a while."

She took a sip of coffee. "Well, I believed you had someone

303

else when I called you about Toots. A strange woman answered your cell phone." She paused. "Now, tell me about your ex-wife." He brought up the subject and she needed to know more. "You said she left you for another man?"

"No, it wasn't a man. She left me for another woman. She is a lesbian." He looked down at the table. "She didn't tell me she felt this way until we'd been married for twenty years and Holly was in high school." There was a bitterness in his voice.

"I'm so sorry." She felt helpless. It must have been a terrible blow.

"Don't be." He smiled at her. "I would never have met you." He took her hand to his lips.

Damn, I wish he'd stop that. He makes me want to rip off his clothes right here, she thought.

"What are you thinking?" He asked.

"You don't want to know, at least not here."

"Then let's get out of here.' Joe threw down a ten dollar bill on the table. "This should cover our tab."

"Where are we going?" Judy asked.

"You'll see," was the only thing Joe said. He kept his hand on her thigh except when he had to shift.

They pulled in a parking place by Kathy's and Mark's.

"Two things before we go in." Joe faced her. "My being four years younger than you isn't going to make a difference, is it?"

Judy hadn't even thought about a difference in their ages. "Kathy's ten years older than Mark. I kinda like younger men. Steve was six months younger than me." She giggled.

"Then will you marry me?"

"I'll have to think about it."

"Don't take too long. I'd like to get married as soon as possible." He walked her to her sister's condo. "I'll save the surprise for another time."

"You're terrible," she said to his teasing.

"Terrible? You're the one who has to think about marrying me." He wiggled his eyebrows. "You ain't seen nothing yet, kid."

He walked her to the door. After a long hot kiss, Judy went inside. She stood for a few minutes, leaning against the door. Her heart took flight. She knew she could trust him.

Once in bed, she lay awake, staring into the dark. She was going to marry him as soon as she could. She recalled his sweetness and the feel of his touch. In her heart she knew she loved Joe despite all the old misgivings. How much did you know anyone? Life was a crap shoot any way you looked at it. Steve died suddenly. Sandra was married to a jerk. Kathy found a great guy.

With her mind made up to tell Joe she would marry him, she rolled over and went to sleep with a smile on her face.

XXVIII

The next morning, the two sisters sat on the balcony and sipped coffee. "Well, did he ask you?" Judy almost dropped her mug. "He asked...and how did you know?"

"Mark told me. Well, what did you say?"

"I said I had to think about it."

"Juuu-dy, you are terrible."

"He didn't trust me, remember? I just had to think it all through."

By now, Kathy was sitting on the edge of her chair. "Come on. Did you decide?"

Judy laughed. "I'm going to marry him. I feel like I'm on cloud nine"

Kathy gave a sigh of relief. "When?"

"He wants to get married as soon as possible."

"Is there any reason not to?"

"No, except I'd like to let the kids and Sandra know beforehand."

"It would probably be nice." Kathy got up and went into the kitchen. Judy followed. Kathy went to the sink where she rinsed out her coffee cup and put it in the dishwasher. "Want to go for a walk? Mark went golfing."

"Sure, I need to get out and stretch my legs."

"Let's get going then," Kathy said. They both went and changed into walking shoes.

They walked as far as the bakery. "This isn't doing much for exercise," Judy said as she took a bite of a French doughnut.

"I know," Kathy chuckled. "But this is a perfect way to enjoy a Sunday morning-coffee and doughnuts. I better bring one home for Mark. These are his favorites."

It was a beautiful day. The mountains were clearly visible on the horizon. She and Kathy didn't talk on the way back.

In the condo, Mark was making himself a sandwich.

"Here, lover." Kathy handed him the white bakery bag.

He opened it for a peek. "Oh, you sure know how to get to me." He wrapped his arms around her and gave her a long kiss.

"While you two make out, I'm going to take a shower." They didn't even hear me, Judy thought. Now that she made up her mind to marry him, she didn't want to wait to tell him. As soon as she could, she'd call him.

Judy dressed in white capris and a teal knit top. She was barefoot when she came out of her room. There was Joe, sitting on the couch. "What are you doing here?"

"That's a fine howdy-do," Joe got up and crossed the room. "I came to ask for your hand and you ask what am I doing here."

Judy felt foolish, but only for the moment it took him to take her in his arms and smother her with kisses.

When they came up for air. He said, "I want to show you my surprise. But, first, have you an answer to my question?" He put his forehead on hers. "I'm waiting."

Judy took a deep breath. "Yes, I'll marry you." There, she'd given her answer.

"Yipee!" Joe twirled her around the room like he did with his mother and Holly. "Hear that! She'll marry me." He finally set her down. "Now, come on. I want to show you the surprise." He grabbed her hand and practically dragged her to the elevator. "Close your eyes until I tell you to open them."

Judy did as she was told. She laughed at the excitement in his voice. The elevator beeped four times. Fourth floor, I wonder what he's up to? They walked down the hall. "Keep those eyes shut." She heard a jangle of keys. Then he scooped her up.

"Can I open my eyes yet?"

"Just one minute." She heard a door slam shut. "Now."

Judy knew where they were immediately. Mark's loft. But there was a difference. It was now furnished. Leather sofas faced the expansive windows. There were end tables and a rocker. In the dining alcove was a table and chairs with a matching sideboard.

"When did you do all this?"

"I had the things delivered yesterday morning while you and Kathy were gone. But if there's anything you want to change, it's alright with me. It won't hurt my feelings" He still was carrying her. "I want you to see this." He started for the loft stairs.

"No, put me down. I'll walk up the steps myself." She could just see them tumbling backwards. He set her on her feet, taking her hand and leading her up.

There was a king-size bed, surrounded with dressers and other furniture. The bed was made, but the covers turned down.

Hmmm, Judy thought, he's pretty sure of himself...and me. No words needed to be said.

After they tried out the bed, Judy curled up with her head tucked under his arm. "This is wonderful." Wonderful was too mild a word, but it was the best she could come up with. He made mush out of her mind...

"Be more specific. The love making?" He gently massaged her breast. She slapped his hand away. "Or the loft?'

"Do I have to make a choice?" She looked up at him.

He started to chuckle. "No, I hope not."

"I'm totally surprised. Did Kathy and Mark know?" Obviously, one of them had to know.

"Only Mark knew I wanted to buy this for you. He knows nothing of what I did."

"Pretty sure of yourself."

"No, just sure you loved me enough to marry me." He kissed her. "Now, I think we should go to your sister's and start making wedding plans. If we stay here, we'll be too distracted."

"Then we better go down to your sister's." After another long kiss, they left.

XXIX

"When did you say you made reservations to fly home?" Kathy said after Judy and Joe asked for help making wedding plans.

"I was going to make them, but didn't." Judy had procrastinated, though she was going to call the airline on Monday.

"Great." Joe grinned.

"What do you think of Joe buying my loft?" Mark came to sit with them at the table.

"Joe's buying the loft?" Kathy squealed. "That means we'll be neighbors." She got up and gave Judy a hug.

"Um, not so fast," Joe said.

All three turned to look at him. "What do you mean?" Judy said.

Joe cleared his throat. "Well, I'd like Judy to accompany me on some of my trips."

He hadn't said anything about that. She didn't want to go off to Brazil's jungle or a Siberian settlement.

He went on. "I've got a job in New Zealand and I'll be gone for six months. You know, have wrench, and will travel." He said to Judy, "Do you think you could live in a resort in New Zealand for six months? I'd never ask you to go someplace dangerous or primitive."

Judy didn't realize she'd been holding her breath. She coughed. "When are you scheduled to leave?" Maybe this was a mistake. Though a six-month honeymoon sounded great.

"They want me there next week, but I can hold them off for a month or so."

"Can we get a wedding together that fast?" Kathy asked Judy.

"You should know, you did it." Judy paused. "I would like to have Sandra and my children there." Joe nodded.

"I think we can do it." Kathy snapped her fingers.

"We could get married at the ranch. Toots would love it," Joe said. "I suppose I should call her and let her know she's getting a daughter-in-law. And call Holly to tell her, she's getting a stepmother."

"And I have to call my family, too," Judy said.

"Now wait a minute," Kathy said. She took a calendar off the wall. "Let's set a date first."

The wedding would be in three weeks. Toots was delighted to be throwing them a wedding. "You get your dress and I'll take care of the rest."

"I'll pay for your tickets so you have no excuse," Judy told each of her family. Sandra said she'd come, but Brad wouldn't. Judy was relieved. Grace and her latest young man would come out, but they'd drive. Andy, Tammy and the kids would take the train. Clark and Tina would be coming, too. Ellyn was the only one who couldn't make it. She didn't think she wanted to go far, now that she was pregnant. So Judy wasn't the only one with good news.

Sandra called a couple of days later. "What about your apartment?"

"I'll send you a list of items I want shipped out here. Grace and Clark can split up the furniture. Clarke can consider it a wedding gift. He and Tina are planning on getting married. And Grace just bought a house and would need extra furniture. The rest can go to the Salvation Army."

"What about the lease?"

"I didn't sign a lease. All I have to do is give a 45 day notice. I think I can take care of the other details from here."

"What are you going to do to keep busy while Joe is away?"

"I'm going with him this time."

"You're going to New Zealand?"

"Only for six months. When he goes to more primitive areas. He suggested I help out at a school. It might be fun. Besides, I want to learn more about the area."

Judy didn't know what to do with herself. Toots was doing all the wedding preparations. Judy and Kathy found the perfect wedding dress for Judy. And a new dress for Kathy. Kathy and Mark were going to be the honor attendants.

Judy took some long walks to keep out of the way. She remembered her and Steve's wedding. The small guest list and the buffet lunch at her parents' home. Their wedding night at a local hotel. They didn't have much money but neither did any of their friends. What they had was their love and the support of family. That life seemed so long ago. She knew in her heart he would approve of her decision.

While Joe was out of town for several days, Judy read everything she could about New Zealand She even rented a DVD.

Joe wanted her to move into the loft with him, but she didn't feel comfortable with that arrangement. She stayed there when he was gone, but kept her room at Kathy's.

A week before the wedding, Judy went to help Toots, even though Toots said she didn't need help. Judy found out why. Maria and several of Maria's friends were doing all the work under Toots supervision.

This not going to be a western style barbeque. No expense had been spared on the food. Little canapés of salmon caviar, and stuffed mushrooms would be served before the ceremony. Everything was built around lobster and prime rib. Asparagus in little bundles and individual molded salads would adorn the tables. Waiters in white coats would do the serving.

Judy chose a simple three tiered cake with real flowers in the middle instead of the bride and groom dolls. Two cases of champagne were brought in. The guests would sit at linen covered round tables under a white canopy. A string quartet would play for the wedding and then stay and play during the entire reception.

Joe came out to the ranch two days before the wedding. "I borrowed a couple of campers to use as guest rooms," he said. "Sandra is going to stay with Kathy and Mark. I let Andy and his family stay in the loft." He paused. "Its okay, isn't it?" Judy nodded. "The rest will stay out here."

"Between you and Toots, I don't have much to do."

Joe leaned over and whispered in her ear, "Save your strength, baby." She felt her face get warm.

XXX

The wedding day was beautiful. A retired pastor who was a friend of Toots performed the morning ceremony. Judy was so nervous, she was sure everyone could see her bouquet shake as she walked down a short aisle. Joe was so handsome in a tux. There were flowers banked on either side of the platform.

Joe took her hand and they faced each other. The pastor read the standard wedding ceremony. "And, Judith, will you keep Joe only unto yourself as long as you two shall live?"

Judy hesitated just a second. Oh, God, please don't take Joe away from me. Then she gave Joe a smile and said, "I do." She would go forward in faith.

The ceremony was short, but Joe's kiss wasn't. There was applause and a couple of hoots, probably from her sons. Judy couldn't remember when she had so many hugs and kisses, along with well wishes. She and Joe held hands during the whole time.

Everyone took time to acquaint themselves with other guests. Toots sat on a glider, watching the festivities. She beamed as though she willed this to happen.

The quartet played for about an hour. The last piece was for the bride and groom's dance. The piece was Blue Moon. It was a bit hokey, but so romantic. There was a blue moon when they had their first date.

The spell was broken when Joe took an old stereo outside to play rock n roll. When he got Judy to do the twist, Holly and Judy's children all rolled their eyes. The only ones to join in the dance were Judy's grandchildren, one of whom could barely walk.

Gradually, people started to leave. Andy and his family caught a late train heading east. Grace and her date had ridden out with Clark and Tina. They all had to be to work on Monday. Holly planned on spending the night with her grandmother. Judy knew Toots would be glad for the company. Sandra was going to spend a couple more days with Kathy and Mark. "I got a better deal if I don't fly on the weekend.'

As the last car rolled down the drive, Toots waved and went into the house.

"Thanks so much for everything, Toots," Judy said. "I'm so lucky to have you for a mother-in-law."

Toots giggled. "That sounds so funny. But I'm so happy to be able to do it. I know you two will be very happy." She paused, "I think your family approves, too."

"I sure do," Holly put her arm around Toots's waist. "Dad deserves the best. And I now have brothers and sisters." She grinned.

"We're going up to the cabin for the night," Joe said. "We'll be back sometime tomorrow. I need to go to town to finish the last minute details before we leave." He slung his arm around Judy's shoulders. "Did someone bring your passport?"

"I have it in my purse. Grace found it in my desk."

"Holly. Toots. We'll see you tomorrow. My bride and I are off to the woods." He gave them each a kiss and led Judy to his truck. "I have to be careful so the bears don't get us."

As everyone had a good laugh, the newlyweds drove off with a trail of dust following. Joe didn't take the back road like they did the first time. This was quicker, but not much smoother. Judy held fast to the grab bar as the truck lurched along. Recent rains had washed out parts of the road.

Joe unlocked the door. "I have a real good lock on this now."

"You mean so the bears can't come in."

"So the bears, or any other creature, can't come in unannounced." He picked her up and carried her over the threshold. "I put a bathroom in." He pointed to a corner which had a sheet hung across. "There's a porta-pottie there. And a washstand. All the comforts of home." He looked down at her. "Well, almost."

Oh, how she loved this man.

Judy looked around. The cabin was clean. A row of water jugs stood on the counter next to an ice chest. The sight of the bed sent a shiver through her.

"Cold?" Joe moved toward her.

She couldn't help but grin. "You could warm me up."

He didn't need any more hints. He pulled her into his arms and kissed her hard as his tongue slipped between her lips. The rest of the night, they made love and dozed between sweet-smelling sheets.

The morning sun woke them up. Judy was grateful she didn't have to go out to the outhouse, though the draped sheet was thin. Joe started the cook stove and put the water-filled coffeepot on to boil. Judy fixed some bacon and eggs for them.

"I forgot how a night of love can work up an appetite," Joe said between bites.

Judy was pretty hungry herself. Then she remembered they hadn't bothered to eat anything after they got there. Better than a gym workout.

"I think everyone had a good time yesterday, don't you?" Judy said.

"I know they did. It was fun. I'm so happy you insisted on having your family all come out. With just Holly, Toots and me, I forget how much a large family measns." He got up and threw a handful of coffee into the boiling coffeepot. Then he set the pot off to one side "I wish we could stay here a few more days."

"We'll just have to come back next year."

"You don't mind?" He took an egg and broke it into the coffee pot. "Ready for some coffee?"

She held out a cup. When the brew cooled down, she took a sip. "This is the best coffee."

"Cowboy coffee." The little lines around his eyes deepened.

"Do you have any idea how much I love you?" She said.

"Show me and I'll show you." He led her to the bed. Judy's heart soared.

The End

Purchase other Black Rose Writing titles at www.blackrosewriting.com/books
and use promo code PRINT to receive a 20% discount.

BLACK ROSE
writing™

CPSIA information can be obtained
at www.ICGtesting.com
Printed in the USA
FFOW05n1815100715

9 781612 965475